Red Clover Inn

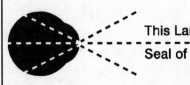

This Large Print Book carries the
Seal of Approval of N.A.V.H.

RED CLOVER INN

CARLA NEGGERS

THORNDIKE PRESS
A part of Gale, Cengage Learning

GALE
CENGAGE Learning®

Farmington Hills, Mich • San Francisco • New York • Waterville, Maine
Meriden, Conn • Mason, Ohio • Chicago

GALE
CENGAGE Learning®

LIBRARY OF CONGRESS CATALOGING-IN-PUBLICATION DATA

Names: Neggers, Carla, author.
Title: Red Clover Inn / Carla Neggers.
Description: Large print edition. | Waterville, Maine : Thorndike Press, 2017. |
  Series: A Swift River Valley novel | Series: Thorndike Press large print basic
Identifiers: LCCN 2017001855 | ISBN 9781410496478 (hardback) | ISBN 1410496473
  (hardcover)
Subjects: LCSH: Large type books. | BISAC: FICTION / Romance / General. | GSAFD:
  Love stories.
Classification: LCC PS3564.E2628 R43 2017 | DDC 813/.54—dc23
LC record available at https://lccn.loc.gov/2017001855

Published in 2017 by arrangement with Harlequin Books S.A.

Printed in the United States of America
1 2 3 4 5 6 7 21 20 19 18 17

To Niamh Amalia,
daughter of my daughter

ONE

The Cotswolds, England

Charlotte Bennett was no stranger to trouble but never had she encountered it in the form of a US federal agent who was exhausted, somewhat inebriated or both. "Agent Rawlings." She paused, debating the wisdom of continuing. "Are you by any chance armed?"

"Armed with a smile."

And smile he did, as if to prove his point. It was a casually sexy smile, his turquoise eyes crinkling at the corners. Charlotte didn't know when and where a federal agent was supposed to carry a weapon, but certainly not while drinking beer at a party the night before her cousin's wedding in a quiet village in England. She couldn't see a weapon but he could easily have one under the jacket he wore over a charcoal-gray lightweight sweater. He had ultrashort-cropped dark auburn hair and looked as if

7

he knew his way around weapons of all kinds.

"No worries, okay? I'm not in the UK on official business. You're safe with me."

He was amused. She could tell. She'd arrived at the party late and had chosen a small table by a window slightly open to the damp June evening. She'd had exactly two sips of her wine, a lovely, chilled white, when he sat next to her on the cushioned bench, placed his near-empty beer glass on the small table and introduced himself as Greg Rawlings. Charlotte had recognized his name as the federal agent Samantha, her cousin whose wedding was tomorrow, had mentioned was a last-minute guest.

Charlotte took her third sip of her wine. "You know, I didn't invite you to join me."

"You can kick me out if you want," he said with a yawn. "I'll go quietly."

He didn't look as if he did anything quietly unless it suited him. "Agent Rawlings —"

"Call me Greg. What's your name?"

"Charlotte. Charlotte Bennett."

"Ah. Another Bennett. Live here or in the US?"

"I'm American but I live in Scotland." *For now,* she added silently.

"Well, Lottie, you need to kick back and relax."

He was having fun. Definitely. She wanted to have fun but she wasn't in the mood, at least not yet. Once she saw Samantha and got into the spirit of the wedding festivities, maybe. But she didn't like weddings.

"It's *Charlotte,*" she said. "Don't call me Lottie again."

Greg Rawlings smiled, his eyes half-closed. "Or . . . what?"

He knew he was sexy. Totally knew it. She returned his smile. "I promised my family I wouldn't get in a bar fight tonight."

"You've been in bar fights, Char?"

"Not in a while. And Char isn't going to work, either. Charlotte. That's it."

"As in *Charlotte's Web?*"

"No. As in my parents liked the name."

"Is Charlotte the spider? I don't remember. I guess it makes sense she'd be the spider, or why would it be her web?"

Charlotte didn't respond. She watched him fight back another yawn. Maybe he wasn't inebriated — maybe he was just tired. He'd sat at her table without invitation, but there weren't enough tables for the number of guests, deliberately so, she knew, because the idea behind the party was for guests to mingle ahead of tomorrow's wedding. She'd assumed he'd had too much to drink and had picked an argument with him.

Maybe *argument* was too strong. She'd walked into the Cotswolds pub and found her way to the private-function room intensely aware she needed a distraction. She'd hoped a glass of white wine would do the trick. Then enter a fit, muscular federal agent with attitude.

Maybe he needed a distraction, too. Sparring with her certainly didn't intimidate him or even seem to bother him. One of those guys who always thought he had the upper hand. She supposed it was a strength in a federal agent, if not necessarily in a drinking mate.

"What are you drinking?" he asked her.

"Chardonnay. What about you?" Charlotte nodded to his almost-drained pint glass. "What were you drinking?"

"Implying I'm done for the night?"

"You should be."

He grinned. "You're blunt." He sat up straighter. "Okay. I *was* drinking Heineken, the last of which is in the bottom of my glass and warm. My buddy Brody is supposed to be fetching me another pint."

"Brody being . . ."

"Brody Hancock. He's the tall guy who

isn't bringing me my beer."

Charlotte drew a blank but had a feeling she should know the name Brody Hancock. "Is Brody a federal agent, too?"

"He's a London-based Diplomatic Security Service agent for the US State Department recently married to the only sister of tomorrow's groom. You know about that, right? The wedding tomorrow? You're not a gate-crasher, are you?"

"I know about the wedding. I'm not a gate-crasher." More like the opposite, she thought. The one who ran from weddings. "Are you a DS agent, too?"

He frowned. "Didn't I say that?"

"You acknowledged you were a federal agent when I recognized your name. I didn't know what kind of federal agent. We didn't get to the details once I realized you might be armed." She had a feeling she was digging a deep, deep hole for herself. "Why don't I find Agent Hancock for you?"

Greg sank against the back of the bench they shared. "That's okay. He'll find me."

"I hope so," she said half under her breath.

"You're blunt, Charlotte. Relax. It's the night before a quiet English wedding."

As if *that* should reassure her. "Bad things often happen the night before weddings."

"That's a dark view," he said, clearly

amused. "Let's start over. I will call you Charlotte and you will quit worrying about whether I'm armed and inebriated. Okay? Hitting the reset button . . ." He paused to shake off a yawn. "What do you do for a living, Charlotte?"

"I'm a marine archaeologist. I'm Samantha Bennett's cousin."

"Our bride-to-be. Blood relative, then?"

"She's my second cousin, actually. Our grandfathers were brothers."

"Both gone now?"

Charlotte nodded. "They died within eighteen months of each other, my grandfather Max first, then Harry. They were both predeceased by their wives. Harry was an explorer and adventurer. Max — well, Max wasn't an explorer and adventurer. He managed Harry's expeditions and such."

"Younger brother?"

"By two years. They both lived into their nineties. They would be at the wedding if they were alive." Charlotte picked up her wineglass, taking the opportunity to lower her gaze subtly to Greg's middle. She still couldn't see any evidence of a weapon. "The Bennetts will be well represented tomorrow."

Greg leaned toward her. "I don't mind you staring at me, but you can throttle back on the suspicions. I'm not going to shoot anyone and I'm not drunk."

"The last words of countless drunks as they pass out under the table."

He grinned, not the reaction she'd expected to her frank comment. "I knew I did right sitting next to you," he said. "I saw you come in and decided you're the prettiest, most uptight person here and needed cheering up."

It was distraction she'd needed, not cheering up. "I only just arrived from Edinburgh."

"Any idea why it's pronounced *Edinboro*? Why isn't *burgh* pronounced like it is in *Pittsburgh*?" He didn't wait for an answer, instead grabbing his glass and polishing off his last sip of beer. He made a face. "I let it get warm. That's bad. I'm off my game. Where do you suppose my fresh pint is?"

"Still in the tap, I hope," Charlotte said.

"Going to tell me why you're so uptight? Did you run into trouble getting here from Edinburgh?"

"No trouble. It was a long train ride." She'd constantly fought the urge to jump off her train and return to Edinburgh. But she hadn't, and now she was here, going tit-for-tat with Greg Rawlings. "I'm relaxing with a glass of wine and going to bed early."

"Where?"

"I don't know how that's your business."

He shrugged. "It's not. Just making friendly conversation. I'm staying here at the pub. My room's right up the stairs. Brody and Heather — that's his wife — are staying at the wedding hotel. She's in the wedding party tomorrow. But you know that, right?"

Wedding party. Charlotte inhaled, pushing back a surge of panic. "I haven't met Heather, but yes, I know who she is, and that she's one of Samantha's bridesmaids."

"You're not in the wedding yourself, are you?"

She didn't answer at once. She scanned the private-function room but didn't see anyone she knew. The party was winding down now, only a handful of guests at the dozen tables and standing around with drinks. Samantha had assured her it would be a simple, informal gathering of friends and family who'd arrived for the destination wedding from New England, Florida, Scotland and London. There was no actual rehearsal. It wasn't critical that Charlotte arrive early, or at all, provided she was on time for the wedding preparations and service tomorrow. She'd texted Samantha from the Oxford train station to let her know she'd arrived. She'd sensed her cousin's relief. Charlotte understood. She didn't have a good track record when it came to weddings.

Samantha had already gone back to the wedding hotel for an early night by the time Charlotte had arrived at the party. She shifted back to the man next to her at her table. "I'm Samantha's maid of honor," she said, hoping she sounded relaxed, matter-of-fact.

"There you go. Being in the wedding explains why you're so uptight."

"Actually, no, it doesn't, because I'm not uptight."

"Nervous? Being in front of a crowd can make people nervous."

"I'm not nervous or uptight. But never mind."

He eyed her as if he was debating asking a follow-up question. "Samantha's a pirate expert and treasure hunter," he said instead. "I'm going to guess that you're not."

"Marine archaeologists are sometimes involved in exploring sunken pirate ships, but you are right, I'm not." She used a tone that she hoped signaled she didn't want to answer more questions about herself. "I'll go find your friend."

"Don't bother. I see him. He's chatting up one of the groom's brothers. Am I starting to annoy you, Charlotte?"

"Let's say initially I felt somewhat protective of you but now I don't."

"Protective of me?" Another wide, amused grin. "I like that."

"Protective only in the sense that I don't want you to do anything to get yourself in trouble with your superiors or to cause trouble for anyone else, especially Samantha, since it's her wedding tomorrow."

"And you? Are you being protective of yourself? You don't want me to cause trouble for you, right?" He leaned back on the bench. "Or do you?"

"I assure you, Agent Rawlings, I can handle whatever trouble you have in mind for me."

He gave her a slow, easy, impossibly sexy grin. "I'll bet you can."

"I walked into that one, didn't I?"

"No comment." He blinked, plainly having difficulty keeping his eyes open. "So. You haven't told me to shove off, because you're protecting me and your cousin but not yourself. Got it."

Charlotte didn't quibble. Greg Rawlings was muscular and broad-shouldered but he wasn't what she would call handsome. Instead he had a magnetic, arresting appeal that worked well with her need for a distraction and probably was a factor in her not sending him on his way.

"You *are* pretty, you know," he said, catching her off guard. "Your brown eyes remind me of a golden retriever I had as a kid."

"I beg your pardon?"

"Did I just say you have eyes like a dog? Damn, I did. He was a great dog, if that helps."

"I love dogs," Charlotte said, keeping her tone neutral.

"Me, too. And you do have pretty eyes."

"Do you always dig holes this deep with people you've just met?"

"Usually deeper."

She didn't doubt him.

"And you?" he asked.

"I've dug a hole with you?" She smiled. "Ah, well."

He laughed, looking less exhausted — and not at all drunk. "Fortunately, my job requires me to keep my mouth shut most of the time. Do you work with Samantha's parents? Aren't they exploring sunken U-boats off the coast of Scotland?"

"They were. That project ended recently. I did work with them, yes, on a contract basis."

"Are you a diver?"

Charlotte hesitated only a fraction of a

second. She doubted most people would have noticed her hesitation, but she could tell by the slight narrowing of his eyes that Greg Rawlings did. "I'm with the Institute of Maritime Archaeology based in Edinburgh," she said, crisp, professional. "Diving is an important part of what I do."

Greg shuddered. "Just the thought of diving gives me hives."

"That's your answer, then. If thinking about diving bothers you, then it's the thinking that's the issue, not the diving itself."

"It's the diving."

She couldn't resist a smile. She had to admit she was enjoying their banter. It was harmless, a little fun before she retired for the night. Maybe he'd sized her up right after all. "I've been diving since I was a kid," she said. "I guess it never occurred to me to get hives over it. I'm fascinated by the world's underwater heritage. There's so much to explore and learn."

"One of our last frontiers," Greg said, obviously not that interested. "I guess space is another. I don't like the thought of space suits, either. I like breathing real air."

She wasn't going to argue with him about the definition of real air. "It's hard to believe Samantha ended up a couple of hours from the nearest salt water, but she loves her adopted town in Massachusetts. England is perfect for her wedding, though, since most of her family lives in the UK. She says it's going to be beautiful tomorrow. Apparently the wisteria is in full bloom."

"What's wisteria?" Greg asked.

"It's a flower."

"Then it's not contagious. Good."

Charlotte sighed. "Very funny." She started to rise. "Good to meet you, Agent Rawlings. I'll see you tomorrow."

Greg placed a hand on her wrist, sending unexpected currents through her. "It's okay," he said softly. "Have another glass of wine. You were here first. I'll go find Brody. I remember when he got his first assignment. He was green as a grass snake. Now he's in his prime, and I'm — Wait, where the hell are we?" He glanced around him, as if he were confused. "Some twee English village, right?"

Charlotte observed him. He was entertained, unconcerned — and deliberate, she decided. Diplomatic Security Agent Greg Rawlings might be exhausted and he might be trouble in many ways, but he wasn't inebriated. He was stone-cold sober. Her initial impression of him had been part right and part wrong.

Mostly wrong.

She gave an inward groan, not so much embarrassed as annoyed with herself. But wasn't being wrong about people par for the course for her these days?

Par for the course with her and *men,* she amended silently.

She did much better with the ghosts she found underwater.

"I have to unpack," she said politely, firmly, as she stood. "Enjoy the rest of your evening."

This time, Greg didn't stop her, and she slipped out of the party room, down the hall and out to the bar. More family and friends had decided to stay overnight than expected, and Charlotte had offered to stay in one of the pub's half-dozen guest rooms, freeing up space at the relatively small wedding hotel.

A room at the pub also allowed her to get her bearings before tomorrow.

Weddings.

She took a breath and sat on a stool at the bar. A quiet drink without any back-and-forth with a federal agent and then she'd collapse into bed. By daylight, she'd be ready to pour herself into her maid-of-honor dress. The long train ride from Edinburgh to Oxford and then a cab to the small English village where her cousin was getting married had left her drained. She'd had too much time to think. Inevitably, her mind had drifted to thoughts, questions and regrets best avoided on her way to a wedding.

"Scotch," she said to the tawny-haired barman. "Smoky and expensive."

"What are we celebrating?"

"We are celebrating that I'm here for my cousin's wedding tomorrow, alone, single and in one piece."

The barman poured a pricey single malt and set the glass in front of her. "Cheers, then."

Charlotte held up her glass and smiled. "Cheers."

Brody Hancock planted a fresh beer in front of Greg and sat across from him. "Do I need to go find that woman and apologize on your behalf?" Brody asked.

Greg picked up the beer. "*That woman* is Charlotte Bennett, Samantha's cousin and her maid of honor."

"Even more reason to apologize."

"Apologize for what?"

"You tell me. I'm going to make an educated guess and say you were jerking her chain."

"She started it by assuming I was drunk."

Brody groaned. "That's so third grade, Greg."

"I know. It's fun, isn't it?"

"For you, maybe."

Greg didn't argue the point with his friend and colleague. Brody was a good-looking guy in his midthirties, dressed for the night in a suit, probably because it was his brother-in-law who was getting married tomorrow.

"You're doing some assuming of your own," Brody added. "You don't know what Charlotte was thinking."

"I do. She told me. She's blunt. She threatened to disarm me." It was an exaggeration and Greg knew it. "I swear."

"How was she going to disarm you, Greg?" Brody asked, sighing.

"I don't know. It could have been interesting to find out."

Brody shook his head. "Don't make me regret getting you invited to the wedding."

"I won't. Relax. That's what I'm doing. Relaxing."

"Sure, Greg."

He realized his eyelids were drooping. Damn, he was beat. He'd been going all out for months. A wedding in the English countryside was just what he needed. "Charlotte's uptight and was looking for a distraction," he said, confident in his assessment. "Fretting about me gave her something to do. If anyone needs to apologize, it's her."

"Somehow I doubt she's the one who needs to make apologies."

"Charlotte Bennett can hold her own. Trust me. And it's Charlotte, by the way, not Char or Lottie or anything else. Charlotte."

"And you're an ass," Brody said with a grin.

"I do a good imitation of one, anyway." Greg considered his encounter with tomorrow's maid of honor. "She's hiding something. I can tell these things."

"You're good, Greg, but even you aren't a mind reader. Enjoy your beer. We don't have to worry about getting in a car and driving on the wrong side on the winding country roads."

Heather, Brody's dark-haired, blue-eyed bride of a few months, joined them. She and Brody had grown up in the same town, an out-of-the-way little place west of Boston called Knights Bridge. Greg had been there over the winter and met a bunch of locals, including Heather's five older brothers. They were all here for tomorrow's wedding — especially Justin Sloan, since he was the groom. Being the youngest and only girl, Heather was another one who gave as good as she got. Brody had never intimidated her. Neither had the animosity between him and her older brothers that had gone back to their teen years. All water over the dam now. On Greg's one and only visit to Knights Bridge, Brody had just returned to his hometown after more than a decade and he and Heather Sloan were doing the dance, wondering if they were meant for each other. But they were. Greg had seen it right away. Love for them had come fast and fairly easily, and he was certain it would last.

Heather set three glasses of water on the table. "Figured it's time for us to switch to H2O," she said cheerfully as she sat next to her husband.

Greg thanked her but stuck with his beer. "We haven't had much chance to talk since I got in from parts unknown. How's married life for you two lovebirds?"

"It's perfect," Heather said without hesitation.

Brody smiled. "Just what I was going to say."

"We're loving London," she added. "Having my family here for the wedding is great. Helps with any homesickness."

"You're not down on the farm anymore," Greg said.

"We have a construction business. My parents live in an old farmhouse, but it's not a working farm."

"It's an expression, Heather." Greg got a kick out of her. "I'm glad you two are happy. I said you would be, didn't I?"

"You're always right, Greg," Heather said, then drank some of her water.

He laughed but he could feel the rawness of his exhaustion.

Brody lifted his water glass. "Are you going to pass out here, Greg? You look like you need toothpicks to keep your eyes open."

"Here would be good but Samantha's marine archaeologist cousin would probably sic the local cops on me." He abandoned his beer barely two sips into it. "I'll stumble up to my room."

"Want me to spot you?" Brody asked.

"No." Greg snorted as he got to his feet. "Spot me. Hell."

He did stumble, though. Imperceptibly, he thought, but there was no denying it. He didn't give a damn. He'd had a rough few months since crawling off his deathbed and going back to work.

How close was I to dying, Doc?

25

Close.

Seconds? Minutes? I want to tell my ex-wife.

His doctor hadn't thought that was funny. Laura wouldn't have, either, but Greg would never tell her. Divorced or not, he was the father of their two teenage children. She'd often grumbled that life as his wife was like being widowed, but she had never wanted him to die for real. Decent of her, considering she'd had a point. He'd left her high and dry too frequently during their marriage. They'd married young and had two kids right away, and they'd never been easy as a couple, not like Heather and Brody. Finally, they'd accepted they no longer were a couple and it was time to move on, end their marriage.

It hadn't been Laura's fault. It damn sure hadn't been the kids' fault.

They lived in Minnesota near Laura's family and liked cold weather. Andrew and Megan had no idea what their father's life was really like. They'd see a Diplomatic Security agent in a movie and think that was it. But it wasn't.

Greg took the blame, every bit of it, for the distance between them, but he knew, at least intellectually, blame and guilt got him nowhere. He wasn't going to let them be an excuse to keep his distance, prevent him from living the life he wanted to live.

He swore under his breath.

No way was he going to bed with all that rolling around in his head. A good night's sleep would help, but it would elude him if he didn't get a grip first. His demons were part of the reason for his admitted exhaustion.

He walked down the narrow hall to the bar, managing not to fall on his face. He spotted Charlotte Bennett at the bar and grinned at her when she fastened her dark eyes on him. She had creamy skin and thick, rich brown hair that hung in waves to just above her shoulders, and she wore a simple, close-fitting black dress and strappy black heels. Greg would bet a million dollars that her shoes were killing her feet, but she'd never show pain. Not the type.

He sat in a booth. It had a worn wood bench. No cushion. Aches that hadn't bothered him in months gnawed at him now. It'd been four months since he'd defied his doctors' predictions and had made a full recovery and returned to duty after being wounded in an ambush late last fall. He'd seen a similar determination in dark-eyed Charlotte, but maybe he'd only been projecting.

The pub had low ceilings and a large open

fireplace, unlit given the warm evening. A votive candle glowed on his table. The place was owned by Ian Mabry, a former RAF pilot engaged to Alexandra Rankin Hunt, an English dress designer with a shop down the street and tangled connections to little Knights Bridge, Massachusetts.

Greg ordered Scotch. "Whatever you recommend that doesn't cost a fortune," he told Mabry, a good-looking sandy-haired guy who didn't seem to miss the RAF. Greg wondered if he'd miss his job when the time finally came to call it quits. He wanted that moment to be on his own terms, not a bullet's terms. But he wasn't contemplating his past or future this weekend, he decided. Especially not tonight, with Scotch on the way.

He settled back and observed tomorrow's maid of honor. He didn't know much about the Bennetts. Samantha's grandfather, Harry Bennett, had earned an international reputation as an adventurer and explorer when he'd ventured to the Antarctic under dangerous conditions. He and some in his party had almost frozen to death. Greg gave an involuntary shiver. He figured he'd done well by not freezing to death in Minneapolis.

Laura, his ex, wouldn't think that was funny, either.

No wonder they hadn't been a "forever" match.

Greg focused on eyeing the curve of Charlotte Bennett's hip under her sleek outfit.

"Do you wear dresses very often given your work as a diver?" he asked, not sure if she'd heard him. Her dagger look as she swiveled to him ended any doubt. He grinned. "No, huh? Did you have that one hanging in your closet or did you buy it special for tonight? Borrow it? Wait. Let me guess. You don't have a closet."

"I'm not indulging you." She swiveled back to her drink, giving him her back again.

"That's not apple juice you're drinking, is it?"

No reaction. Greg decided to shut up before Ian Mabry tossed him out for being an ass. The pilot/barman delivered the Scotch himself, a smoky-but-not-too-smoky single malt from, according to Mabry, an Islay distillery.

"So it's *Eye-la* not *Iz-lay,*" Greg said.

Mabry smiled. "I have a feeling you knew that."

The Englishman withdrew before Greg told him yeah, he'd known. About a decade ago he'd mispronounced *Islay* in front of a UK-security type who'd relished trying to make him feel like a dumbass. It hadn't worked, and they'd become friends, drinking expensive Scotch to nonexcess and deliberately mispronouncing one booze name after another.

Greg debated asking Charlotte to join him. Probably not a good idea.

One sip into his Scotch and his fatigue blanketed him, suffocating him. He should have seen it coming, but he hadn't, instead distracting himself by teasing an obviously smart, tough marine archaeologist.

He could have tackled the fatigue, fought it off and forced himself up to his room, but he took another sip of Scotch.

And he was done.

Toast.

His weariness took him under. He didn't fight it. There was no reason to fight it. Everyone around him was safe, and he was off duty, secure, in a quiet English pub.

Next thing, he felt something frigid-cold and wet on his neck and then rolling down his back. He bolted upright and noticed Charlotte had moved onto the bench next to him.

He shivered, the wet cold reaching the small of his back. "That was too cold to be your tongue."

"It was ice."

"They have ice here?"

30

"I asked for ice for my glass of water. I was tempted to pretend I didn't see you pass out." She dumped the rest of her handful of melting cubes into his Scotch. "You're done drinking."

"You just ruined the rest of my excellent single malt."

"That was the point. Come on. I'll help you up to your room."

He debated protesting, but instead he stifled a yawn, his eyes half-shut. The ice had given him a jolt but he was still struggling to stay awake. He could have made it up to his room on his own, but damn. Having attractive, sexy Charlotte Bennett help him? An opportunity not to be missed. He figured he couldn't go wrong.

"I am feeling a bit woozy," he said.

"I wonder why."

"I haven't had too much to drink."

"Doesn't matter." She slid an arm around his middle. "Up you go."

She inhaled sharply as she tightened her hold on him. He liked to think it was because she was reacting to being in such close contact with him, but maybe he smelled or something. He offered no resistance as she helped him to his feet, using her legs for leverage. He was a big guy but she clearly knew what she was doing. Another good tug, and she had him on the other side of the table, near the base of the stairs.

"Not bad," he said.

"I'm used to dealing with inebriated divers."

"You're a tough cookie, aren't you?"

She gave him a steely look, the kind he'd given countless times in similar situations. "You need to call it a night, Agent Rawlings."

"You aren't going to dump more ice down my back, are you?"

"Would it help get you up the stairs to your room?"

"There are better ways."

Her cheeks reddened but it could have been exertion. Probably unhelpful that he was thinking in physical terms, but maybe she was, too.

"You're going to have to help me," she said. "I can't carry you."

"No piggyback ride?"

"Not unless you . . ." She shook her head. "No. No piggyback ride."

She steadied her arm around him and edged him to the stairs, then took his right hand and planted it on the rail. He glanced at her. "You'll catch me if I fall backward?"

"I'll get out of your way."

"Heartless."

"Practical. We'd both stand a better chance of not getting hurt."

He looked up the steep, narrow stairs and grimaced. "Sure you can't carry me?"

"Positive." Charlotte smiled with understanding. "Might as well be the last few yards climbing Everest, huh?"

"But it's not. It's a set of stairs in an English pub."

"This is true."

He made no comment. As he started up the stairs, she eased her arm from around him and placed her hand on his hip, obviously hoping that would help stabilize him. "Are you sure you can manage?" she asked him.

"Absolutely. I can do stairs."

He faltered only once but Charlotte didn't have to intervene. When they reached the second floor, he grinned at her. "Are you sorry I didn't fall backward and get tangled up with you?"

"No."

Her brown eyes were enough to melt him. His grin broadened. "I bet you're not as cool and heartless as you're making out right now."

"Let's just get you to bed."

"Sounds like a plan."

"You know what I mean, Agent Rawlings," she said, starchy.

"Brody and Heather have gone to the wedding hotel. I'm at your mercy. Brody would have left me under the booth. Nowhere near as fun as having you put me to bed."

She sighed. "What's your room number?"

"Crisp and efficient, aren't you, Charlotte Bennett?" He pointed vaguely. "It's the second door on the right."

"Key?"

"I can manage the key."

"Actually, I'm not sure you can, and I suspect you aren't sure, either."

He decided he must look even worse than he felt. He reached into his jacket for the old-fashioned key and handed it to her. She nudged him down the hall, but he was more awake, or at least more alert. Maybe it was having a wall next to him should he collapse, or maybe mounting the stairs had perked him up. Whatever the case, they arrived at his door without incident.

"Where's your room?" he asked her.

"Down the hall."

"Do we have connecting doors?"

"No. There's a room between us."

"Ah."

"I don't know if you're teasing or just

34

making small talk in an awkward situation, but it doesn't matter. Two seconds and you'll be in your room and can get some rest before tomorrow. I don't want you to make a scene."

She shoved his key in the lock. One try and she had the door open.

"Efficient," Greg said.

She tucked the key into his jacket pocket and held the door open. "In you go, Agent Rawlings."

"Greg. Gregory is fine, too. So is Agent Rawlings, but it's too formal now that you're in my hotel room."

"I'm not in your hotel room."

"Right. It's a pub that lets rooms. It's not a real hotel or even a B and B or an inn."

"I'm not in your room, period."

He felt a wave of fatigue and forced himself to stay upright. He attempted a grin. "You're not going to make sure I get to bed without collapsing?"

"Tell you what," she said. "I'll wait outside the door, and if I hear a thud and think you hit your head or otherwise hurt yourself, I'll call for an ambulance."

Greg stood straight, leveling his gaze on her. "I'll be fine, Charlotte. I'm not sick or drunk. Thanks for your help."

The pink returned to her cheeks. "You're

exhausted," she said finally. "Get some sleep. See you at the wedding."

"How's your maid-of-honor dress?"

She ignored him and left, shutting the door quickly — not in his face but it was close.

Greg managed to make it to the bed before he collapsed.

No thud for Charlotte to call backup.

Charlotte didn't breathe normally again until she reached her room, shut the door and kicked off her shoes. She didn't know how she'd made it up the stairs in them. Her feet *ached*. Adrenaline had undoubtedly helped keep her from feeling any pain.

She stared at the locked door next to the closet door. She'd lied. Her room did adjoin Greg's room, and it did have a connecting door — inaccessible by either one of them without the key. There'd been no point in telling him and getting his imagination fired up. He needed sleep, and so did she, if for different reasons.

Her room was adorable, decorated with warm fabrics and simple furnishings. A small window looked out on the village street, dark and quiet now. She didn't hear any noise from the pub below her. She supposed the barman would have dealt with

Greg if she'd left him in the booth. Presumably, she'd see him at the wedding tomorrow, and then that would be that. They'd be on their separate ways.

She peeled off her dress. Her maid-of-honor dress was at the wedding hotel. She appreciated Samantha's asking her to be her maid of honor and didn't regret saying yes — but she'd come close to saying no. Unsaid between them had been the reasons why. "You're who I want as my maid of honor, Charlotte," Samantha had told her. "You're as close to a sister as I have, and you're my best friend, but I'll understand if you just want to be a guest."

"Thank you, Sam. I'm honored. I'd love to be your maid of honor."

Charlotte had meant every word, but she also knew it wouldn't be easy to walk down that aisle tomorrow without memories bubbling up. She'd just have to work at stifling them. It wasn't her wedding. It was Samantha and Justin's wedding, and Charlotte wanted to do her part to make it a wonderful day for them.

She washed up, slipped into her nightgown and crawled under the cozy duvet in the double bed. She listened, but she didn't hear anything from the adjoining room. Greg Rawlings was similar to other alpha types she knew in her work. While she appreciated the training and dedication that no doubt went into his job as a DS agent, she was well aware that even tough guys bled, got sick and messed up. The problem wasn't that she wanted to believe they were indestructible. *They* wanted to believe it.

She shut her eyes, giving in to her own fatigue. Even after her long day, she had no sign of a headache.

Progress.

But she didn't want to make too much of it, and she knew getting rid of her headaches didn't mean she'd ever dive again.

She put that thought out of her mind and pictured Greg instead, half-asleep, genuinely exhausted and yet still capable of teasing — and, no doubt, of getting himself to his room.

She put him out of her mind, too. She'd done her bit for him, but Greg Rawlings was a fit, capable man.

The Diplomatic Security agent in the next room wasn't her problem.

Two

Greg managed to take a shower, pull on jeans and a sweatshirt, and tie on a pair of running shoes when he woke up at oh dark thirty. He'd been wiped out when he'd arrived in London yesterday. Mop-the-floor-with-him exhausted after months of non-stop, high-intensity, high-stress work. Not an excuse for passing out in an English pub, but no harm, no foul.

As he started down the steep stairs, he remembered more of his encounter with Charlotte Bennett last night than he wanted to remember.

"Should have had more to drink."

Breakfast was set up in the same room as last night's party. Eric Sloan, a police officer and the eldest of the Sloan siblings, invited Greg to join him. Greg had met him briefly in February. Eric resembled the rest of the Sloans: dark haired, blue eyed, strong. Straightforward. Another Sloan trait. It was still the middle of the night back home in New England, but Eric looked wide-awake. Probably used to odd hours. He, too, had on jeans and a sweatshirt.

Greg sat at Eric's table by a partially open window, exchanged a couple of pleasantries, ordered coffee and then got up again and went to the cold buffet table.

He returned with Weetabix and cut fruit. "I've never had Weetabix," he said. "Have you?"

Eric shrugged. "It's like Shredded Wheat?"

"Sort of. I think it's one of those things you can do anything with. Add fruit, peanut butter, cream cheese, hot milk, cold milk. Probably can make tacos out of it."

Eric didn't look amused or interested. He had coffee. Black. Nothing to eat yet.

"Brody and Heather made it back to the wedding hotel?" Greg asked.

"As far as I know. Just my brother Christopher and I are here. The rest of my family's at the hotel, too."

"Christopher's the full-time firefighter?"

"Yes. The youngest brother. Justin's a volunteer firefighter." Eric drank some of his coffee. "I skipped the buffet. Just having the hot breakfast."

"There's a hot breakfast?"

A slight smile. "You aren't restricted to

40

Weetabix."

Suddenly starving, Greg ordered a full English breakfast minus the black pudding. He wondered if Charlotte would be down for breakfast before leaving for the wedding. Since she'd come in from Scotland, she was on the same time as the Cotswolds and wouldn't be jet-lagged. Early riser? Late riser? He gave himself a mental shake. Last night was *over.* Time to behave.

"You'll enjoy staying at the inn for a bit," Eric said.

Greg tore open his Weetabix. What inn? Had he zoned out and missed something? He dumped the two biscuit-like triangles into his bowl. "I have some time before I need to be in DC for my new assignment," he said, neutral.

"Great," Eric said. "Brody says you like to camp. You can pitch a tent out back if you want. The inn could have bats."

Bats. Still clueless, Greg added some of his cut fruit to the Weetabix. "Good location?"

"It's within walking distance of the village but feels more remote."

Okay, getting some specifics. This village? Another village in the Cotswolds? Was this mystery inn located in England? Was staying there Brody and Heather's idea? Greg

41

was stumped. He had no memory of discussing an inn, with or without bats, with anyone, ever.

"It has an open field on one side," Eric added. "Makes sense given its name."

The waiter set a coffee press on the table as Greg poured cold milk over his fruit and Weetabix. Maybe he should have waited and had some coffee before going to the cold-buffet table. "I don't remember the name of the inn . . ."

"Red Clover Inn."

"Cute name," Greg said, desperate now. What had he done? He cleared his throat. "Homey sound to it."

"Justin and Samantha want to keep the name. I don't care one way or the other. It sounds more like it should be out in the country rather than a half mile from the village. We bought it on a whim. The owner died without a proper will and there was a family squabble. It took some time to get sorted out. They couldn't wait to sell the place."

The Sloans hadn't struck Eric as people who did things on a whim, but Heather Sloan had married Brody after a short romance and now Justin Sloan was marrying Samantha Bennett after meeting her in a fire last fall when she'd slipped into

Knights Bridge in search of pirate treasure.

People who knew their own minds, maybe.

But . . . wait . . . the Sloans owned this inn?

Greg poured his coffee and set the press down. He was an elite federal agent who protected ambassadors and other dignitaries in and outside the United States, and he damn well could figure out that Eric was talking about Knights Bridge, his hometown in rural New England, about two hours west of Boston. Greg hadn't expected to return to Knights Bridge except maybe to visit Heather and Brody when they built their place on the lake where Brody had grown up. And that was a big maybe.

Greg tried the Weetabix. It was fine. Good, in fact. "Definitely waited too long to give this stuff a try." He was buying time. Given Eric's narrowed eyes, Greg suspected the guy's cop instincts had clicked into gear. He ate more of his cereal. Hard to look suspicious eating cereal. "The fruit helps. The inn sounds like a great family project."

"We'll see. It's a regular country inn. Or it was. It hasn't been anything for a while."

Glad his mouth was full and he didn't have to respond, Greg waited for Eric to head to the cold-buffet table. He got out his phone and surreptitiously texted Brody.

I'm staying at an inn in KB?

Brody's answer came right away. Yes.
Greg grimaced. Why?

You're at a loose end. You're looking after the
place.

How long?

While Justin and Sam are on their
honeymoon.

A week?

Maybe two.

When did I agree to this?

Text last night after I got back to my hotel.

I was asleep.

Ha.

Greg drank some of his coffee. His head was going to explode. He didn't want to mess up anyone's honeymoon, but he'd obviously been impaired when he'd agreed to this mission, or whatever it was. He typed again: Animals?

Bats, mice, spiders. No pets or farm animals.

That meant no cat or dog or pet gerbil to look after, just the place itself, which presumably had been uninhabited for a few years and would be fine without him playing caretaker. He could bow out. Two or three days, never mind longer, next to a field of clover — there had to be clover, right, considering the inn's name? — would send him over the bend. He didn't do well sitting still.

He had time to come up with a face-saving excuse and ease out of this thing.

Eric returned to the table with fresh fruit. Their hot breakfasts arrived. Greg dove in. Weetabix would do but even better was a plate of fried eggs, grilled mushrooms and tomatoes, sausages, bacon, fried bread and baked beans. Even with wedding food in his near future, he figured stoking up now was a good idea. He needed his full faculties. Fatigue and a slight hangover wouldn't help him work out how to get out of this Red Clover Inn deal without pissing off a bunch of Sloans, not to mention his friend Brody.

Christopher Sloan joined them. He, too, seemed to Greg like a solid sort. He'd come to England alone for his older brother's wedding. The Sloans had struck Greg as a tight-knit lot. That didn't mean there weren't occasional tensions between them.

He didn't bring up Red Clover Inn and instead asked Christopher his plans while in England.

"I got here last weekend," Christopher said. "I had a great time. Good break. I go home tomorrow. Have to be back at work on Monday."

Eric was also headed back tomorrow. Greg relaxed. There'd be enough Sloans around to look after this old inn of theirs. They didn't need him.

After breakfast, he went up to his room.

He glanced down the hall but Charlotte's door was shut tight. He knew she'd lied about staying down the hall. He'd heard her going into the room adjoining his. In her place, he probably would have lied, too, what with his behavior last night.

He'd been tired as hell, and in a mood.

Had she ever been to Knights Bridge now that her cousin was making her home there, marrying a local?

"None of your business, pal," Greg muttered, going into his room.

He could bolt. No one would miss him at the wedding. He'd been invited only because he'd made a stop in England to see Brody and Heather on his roundabout way to Washington.

But as he debated grabbing a cab and fleeing the Sloans and Bennetts, he got dressed for an English country wedding.

The wedding hotel was charming, located a few miles from the village in the rolling Cotswold countryside. The informal ceremony was held outdoors in a garden brimming with roses, which Greg recognized, and climbing purple flowers he assumed were the wisteria. Samantha Bennett wore a gown designed by Alexandra Rankin Hunt, Ian Mabry's fiancée. They were guests at the wedding. Alexandra, an elegant, attractive woman, had her own tangled ties to Knights Bridge through her great-grandfather, an RAF pilot who'd ventured to rural Massachusetts on the eve of World War II. He'd fallen in love with a young American woman, now in her nineties and living in little Knights Bridge. He'd meant to come back for her but had been killed over the English Channel early in the war. Greg didn't have all the details. Brody had tried to explain a few of the connections of his hometown as he and Greg had found a place to stand for the short wedding service.

Greg might have felt out of place at the simple but elegant wedding, but he wasn't the type. He appreciated rugged Justin Sloan's love for Samantha and, likewise, his awkward pleasure at expressing that love in front of his family and friends. Greg thought back to his own wedding. He and Laura had been young, filled with hopes and dreams.

I'm seeing a great guy here in Minneapolis. I wanted you to know.

Laura, a couple of weeks ago. Their divorce had been finalized months ago and Greg was glad she was getting on with her life. No problem there. The problem was his own life. Getting wounded in an ambush on the job and its isolating nature hadn't

48

helped him with his personal life, but the biggest issue, he knew, was inertia. Laura had always been there. He'd taken their life together for granted. He didn't want to make that same mistake again.

After the service, he noticed Charlotte Bennett laughing with the bride and groom. Her maid-of-honor dress was a deep coral, its cut perfect for her curves. She didn't look as cool and judgmental as she had last night. The warm color of her dress and the lush late-spring garden setting probably softened her hard edges. According to Brody, her parents were in Australia on an underwater salvage project and couldn't make it to the wedding.

Interesting family, the Bennetts.

Greg congratulated the happy couple and found his way to the bar.

A beer, a table in the shade, a breeze stirring in a trellis of peach-colored roses — despite not having a woman at his side, his life, he decided, was pretty good. At least right now, at this moment. He felt some of the weariness and rawness of the past months lift. He was able to focus on his surroundings without being poised for threats. Instead he could sit back and enjoy the beauty of the place. Warm-pink roses in addition to the peach-colored ones, bumblebees, pots of herbs and flowers. Nice. Damn nice, in fact.

He observed Charlotte as she greeted guests and relatives. She struck him as a woman who preferred to be here, at her cousin's wedding, alone. Her body language said loud and clear she didn't want or need a man on her arm. Was she getting over a relationship? Thinking about sunken U-boats? Greg knew better than to speculate but figured there was no real harm in it while he was drinking a beer and smelling the roses.

Brody joined him. "You look awake and sober."

"I was awake and sober when you saw me last night."

"Sober, maybe." Brody pulled out a chair and sat down, loosening his tie. "Great wedding. Heather says she doesn't regret that we didn't have a more formal wedding."

"She'd tell you if she did," Greg said, noticing Heather making her way toward them.

"True," Brody said. "Sloans don't hold back their opinions."

"You wouldn't have it any other way."

"Also true. When do you head to Knights Bridge?"

"Haven't figured that out. I haven't even

decided on my flight out of here. Probably Monday but I could leave tomorrow. I don't have anything I need to do in London. Do you know this Red Clover Inn?"

"I remember it from when I was a kid. Quiet place. It did a good business with fishermen and graduations at local colleges. Do you fish, Greg?"

"No."

"Lots of rivers, streams and lakes in the area, and the reservoir allows fishing."

"Great. I'll keep that in mind if I get bored."

"You'll get bored," Brody said with a grin.

"I'm not staying two weeks. There are plenty of Sloans who can look after the inn. I like that I can help out but I figure my bleary eyes last night at the party are half the reason the idea came up."

"You always have bleary eyes these days, Greg."

"Point taken."

"You could use the break."

"I guess. Anyway, I need to see my kids. They've got stuff going on this summer. It's not like when they were little." He drank some of his beer. He could hear a bee humming in the roses. "Maybe I'll invite them out to Knights Bridge before their summer gets crazy. We can pop down and do a few days in DC, too. See the sights there. There aren't any sights in Knights Bridge."

"Rivers, streams, lakes and a reservoir."

"So you said."

Brody stretched out his legs, drank some of his beer. He, too, seemed to be enjoying the bucolic setting. "You all could tour Emily Dickinson's old house in Amherst. You read her in high school, right? Nineteenth-century poet. Historic Old Deerfield and Old Sturbridge aren't far."

"*Old* being the operative word here. Make a list. We'll see."

"It can feel like time stopped in Knights Bridge," Brody said.

"But it hasn't. It marches on there just like everywhere else. Can't stop the clock."

"Cheer up. Hell, Greg. It's a wedding."

"What? I am cheerful."

Brody just shook his head. Greg followed his friend's gaze to Heather, who kept stopping to greet other guests. Finally she made it to their table and sat next to Brody, grabbing his hand. "What a great day," she said.

Eric Sloan, the best man, stood to toast the bride and groom, followed by the maid of honor, neither of whom let anyone's champagne get warm. Succinct was fine with Greg but he was intrigued watching Charlotte address the gathering with such

52

poise and graciousness. Not exactly his experience with her. He could hear her laugh of affection and delight when she hugged her cousin after the toast. Maybe he'd been a bigger jerk last night than he'd realized and he'd misjudged her.

"Got what you deserved, my friend," he said under his breath.

A few minutes after the toast, Charlotte made her way over to his table. It was fun watching her move. He could see she was fit, but he'd had an up-close-and-personal taste of just how fit last night. All that diving had worked wonders.

She didn't sit. She greeted Brody and Heather warmly, then turned to Greg. "I see you made it to the wedding."

"Wouldn't miss it. You ever come eye to eye with sharks while you were diving?"

"I beg your pardon?"

He pointed his champagne glass at her. "I bet you could take on a shark. You're in good shape. Into CrossFit? I know some guys who are. It's smart to stay in shape when you dive for sunken treasure for a living. You never know what you'll run across underwater."

"I don't dive for sunken treasure."

"Right. You're a serious scholar. Not going to tell me about sharks?"

She touched a fingertip to a rosebud. "We're at a wedding, Agent Rawlings."

"So we are." But his inappropriateness didn't fully explain the sudden strain in her voice. He'd struck a nerve. He changed the subject. "Are the younger bridesmaids your cousins, too?"

"Ann and Eloisa, yes. They're the two youngest of Caleb Bennett's four children. He's Harry's younger son. He's a professor of maritime history and his wife's a rare-books specialist. They live in London. Samantha and I are closer in age than she is to her first cousins. We have similar interests."

"Cool."

"I went on too long?"

"No. I should have said more in response?"

"You seem bored."

Greg shook his head. "Not bored. You're here on your own, right?"

"What? I just explained I have family here."

"I meant a guy. A date. Didn't it say 'Charlotte Bennett plus guest' on your invitation?"

She frowned. "You're direct."

"I like to be clear."

"Mm. That must be it." She sounded

dubious. "Yes, I'm on my own."

"Why don't you sit down, have a beer with us?"

She glanced at Brody and Heather, who were chatting with Adam, the stonemason Sloan brother. She turned back to Greg and shook her head. "Thanks but I've had champagne already."

"Back to Edinburgh soon?"

"I haven't decided. As I mentioned, I worked with Sam's parents on a project to discover and explore sunken World War II submarines off the British coast, but it's wrapped up. I'm not under any pressure to get back to Edinburgh."

"What's next?" Greg asked.

"We'll see."

"Who's we?"

"A figure of speech, Agent Rawlings. Did you get a good night's sleep?"

Dodging him or just making small talk? He shrugged. "Perfect. I sleep fine when I sleep."

"That makes no sense."

"Does to me. How'd you do? No tossing and turning after putting me to bed?"

"No tossing and turning."

Brody shifted in his chair and frowned at Greg, who ignored him and studied Charlotte instead. She wasn't telling the truth but the makeup job for the wedding would have dealt with any obvious signs he could point out to her of a bad night. He let it go.

He set his glass on the table. "Samantha and Justin are an unusual pair. Think they'll be together in five years?"

Charlotte looked as if she wanted to throttle him. "You don't say such things at a wedding, you know."

"Okay."

She narrowed her gaze. "I see that you're on your own, too."

"I was shoehorned onto the guest list when I turned up in London."

"I see." Charlotte straightened. "I hope you enjoy yourself."

Greg watched her weave back through the tables to the Bennett family. She seemed to have an easy relationship with Samantha's parents and her uncle and aunt and their four kids, the eldest of whom, Isaac, was, according to Heather, starting at Amherst College that fall. It wasn't far from Knights Bridge and it was Harry Bennett's alma mater. Greg wondered exactly what Max Bennett, Charlotte's grandfather, had done with himself. Packed Harry's adventurer bags for him?

"My last family wedding, my sister threw up in the men's room," Greg said, address-

56

ing Brody, who had hardly touched his champagne. "I cleaned up after her since it was her first drinking offense, at least that I knew about. She's a piano teacher in Manhattan."

"Whose wedding was it?" Brody asked.

"My cousin Johnny. Three, four years ago. He's a paramedic. Wife's a nurse. They have a toddler — a little boy — and another baby on the way. They're living the life my mother wanted me to live."

"You have two kids."

"Yeah. I do. I didn't stay within ten blocks of her, though."

"Instead you're living the life you wanted to live."

"Made my choices." Greg's gaze landed on a trio of Bennetts up by another trellis of roses. "Think Charlotte is in a champagne-and-dancing mood or a wallflower mood?"

"Only two options?"

"She looks uncomfortable. Something's bugging her."

"There's what you know, and there's what you think you know," Brody said. "That's something you think you know."

"Nope. I know."

"She told you?"

"Didn't have to."

"Greg . . ."

He waved a hand. "Forget it. Let's eat."

"Weddings are for champagne and dancing," Charlotte said after the lunch dishes were cleared and she'd made her way to Greg's table. Her comment caught him by surprise. She smiled, obviously relishing that fact. "Do you dance, Agent Rawlings?"

"If I have to. Is that an invitation?"

Her brown eyes sparked. "Well, why not? You don't have to dance with me. There aren't many unattached guests but I can get my cousin Isaac —"

"Can't let you dance with your cousin."

Greg was on his feet. Brody's eyebrows went up. "I don't think I've ever seen you dance, Greg."

"It's been a while but it's like riding a bike." He slipped an arm around Charlotte's waist and turned to her. "Don't worry. I won't step on your feet."

"I might step on yours," she said.

Greg eased Charlotte onto the makeshift dance floor on the garden terrace. "I don't know about this prissy Jane Austen music they're playing," he said.

"At least you don't have to wear tights."

"You'd like that, wouldn't you? All us guys in tights."

"Not if I had to wear a Regency gown."

"You look fine in your maid-of-honor dress," he said, feeling the soft fabric under his hands.

"Alexandra's an incredible designer."

"Want to kick off your shoes and pretend we're on *Dancing with the Stars*?"

"What?'

Next to them, dancing with her new husband, Samantha laughed. "She has no idea, Greg. She doesn't watch much television."

Neither did he. Finally something they had in common, even if he had heard of *Dancing with the Stars.*

The harpsichord music or whatever it was ended and switched to rock — or something. It wasn't loud, but Greg could make out a beat and that worked for him. He didn't recognize the song playing but Charlotte looked as if she didn't, either.

"I love to dance," she said. "I don't get much opportunity. I've never had a lesson. I really might step on your feet."

"Just follow my lead," he said.

"You've had lessons?"

"My grandmother insisted. I did lessons at Lady Bella's Ballroom Dancing School when I was twelve."

"Torture?"

"Getting shot was nothing in comparison."

He felt her stiffen. "Don't make jokes about such a thing."

"Only way to get through it. For me, anyway."

And that was all they had a chance to say. He had to concentrate or he'd bump into someone or trip over his own feet trying to avoid hers, and the music, the atmosphere — everything was great. Pretty, uptight Charlotte Bennett didn't exactly loosen up, but she was smart and fit and seemed to enjoy herself.

"Woo-hoo," Brody, hopelessly obnoxious, shouted from his table. "Go, Greg."

Charlotte flushed, whether from the attention or exertion, Greg couldn't tell. "Ignore him," he said in a low voice.

But the Bennetts noticed she was dancing and gave way, creating a semicircle around her and Greg. In another moment, they had the dance floor to themselves. Samantha was clapping. "You go, Charlotte!"

"Families" was all she said, with a slight smile.

It took some work but Greg, remembering his instructions from back in the day, took a firm lead, getting her to focus on him and not their audience. He had no trouble focusing on her. Nothing to do with dance lessons, either.

When the song ended, everyone clapped. Charlotte laughed, waving to her family, taking a slight bow. "Thank Greg for keeping me on my feet."

"Thank you, Greg," the young Bennett cousins chimed in unison.

He kissed Charlotte on the cheek. "*Dancing with the Stars* is next for you. Look it up."

Another song started, and she smiled. "One dance was plenty for me in these shoes."

"Told you to kick them off."

"I will should I ever dance again in this lifetime. It was fun. Was it fun for you, too?"

"More fun than a 10K run in the desert for sure. I resisted looking down your dress and patting your butt, seeing how your family was watching."

She sighed. "Good of you."

"I know deep down you're disappointed. Rest assured that I was tempted, but I'm a man of great discipline and control."

"As evidenced last night when you passed out in the pub."

"I fell asleep. There's a difference. More fun to dance than to explore sunken wrecks?"

"That's my work."

"And your work is your life, isn't it?"

She didn't answer and instead excused herself to go in search of strawberries and chocolate. Greg headed back to his table. Brody didn't make a smart remark, even without Heather having a hand over his mouth to keep it shut. "Nice job," he said when Greg sat down. "Top agent and a top dancer."

"You're always full of surprises," Heather said. "Samantha mentioned that Charlotte's heading home to the US for a bit and plans to stay at the old inn my family is renovating. Justin and Samantha are in the process of moving in from the cabin where they've been staying. It'll be good to have someone look after the place while they're on their honeymoon. Charlotte will be on her own. A good chunk of my family's staying in England to see the sights, but I'm sure she'll find ways to amuse herself. I gather she's been working nonstop for months."

Brody's eyes narrowed on Greg. "Have you backed out of going?"

"Nope. Knights Bridge sounds good. Better and better."

His friend's gaze darkened. "Greg . . ."

"Relax. I'll behave."

Heather frowned. "What are you two talking about? Did I miss something?"

"Not a thing," Greg said.

"I'll explain later," Brody said. "Let's go find your nephews before they tear up the place."

Greg wandered to the outdoor bar. He was ordering a beer when two buff men in their midthirties arrived. They weren't wedding guests. They greeted Samantha and Justin, apparently wishing them well, and then spoke for a few minutes with Malcolm and Francesca Bennett, Samantha's parents. As they started out, the taller one, a serious stud of a guy, shot Charlotte a scathing look. She went deadly pale. Ten seconds ago, Greg would have said it was impossible. The Bennetts were all watching her and the guy, as if they were holding their breath for something to erupt between them.

Then it was over. The two men left without incident.

Greg, trained to observe a crowd, wasn't sure how many people noticed the tension between Charlotte and the drop-ins. Brody Hancock and Eric Sloan probably would have if they'd been paying attention.

Pint in hand, Greg eased next to Isaac, the Amherst-bound Bennett. "The swaggering studs," Greg said. "Who were they?"

Isaac grinned. "They did swagger, didn't they? They're contract divers. They did a few dives on the submarine project with Uncle Malcolm and Aunt Francesca. The tall one with the dark hair is Tommy Ferguson. I don't know the other guy's name."

"How do you know Ferguson?"

"He's the SOB who left Charlotte at the altar. No, wait. It's the other way around. She left him at the altar."

"When was this?" Greg asked.

"Last spring. I think it was spring. I was still in school. My junior year. So it's over a year ago now."

Greg took a drink of his beer. Well, this was interesting. "Our boy Tommy was in his tux, waiting for his bride-to-be to walk down the aisle, and she bolted?"

"She never showed up. It's okay. They both say it wasn't meant to be. Tommy's over it."

Tommy didn't look over it, but Greg let Isaac return to the wedding festivities. He wandered back to his table. People were starting to make their goodbyes. Heather and Brody were going back to London. Greg didn't know how many Sloans were showing up at their apartment. He'd stay at the pub again tonight. Then what?

Rural New England. The Red Clover Inn.

Bats, mice.

One Charlotte Bennett.

Time to book his flight. A few days in little Knights Bridge could be fun after all.

THREE

Charlotte stood by the window in Samantha's room on the second floor of the hotel, overlooking the garden terrace where the wedding ceremony and reception had taken place a few hours ago. It was back to normal now, extra tables put away, tablecloths and decorations gone, wedding vases exchanged for pots of herbs. Samantha had changed out of her wedding dress into comfy travel clothes. Charlotte had switched her maid-of-honor dress for jeans and a sweater.

"The front-door key is hanging on a hook by the socket for the hose," Samantha said as she tossed clothes into a suitcase open on the bed. "You can't miss it. Neither could a thief, but thieves aren't interested in Red Clover Inn. It's not a dump, I promise. It's just that it doesn't look as if it holds anything of value."

"No pirate treasure tucked in the attic?"

"I wish. The quarreling heirs to the last

owner would have discovered and claimed anything of value before they sold the place. Not that I blame them. Justin and I are moving our stuff into the innkeeper's suite on the main floor. We'll live there during renovations. We can't wait to get started, but we got a bit ahead of ourselves with our work schedules and the wedding."

"Totally understandable," Charlotte said.

"We'll have more time when we're back home. Are you sure you want to house-sit?"

"I am. I wouldn't have offered if I wasn't sure."

Samantha walked over to the closet. "Weddings can do funny things to people's heads."

"Especially my head," Charlotte said.

Her cousin looked horrified. "I didn't mean that! Charlotte . . ."

She smiled. "It's okay. Imagine if you'd bolted today. We Bennett women would have had a tough reputation to live down when it comes to weddings. But you had the right guy waiting for you. I'm really happy for you, Samantha. Don't spend half a second worrying about me. It'll be fun to stay at your inn for a few days. Then I can head to Washington and sort out Max's house. The last renters moved out in May. I need to decide what to do."

"Time to fix it up or sell it?"

"Or both."

"I miss Max and Harry," Samantha said simply. She pulled a top out of the closet, rolled it up and placed it in the suitcase. "You can let us know about any quirks or issues you discover at the inn. We've cleaned up the place and put fresh sheets and towels out in a few of the rooms in case family or friends want to stay, but nothing formal. Mostly we were just getting a feel for the place. We can manage without someone there — there's no dog to walk or anything and we have family in town — so no problem if you change your mind."

Charlotte moved away from the window. "It sounds like a great place to unwind."

"I can't wait for us to be in Knights Bridge together."

"It'll happen, probably sooner rather than later. Don't worry about a thing, okay? Your wedding was the best, Sam. I'm glad I was a part of it. Thank you."

"It was everything I wanted it to be."

"That's fantastic. I imagine you're ready for your honeymoon now."

Samantha laughed. "Definitely. I'm so happy, Charlotte. I didn't think it was possible to be this happy. Justin and I are perfect together. Harry always said I'd end up with someone who surprised me."

"He and Max would have enjoyed today," Charlotte said, no question in her mind.

"Harry wouldn't have believed the good weather. He always said it rained all day, every day whenever he was in London."

"He had a gift for hyperbole."

"No kidding." Samantha shut her suitcase. "I didn't realize Tommy would stop by today. Mom and Dad didn't, either. They saw him a few weeks ago. He'd heard I was getting married. They're so polite — they'd never tell him to stay away. I hope it wasn't too awkward for you."

"No problem. We both moved on within four seconds of our wedding that wasn't."

"Just as well." Samantha reached into a small bag on the dresser and withdrew a set of keys. "Here are the keys to Harry's house in Boston in case you want to stay there or just have a look around. Feel free to use his car. We like to run it periodically. My folks and Uncle Caleb are still figuring out what to do with it and the house but might as well enjoy them for now."

"I shall seize the moment," Charlotte said lightly. "Leave Red Clover Inn to me. Relax and enjoy your honeymoon."

"Ten days in Scotland. Justin's never been. He'll love it. We leave tonight to get a head start on the drive north."

And no doubt to get away from lingering guests — including a slew of Sloans. As much as she and Justin loved their family and friends, it was time for each other. "We'll have that get-together soon," Charlotte said, hugging her cousin. "Have a great time on your honeymoon."

She left Samantha to her packing. She ran into Justin in the lobby. He'd changed out of his tux and was as eager to be on his way to Scotland as Samantha was. "I won't keep you," Charlotte said cheerfully.

Isaac gave her a ride back to the pub. He was bussing tables at a London restaurant for the summer, before heading to New England for college. He hadn't decided on a major — except that it wouldn't be in maritime anything. "Sorry," he said. "Whatever I end up doing, it won't have anything to do with sunken wrecks. I'm not a big fan of the water."

"Don't be sorry. It's good to keep your options open at your age."

"Did you always want to be a marine archaeologist?"

"A diver," she said. "I always wanted to be a diver and explore what's under the ocean."

He shuddered as he pulled to a stop in

front of the pub. "I'd stay up in my warm ship and let a mini submarine or a robot do the exploring."

Charlotte laughed. "You always were a smart kid. It's still hard for me to believe you're old enough to drive, and now you're off to college. Stay in touch, okay?"

"You, too."

As she headed into the pub, she noticed the sky had turned grayer, rain likely on the way. She'd checked out of her room before she'd left for the wedding but hadn't taken her bag. Now that she was alone, she wanted to have a pint and lick her wounds. *Tommy.* What had she ever seen in him? A whirlwind romance, a brief engagement, a slapped-together wedding . . . and cold feet.

Not cold feet. She'd come to her senses.

She sat at the bar and ordered a beer. She had a few minutes before she had to get herself to the train station. She'd be back in Edinburgh tonight and would figure out when she would leave for Boston. Right now, the sooner the better worked for her, but she'd wait until she got home to decide. Samantha hadn't had a single photo of Red Clover Inn, but she'd given Charlotte directions.

She hadn't expected to see Tommy today. She knew Malcolm and Francesca had

71

hired him for a few dives earlier in the year. Everyone had worked hard to wrap up the U-boat project, and Charlotte was a professional. She hated the idea that friends and family might feel they needed to keep her and her former fiancé apart. She didn't want them tiptoeing around her. She and Tommy were grown-ups. They could manage.

But when he walked into the pub and sat on the stool next to her at the bar, her heart sank. She didn't want today to end this way, with the man who'd once proposed to her trying to get under her skin. Because that was what Tommy did. He thrived on it.

"Well, Charlotte," he said, cocky as ever, "I see your life hasn't changed."

"Work, family, fun."

"Uptight, alone, superior." He winked at her. "Kidding."

"Right. Kidding. I have a cab coming. I don't have time to chat."

His gray eyes settled on her. Speaking of superior, she thought. "How are you?" he asked.

"Great. It was a beautiful wedding."

"Not going to ask about me?"

"As I said —"

"No time. Thought you might like to know I'm heading home to the States to take a permanent diving job in South Florida."

She pushed her beer glass aside. "Good luck."

"I heard you had a close call in April. I'm sorry."

Of course he'd heard. Theirs was a small world and Tommy had known the amateur diver she'd rescued, resulting in a dangerous bout of decompression illness that continued to haunt her. "One of those things." Her throat was tight but she didn't think her voice sounded strangled. "I really have to go."

"Things will be different for you now if you can't dive again —"

"Not your concern, Tommy."

"There's that barbed tongue." He paused, staying calm. "I'm trying to be nice. I'm a concerned colleague, a fellow diver who's had a few close calls of his own. But you can't let bygones be bygones, can you? You'd think I wronged you, when the opposite is true. You wronged me."

"You know why I did what I did. I understand that today probably stirred up hard feelings, but we've both moved on, Tommy. Don't drag me into the past with you."

"I'm not dragging you anywhere, Charlotte. Trust me."

73

She dug cash out of her bag and left it for the beer she'd ordered. She didn't look at Tommy as she jumped off the stool and reached for her suitcase at her feet.

"Here," he said, getting to his feet. "Let me get that for you. You don't want to do anything to impede your recovery. I know how much diving means to you."

"I'm fine, thanks."

He put his hand over hers on the suitcase handle. "Don't let stubbornness and pride get in the way of common sense."

She stiffened. "Let go, Tommy."

"Independent Charlotte. You don't need anyone's help, do you?"

Before she could react, Greg Rawlings materialized at her side. "Time to order a pint and relax, Tommy," Greg said in a steady, low voice.

Tommy shrugged. "Not interested in a pint." He let go of the suitcase and Charlotte's hand and smiled at her, unapologetic. "See you around, Charlotte."

Greg leaned against the bar and watched her ex-fiancé head out through the main pub door. Then he shook his head and sighed. "Nothing takes that swagger down a notch, does it?"

Charlotte rubbed her hand. "Not much."

"Did he hurt you?"

"No." She shook out her hand. "It's tension more than anything else. Thanks."

"First time you've seen him since you left him at the altar?"

"I suppose I'm not surprised you know about that. Yes. First time. Getting stood up on his wedding day didn't take his swagger down a notch, either."

"An interesting life you lead, Charlotte Bennett."

"It's a Bennett rule. Can't be boring. Are you heading back to London?"

"I'll hang out here another night. I don't know about London. Heather and Brody are expecting an assortment of Sloans in to see the sights." He sat on her vacated stool. "I assume that's your suitcase and you're leaving."

"I'm taking a late train to Edinburgh."

"Guess I'll have to put myself to bed tonight."

Charlotte smiled. "I have a feeling you'll manage just fine. When do you have to be back at work?"

"I'm starting a new position. No firm start date."

"Can you say where it is?"

"Washington. DSS Command Center."

She waited for him to elaborate but he didn't. "My grandparents' house is in the

DC area. Well, it's my house now that they're gone. I rent it out. Max loved living in the city but I think my grandmother missed New Hampshire. They both grew up there." Charlotte waved a hand. "I'm talking too much. Today was my first wedding since Tommy and I . . ." She took a deep breath. "Have you ever been posted in London?"

Greg didn't answer at once, looking at her as if he wanted to say something besides what he knew he would end up saying. "I worked in London for two years when my kids were small. It was good. I haven't always been able to have my family with me."

"Your family —"

"Andrew is fifteen and Megan is thirteen. Laura — my ex — and I had an amicable divorce. We got married young, had a couple of kids and drifted apart given my job and life in general. We're okay with each other and we share two great kids. That's it."

"Your life in a tidy paragraph?"

"Yep."

It was how Greg Rawlings thought, Charlotte realized. He didn't dwell on details and things he couldn't control. "Tommy and I wouldn't have had an amicable divorce," she said lightly.

"You figured him out in the nick of time."

"Yes, I did. Tommy Ferguson was never going to be the love of my life."

"Is that what you want, someone who'll be the love of your life?"

"Don't we all?" She took in a sharp breath. "I must have had too much champagne at the wedding. I'm saying too much. I need to get going or I'll miss my train."

"No problem," Greg said. "If I can't manage to get myself up to my room without you, I'll just sleep in a booth."

"You aren't embarrassed about last night, are you?"

"Should I be?"

Charlotte laughed, shaking her head. "Sometimes I wish I could be as oblivious as you are at least pretending to be right now. Thanks for intervening with Tommy. He wouldn't have gone too far, and I'd have handled him if he'd tried, but I appreciate the help."

"You could have flipped him on his ass?"

"More likely I'd have called the barman."

"Smarter, I guess. Not as much fun."

"You're an interesting man, Agent Rawlings. Best of luck with whatever's next for you."

She lifted her bag and started out the door, glancing back at Greg Rawlings, trying to ignore a pang of regret that she wouldn't see him again. She couldn't explain it but it was there. Maybe he'd find a way? Maybe he was feeling the same thing?

What was she thinking?

Fortunately, her cab was waiting. Next stop was the Oxford train station. She'd be in Edinburgh tonight and on her way to Boston and Knights Bridge in a day or two.

Samantha and Justin were a special, wonderful couple, but Charlotte's opinion of weddings hadn't changed in the past twenty-four hours.

Best to avoid them.

An hour after Charlotte left for Edinburgh, Greg stood on a footbridge on a marked trail that had taken him through the village, down a twisting lane and into woods. The wooden bridge spanned a shallow stream, the coppery water coursing over rocks and mud. He'd changed out of his wedding clothes into khakis and a polo shirt and jacket but he hadn't bothered with rain gear. Might prove to be a mistake given the darkening clouds.

He dug out his phone and called his son in Minnesota. Fifteen and he had his own phone. Not unusual these days.

"Hey, Dad," Andrew said. "What's up?

How was the wedding? Are you still in England?"

"Still in England. Wedding was good. Nice setting, great food, great people."

"Did you dance?"

Greg heard the teasing note in his son's voice. "As a matter of fact, I did."

"Wish I'd been there to see that. Did you dance by yourself or with someone?"

"I don't dance by myself. What are you up to?"

"Nothing."

"Whenever I said I wasn't up to anything as a kid, my mother handed me a broom."

His son chuckled. "Good thing you're in England, then."

"What's your sister up to?"

"Nothing much."

"I bet your mom has two brooms."

"She's not here. She's at a movie with . . ." Andrew stopped abruptly. "Never mind."

"With Richard," Greg said. "I know. I texted her earlier. I hope they're having a good time. Listen, I'm on my way to Washington via New England. What if you and Megan join me for a few days? It's okay with your mom. I have some time off before I start my new job. New England would be different. I'll be staying at a small-town inn that's being renovated."

79

"I've never been to New England," Andrew said.

"We'd have the place to ourselves. You and Megan can each have your own room."

"Sounds cool. What's there to do there?"

"Beats me."

His son laughed. "Good thing you're not a salesman, Dad."

"I was there for a few days in the winter. It's a pretty town. We can hike, go fishing — swim if you're brave since it's only June and the ice just melted."

"Ha. This the town where Ambassador Scarlatti lives?"

"Yes, it is."

Greg was impressed his son remembered the retired ambassador, a smart, interesting if also occasionally overdramatic man who owned a house on the same Knights Bridge lake where Brody Hancock had grown up. Vic had encouraged Brody to join the Diplomatic Security Service. They were the reason for Greg's wintry visit to the small New England town.

"Ambassador Scarlatti lives on a lake, doesn't he?" Andrew asked.

"Echo Lake," Greg said.

"He'd let us go swimming and kayaking?"

"Probably. Brody owns the land where he grew up. We can go out there, too."

"This is sounding better and better," his son said.

"I can teach you how to fly-fish."

"Do you know how to fly-fish?"

"Yeah. You bet." He had no idea how to fly-fish, but how hard could it be? "We could ride bikes, too. This inn must have bikes, or we can borrow some. I know people in town."

"That'd be good," Andrew said, sounding more enthusiastic.

Greg didn't mention he hadn't been on a bike in years. They chatted a few more minutes. Megan was out with friends, so Greg postponed calling her. She had her own phone, too. Laura had been amenable to them flying to Boston. He'd pick them up at the airport and they'd hang out together for a few days. Going to Minnesota himself was less and less an option. Laura needed space, and he didn't live with her anymore. The kids were old enough to come to him or he could pick them up at home and take them somewhere. No staying on the sleeper sofa. He and Laura weren't going to have that kind of postdivorce arrangement.

"Okay," Greg said. "Let's make Knights Bridge happen."

"Knights Bridge?"

81

"That's the town where we'll be staying. It's west of Boston. Look it up. It's small but it's got to be on the map." He paused. "I think."

"Great, Dad."

Greg heard the sarcasm in his son's voice and grinned. "I'll get back to you with details."

When he disconnected, Greg felt both a sense of satisfaction and a sense of loss. He wished Andrew and Megan were with him now, in the quiet English countryside. He was accustomed to being apart from his kids but that didn't mean it was easy. In some ways, they were better at dealing with his absences than he was. It was the life they knew.

He crossed the stream and continued on the dirt trail through the woods to a grassy field and finally onto a paved lane. Enjoying the quiet, the mystery of where he'd end up since he hadn't consulted a map, he followed the lane toward the village, past fenced fields dotted with sheep and a large stone farmhouse. Dusk came late this time of year. He wasn't concerned about getting caught in the dark too far out in the countryside.

Charlotte would be on her train by now. It would take five or six hours to get to

Edinburgh. Greg supposed he could have told her about his plan to head to Knights Bridge. Maybe he should have told her, considering what he'd learned about her plans, but she'd been preoccupied with her encounter with swaggering Tommy and in a hurry to get out of there.

A rationalization for his silence, maybe, but why get her worked up? Let her get home and figure out if she wanted to change her mind about Knights Bridge. Why influence her decision?

And if she *did* change her mind?

Greg tried to ignore the tug of regret he felt. He was looking forward to staying with her at the abandoned inn in the same little New England town. From what he'd gathered, there was plenty of room.

"Could be fun," he said half-aloud as the lane curved into the quaint, pretty village.

He hopped onto a low stone wall and admired the view of rolling farmland and traditional Cotswolds yellow-stone houses, breathed in the fragrant June air. He thought he smelled rain. He didn't mind. He welcomed the prospect of rain after months in a hot, dry climate.

When he reached the pub, it was filling up with locals. Greg could have gone back to London with Brody and Heather, but he was content to sit at the bar and order a beer.

Ian Mabry drew the pint himself. "You don't look as tired as you did last night," the former RAF pilot said.

"Not saying much. How's life after the military?"

"It's grand. I'm marrying the woman of my dreams and I'm back home, here, running this place. I was ready to move on to something else." He set the beer in front of Greg. "You're a Foreign Service officer, aren't you? Diplomatic Security?"

Greg nodded. "Just wrapped up an overseas assignment. I'm taking a desk in DC next."

"Not enthusiastic?"

"I never saw it coming."

Mabry grinned. "A promotion, then?"

Greg raised his beer. "You got it."

"From what I hear, you've done everything as a DS agent. You know the ropes. You have credibility." Ian Mabry looked as if he'd considered similar options in his day as an RAF pilot. "A promotion was inevitable, wasn't it?"

"That's what they say."

"You believe you can do more good staying in the field."

"It's what I know."

"You'll bring that experience to your new job."

"Does your background as a fighter pilot help with running a pub?"

"You've no idea," Mabry said with a laugh.

Greg tried his pint, savoring the first swallow after his walk. Mabry's upcoming marriage no doubt was making his transition from active duty to civilian life easier. Greg didn't have family in Washington. A handful of DSS colleagues he considered friends and a few he planned to avoid or tolerate. He'd never been good playing bureaucratic games but it wasn't that kind of desk job.

"It's a promotion, pal," he muttered. "Be happy."

He finished his beer, realized he wasn't hungry after all the wedding food and headed up to his room. As he shut the door, he heard raindrops slapping his window and then a rush of rain. He walked over to the window and opened it, welcoming the smell of the rain and the cool breeze. Rain sprayed him in the face. He smiled.

His peaceful interlude was interrupted with a text from Brody.

Back in London. You?

Chasing raindrops.

Greg?

I'm good. Quiet here. I like the rain.

Don't agree to anything else and then forget.

Will do. Hi to Heather.

She says hi back.

That was it. The check-in to make sure he wasn't dancing on the tables or passed out behind the bar. Greg understood. He'd arrived in England clinically exhausted, and he hadn't covered himself in glory with his behavior last night.

Tonight would be different. He'd read a book in his room, listen to the rain and hit the sack early — and, once again, alone.

FOUR

Edinburgh, Scotland

Charlotte awoke early given her late bed-time, walked to a tea shop near her apartment and indulged in fresh scones, jam and cream. She'd arrived home at midnight and fallen into bed, more agitated than tired. She'd slept little on the long train north, instead reading and contemplating her life — a consequence of seeing her family, being at a wedding and the long train ride itself.

And Tommy.

She added a dollop of clotted cream to her scone. He'd had some nerve showing up at the wedding and then confronting her, but he'd never been good at reading social cues. She remained convinced he'd sought her out at the pub deliberately to get under her skin. Even if it hadn't been his intent when he'd stopped at the wedding, he hadn't been able to resist the temptation.

The scene was perfect, just what she needed. The nightmare that had been her brief, volatile relationship with Tommy Ferguson was behind her, and good riddance to it. She drank some of her tea. Still no hint of a headache. If her encounter with Tommy hadn't triggered one, then maybe she was done with that particular fallout from her diving accident.

Weddings being what they were for her these days, she felt unsettled, self-conscious and slightly awkward, as if she'd done something wrong. She wasn't usually introspective. If she had to have dreams tonight, she preferred them to be about Greg Rawlings and his taut abs, but she'd thought about him enough in the past thirty-six hours.

She'd booked her flights while on the train. She'd leave tomorrow for a two-week stay in the United States. She'd arrive in and leave from Boston but could easily change her return date or departure city and absorb any penalties. In addition to spending time in Knights Bridge, she'd fit in a trip to Washington to see about Max's house. She had no firm schedule. That was new to her, but she tried to think of it as liberating rather than unnerving.

She took a meandering route back to her

New Town apartment. A Samantha Bennett–Justin Sloan kind of love wasn't in the cards for everyone. Any uncertainty she'd had about their relationship had evaporated yesterday. Unexpected and unconventional they might be, but Charlotte didn't doubt that she'd be congratulating her cousin and her husband on their anniversary for decades to come. She didn't want to believe she'd had her one chance at true love and had blown it by picking the wrong man, but she knew, deep down, that was exactly what she believed.

"Doesn't matter," she whispered to herself.

She had a good life in a beautiful city. That was what counted.

But if you can't dive, Charlotte? Then what?

She shook off the question, as she had dozens of times since April. In the months since she and Tommy had parted ways, she'd focused on her work, letting it take over her life, and now she didn't even have it, at least not in the same way. She'd spent a semester in Edinburgh as a graduate student and then returned three years ago when she started her job at the institute as a marine archaeologist and diver. The submarine project with Malcolm and Francesca Bennett had been exciting and all-consuming, and even before her accident, Charlotte had wondered what was next for her.

It had been such a *stupid* accident. A private excursion, not part of her job. If only she'd stayed home that weekend . . .

She swept her fingertips across a black iron fence, touching raindrops. Would Greg Rawlings like Edinburgh? Had he ever been here? She pictured herself walking hand in hand with him on a quiet, gray Sunday morning. It was a fun image, but she suspected her reaction to him had been sparked more by the romance in the air than anything they had in common.

Weddings, she thought with a shudder.

She didn't want to stereotype him, but she had experience with his type. DS Agent Rawlings was a rough-and-tumble sort. He had an irreverent sense of humor, an obvious penchant for risk and, no doubt, considerable experience in dangerous conditions. The man was sexy as hell, but they had very little in common. Just as well she'd likely never see him again. The only scenario she could think of was if she happened to visit Samantha and Justin in Knights Bridge at the same time Brody and Heather were in town and Greg stopped to see them.

"Not likely," Charlotte said, surprised at

how much the improbability bothered her.

The drizzle turned to a gentle, persistent rain. She kept an umbrella in her tote bag but didn't bother with it since she was only a block from her apartment. She picked up her pace and ran up the steps to her front door. Once inside, she hung her jacket on a hook where it could drip into her copper boot pan, shook the rain off her hair and went into her tiny bedroom, if not in a great mood at least less off balance than when she'd left for her scones — and decidedly more awake.

She unpacked her suitcase from the wedding and set it on her bed to pack again, but she was drawn to the window that looked out on her cobblestone courtyard. Her throat tightened with unexpected emotion as she took in the window boxes bursting with late-spring flowers, glistening as a ray of sunlight broke through the gray and chased off the drizzle. Edinburgh was so different from what she'd known growing up in the Washington suburbs, with summers on the Bennett family farm in rural New Hampshire. She loved her work with the institute.

You are at high risk for a recurrence of decompression illness if you dive again.

How high?

Very.

Her doctor had made clear a recurrence, although unpredictable, could be even more dangerous than what she'd experienced in April.

It's not worth the risk, Charlotte.

Are you advising me never to dive again?

Yes.

She turned from the window. Maybe the risk factors had changed now that she'd recovered. Maybe her doctor would reconsider, or she could get another medical opinion.

She opened her closet.

Edinburgh was home now.

She'd be back.

FIVE

The Cotswolds, England

At first Greg thought his bedside clock had stopped but his phone showed the same time. "Damn," he said, setting his phone back on the bedside table. "Noon?"

He couldn't remember ever sleeping until noon without a good reason, such as recovering from surgery for a gunshot wound, landing in a wildly different time zone or working all night. Even when, on the rare occasion, he'd had a bit too much to drink, he'd never slept until noon. He was a morning guy. Up with the crows.

"It's this promotion," he said, throwing off his duvet and sitting on the edge of the bed. It wasn't in the top ten of comfortable beds he'd slept in, but it wasn't in the bottom ten, either. Since he'd conked out until noon, it'd obviously done the job.

He rolled to his feet without a hint of stiffness or the deep fatigue he'd experienced when he'd first arrived in England. He peeked out the window. Gray. Wet. Not much wind. A good day to sleep in, except he had a plane to catch. He'd booked his flight last night and would be in Boston . . . well, he wasn't sure. Sometime today.

He took a shower, got dressed and went downstairs. Breakfast was done. He didn't see anyone else from yesterday's wedding festivities. He ordered coffee and talked the waiter into bringing him toast and bacon and delivering it to him out back on the terrace. The waiter sent him off with a towel after Greg had assured him he didn't mind the wet conditions. The rain had stopped. Fresh air was good before getting locked up in a plane for seven hours.

Since he was the only one on the terrace, he had his pick of tables and chose one by an urn of flowers. He dried off a chair and the tabletop and sat. He recognized pots of herbs, if only because they looked like herbs he'd seen in the grocery store. He'd always thought he'd have a garden one day. No idea why he'd thought that, since his family hadn't exactly been gardeners. He'd never been around long enough to grow vegetables at home with Laura and the kids. He'd mow the yard and trim trees, and then he'd be off again.

His coffee arrived, hot and steamy, perfect in the damp, chilly conditions. The air felt great to him. He didn't care he was the only one out here. Liked it, in fact. The waiter returned with toast and bacon, and Greg took his time, enjoying the good food, the quiet.

As lives went, his wasn't a bad one.

He decided dessert was in order since he was having lunch and breakfast in one meal and ordered scones. Glorified biscuits in his world, but he didn't want anything that would haunt him on the plane. Unless he'd dreamed buying a ticket, he was booked on a London-to-Boston flight that afternoon. No time to waste, he thought, slathering raspberry jam on a warm scone. He planned to head straight from Boston to Knights Bridge. Maybe or maybe not he'd run into Charlotte Bennett. He figured not. She could end up arriving after he left — if she arrived at all. People did all sorts of impulsive things at weddings, and agreeing to house-sit at a country inn struck him as impulsive, something a practical, tough-minded woman like Charlotte would roll back once she returned to familiar surroundings. The ex-fiancé showing up and memories of her aborted wedding wouldn't have helped with her impulse control. She'd been in fight-or-flight mode. Inn-sitting in New England was pure flight.

Greg was content to let more dust settle on his divorce. Focus on his kids. Head to DC and find a place to live. Learn his new job. That was what he needed to do. He'd gone out to dinner a few times since his split with Laura and his recovery from his gunshot wound but nothing had panned out. He hadn't been ready, he hadn't had much free time and he'd had a hard assignment in an isolated location to complete.

Excuses, Brody would say, and he'd probably be right.

Greg finished his scones, went back upstairs to his room and packed. When he returned to the bar, he settled his bill. By the time he headed outside, his ride was waiting for him, in the form of Ian Mabry.

"Least I could do, mate," the Englishman said.

"Thanks."

"Heathrow?"

"Yep. No rush. I don't care if I miss my flight."

"On your way to Washington?"

"Via Boston and Knights Bridge."

"Ah," Mabry said. "Watch yourself in Knights Bridge. I went there for a wedding and now I'm planning my own wedding."

"Your first?"

"And only."

That's what Greg had thought at his wedding, but he kept that tidbit to himself.

He got in the car. He watched the English countryside pass by. He'd be seeing Andrew and Megan in a few days. He'd booked their flights, too. That would help on the long trip across the Atlantic. Maybe he'd find a book on diving and marine archaeology so he'd have something to talk about with Charlotte if she ended up at the Red Clover Inn after all.

"What?" Samantha gaped at her husband of twenty-four hours. He was behind the wheel of their rental car. He hadn't seemed to have any trouble adjusting to driving on the left. Just as well he was driving because she'd have run off the road at the news he'd just laid on her. "Greg Rawlings is staying at the inn? The DS agent? Brody's friend?"

Justin handled a tight curve with ease. "Maybe."

"Maybe or likely?"

"I don't know. He could be on his way now. Heather didn't say. I don't think she knows his plans. She's got her hands full with Brandon, Maggie and the kids arriving in London."

Samantha got herself under control. Brandon was Justin's younger brother, also a carpenter and the third of the Sloan siblings. He and his wife, Maggie, a caterer, had two young sons. They'd left the wedding hotel that morning for a few days in London with Brody and Heather. Samantha and Justin had slipped out last night, spending their first night as a married couple at a tiny inn an hour up the road.

"Tyler and Aidan want to meet the queen," Justin added.

Samantha smiled, thinking of the two boys, now eight and six, on the loose in London. "Knowing Brody, he could arrange it," she said.

"They'll be happy seeing the changing of the guard at Buckingham Palace. Maggie and Brandon figured they might as well see some sights if they were coming all the way to England for our wedding. Makes sense."

"They love a good adventure."

Justin slowed to let another car bypass them on a straightaway. They were in no hurry, Samantha thought. They were officially on their honeymoon. They had plenty of time to get to Edinburgh, their first stop in Scotland on their ten-day trip.

"I should have mentioned Charlotte would be house-sitting," Samantha said, calmer. "I didn't think of it. It's a maybe, too. I haven't heard from her. She could have decided to go straight to Washington and see about Max's house."

"Weddings can make people agree to things they later have to wriggle out of. Rawlings was beat. I don't know when I've seen anyone that tired. Eric says it was fun watching him try to provoke Charlotte. She had no trouble holding her own with him."

Of that, Samantha had no doubt. "It's fine if Greg stays at the inn. It could be awkward if Charlotte shows up, too, but they'll work it out. There's loads of room."

"Seriously, the guy was bone tired," Justin said. "He could end up staying at the pub and sleep and drink beer all week."

"His type gets restless after forty-eight hours. He'll rally."

"Then maybe he'll stay at the pub and hike and drink beer all week."

Samantha smiled. "Ever the optimist."

"I wouldn't say optimist. Realist. You saw what Greg Rawlings was like when he was in Knights Bridge last winter. He's an adrenaline junkie who thrives on action. Not much action at an old country inn that hasn't been in use for a few years."

"There are cards and musty board games in the library."

Justin grinned at her, his eyes a dark blue in the gray light. "He won't last if he does show up in Knights Bridge. How long do you think Charlotte would last?"

"Not for days and days, maybe, but she looked ready for a real break."

Justin nodded thoughtfully. "I agree."

Samantha tilted her head back, eyeing this man she loved. Justin was solid, a concrete thinker who didn't beat around the bush. She appreciated his bluntness and had seen him get better control of it in their months together, just as she'd gotten better control of her tendency to think she had to do everything herself and couldn't trust anyone.

She trusted Justin Sloan with all her heart.

"Charlotte needs some downtime," Samantha said. "She wouldn't get into any details with me, because it was my wedding day, but I could tell."

"Greg is a federal agent. If he and Charlotte end up at the inn together, it's not as if she'd be holed up with an ax murderer. They're adults. The inn's got a dozen guest rooms and plenty of other rooms — way more space than I had growing up with five siblings. They can spread out. It'll be fine."

"You saw them dancing together yesterday?"

"I did."

"It was her first wedding since she abandoned Tommy Ferguson at the altar."

"She was happy for you, Sam. That's what mattered to her."

Justin downshifted, slowing to a near crawl as they approached another pretty English village. They were taking a scenic route north. Samantha didn't know the details, didn't have a map. She wanted to relax and enjoy the scenery. But here she was, worrying about her thirty-six-year-old cousin. Normally she'd never worry about Charlotte. No one did. She was ultraindependent, competent, good at so many things and yet not one to draw attention to herself. Not showing up for her wedding had been out of character in that sense. In character in the sense that Charlotte Bennett took decisive action once her mind was made up about something.

"Do you want to warn Charlotte?" Justin asked.

Samantha thought a moment. "No. There are too many variables. I don't want to get her worked up about something that might not even happen if she's about to get on a transatlantic flight."

"This is what life's like with our two families." Justin brushed his fingertips on her cheek as they stopped for a traffic light. "Welcome to the Sloans and the Bennetts."

"I love you, Mr. Sloan."

"And I love you, Mrs. Sloan. Shall we enjoy our honeymoon?"

"Every minute."

Six

Knights Bridge, Massachusetts
As Greg switched off the bedside lamp in his corner room at the Red Clover Inn, what felt like a million years after breakfast on the wet terrace of his Cotswolds pub, he could hear scurrying in the walls.

Mice.

He crawled under the top sheet and lightweight blanket on his lumpy double bed. Built in 1900 as an inn, the place nonetheless had the feel of a large, rambling house. It was run-down but not in disrepair, at least from what he'd seen so far. He'd arrived after dark and had turned on a few lights and headed upstairs to find a room. He didn't have a good fix on the inn's layout, but he didn't need one. All he'd needed was to peel off his clothes and fall into bed. Everything else could wait. Red Clover Inn was about what he'd expected.

He'd chosen a corner bedroom on the

second floor. Someone had left a set of sheets and a cotton blanket folded at the foot of the bed. He hadn't minded making the bed himself. It wasn't as if he could call housekeeping. He hadn't bothered to get every tuck just right. Nobody cared. It wasn't a real inn.

He'd opened a window and settled in, lying on his back in the pitch dark, relishing the late-spring breeze.

And then came the scurrying.

Whatever.

If the mice stayed in the walls, they weren't his problem.

The scurrying stopped, at least for the moment. He'd considered changing his plans and checking into an airport hotel when he'd landed in Boston, but he'd had coffee while he waited for his luggage. Good to go. A flight delay, a guy snoring next to him for six hours, one fateful wrong turn coming out of the tunnel from Logan Airport — it'd been one of those travel days best forgotten.

He'd half hoped Charlotte had beaten him here but no sign of her. He was alone.

It was almost morning in Edinburgh.

Greg couldn't keep his eyes open. He sank into the mattress — for all he knew, it had been new in 1982 — and relaxed, letting

his travel fatigue and twitchiness ooze out
of his body. He didn't hear any squeaks or
telltale sounds of flapping wings that would
indicate bats were about. A bat on the loose
he'd have to deal with. Mice . . . He could
go to sleep with mice doing their mice thing
in the walls and ceilings.

How would Charlotte do with mice and
bats?

No mystery. He knew.

She'd have no problem.

Hours and hours after she'd left her cozy
Edinburgh apartment for her westward
journey, Charlotte relished the first sips of
her coffee at Smith's, a small restaurant in a
converted house just off Main Street in
picturesque, totally adorable Knights
Bridge, Massachusetts. She was already in
love with the tiny New England town.

In love.

She smiled, relaxing, at ease now that she
had arrived. She'd be fine unwinding at Red
Clover Inn for a few days. No wonder Samantha had decided to make her home
here. Even without hunky Justin, Knights
Bridge was home-worthy.

Charlotte cautioned herself against over-
reaching with her expectations. She didn't
want to set herself up for a crash later when

she started noticing Knights Bridge's warts. So far, though, her inn-sitting adventure was working out even better than she'd expected.

Smith's first customer on the early Monday morning, she ordered a three-egg omelet with green peppers, onions and ham, home fries, local cob-smoked bacon and multigrain toast.

Just what she needed to get her internal clock onto her new schedule.

As she drank her coffee, she became aware of someone sliding into her booth across from her.

She blinked. *No.*

But it was true. Greg Rawlings had materialized in the little restaurant as if out of thin air. Maybe *actually* out of thin air. How else could Charlotte explain him? She hadn't heard the front door, felt a breeze — anything.

"Don't say a word," she said. "You're not here. You're not real."

"I'm not?"

"I conjured you up in a caffeine-deprived, jet-lagged haze. People can hallucinate after a long trip, a wedding, too many hours without coffee. It's not possible that Diplomatic Security Agent Rawlings is here with me in a Knights Bridge café."

Unfazed by her dismissal of him as a figment of her imagination, he motioned for the waiter to bring coffee, then turned back to her. "It's a stretch to call this place a café. I like it, though."

The waiter, a local teenager, brought Greg coffee, a sign that, in fact, Charlotte hadn't dreamed him up. Maybe she was in a somnambulant state. Maybe she wasn't really awake, or her flight yesterday had messed with her head due to her recent decompression illness.

"We need to work on your situational awareness," Greg said, lifting his mug.

"I see you drink your coffee black. Is that only when you're conjured up, or do you add cream in real life?"

"Always black. Never any cream. I don't drink latte, cappuccino, café au lait, flavored coffee. Just coffee."

"Of course. Not surprised." She blinked. Then blinked again. "Nope. You didn't vanish."

"You're a riot, Charlotte. Okay if I order breakfast or do you want me to pretend to be invisible?"

"I doubt you'd succeed."

"You'd be surprised. I can be invisible when it suits me."

"Order breakfast," she said. "I'm not

107

imagining you?"

He shook his head. "You are not imagining me."

"I suppose we do need to work on my situational awareness. I didn't notice you come through the door."

"You also didn't notice you had company at Red Clover Inn."

She *really* needed more coffee and a few more hours' sleep. "Company?"

"Correct. The car in the driveway was your first clue. Second was the house key missing by the hose spigot. Third was finding the back door unlocked."

She ignored the quickening of her heartbeat. "How do you know all this?"

"Because I'm the one who used the key and left the door unlocked. Apparently we're both inn-sitting this week."

Charlotte gaped at him. She had no words.

Greg settled back on his cushioned bench. "I bet that doesn't happen often — you not knowing what to say. I was up early and heard your car purring outside my window. Whose Mercedes-Benz?"

"It belonged to my great-uncle Harry. Samantha is sorting through his house in Boston. He . . ." She stopped, breathed. "Why didn't you let me know you were there?"

"You were only inside for a minute and I didn't want to scare the hell out of you. I needed to get dressed. I'd just come out of the shower and only had this threadbare towel tied around my waist."

The image of him in only a towel did Charlotte in. She covered for herself by grabbing her water glass but then took a huge gulp, a dead giveaway.

"Easy," he said. "You don't want to choke."

She set her glass on the table. "I was hungry and I wanted coffee. That's why I didn't stay. I saw this place on my way to the inn and decided to walk here and have breakfast."

"You had no idea anyone else was at the inn?"

"No. I thought the car belonged to Justin or Samantha or some other Sloan. I didn't think twice about the key. I emailed Samantha before I left Edinburgh yesterday that I was coming. I figured someone had opened up the place for me."

"Not bad reasoning — not that you're looking for my approval."

"Not that I am," she said.

Their waiter arrived with more coffee and took Greg's order of plain pancakes — no blueberries or chocolate chips — with pure maple syrup, lots of butter and a side of sausage links.

Charlotte could feel her mouth water. "Now I wish I'd ordered pancakes," she said as the waiter withdrew.

"My cure for jet lag. You can have some of mine, unless it's a skimpy order. Then you're on your own."

"It's lunchtime in Scotland. My internal clock is nagging me to eat."

"You haven't had anything today?"

She shook her head. "I try to eat according to the time zone I'm in. It helps me reset my internal clock. I spent last night at Harry's house. It's quite a place. I could always stay there this week. I love Boston. I just was intrigued by Samantha's new town. I woke up at four and got on the road, and here I am."

Greg raised his turquoise eyes to her. She noticed deep marine flecks that matched the color of his lightweight sweater. He didn't look nearly as tired as he had the other night in England. In the cool morning East Coast light, he looked in control. *Sexy.* It took a lot for her to react to an alpha type, but she was jet-lagged.

"Did you know I was en route here?" she asked.

"Sort of."

"It's a yes-or-no question."

"I had an idea you might be en route but I didn't have any details. We could have landed here at different times and missed each other altogether. You could have changed your mind at the last minute or stopped in Iceland for a few days."

"Iceland's gorgeous," she said.

"Agreed."

"When did you arrive in town?"

"Midnight." He smiled over the rim of his coffee mug. "I managed to get myself to bed without incident. Barely, but I did it."

"You're having fun with the mess we're in, aren't you?"

"Oh, yeah."

His sense of humor was contagious, and by his standards — by her own standards — landing at Red Clover Inn at the same time wasn't much of a mess. It didn't seem to bother him at all.

Their waiter delivered their breakfasts. Charlotte could have wolfed hers down but she forced herself to take her time. She picked up her fork and knife. "I had half a cup of instant coffee before I left Boston. I swear Harry brought it to the Antarctic with him." She cut into her omelet. "I thought I'd never see you again."

"Hoped you would or hoped you

wouldn't?"

"I looked at the facts and drew the conclusion that the odds were against it. Hope . . ." She paused. "Hope doesn't factor into my life that much. I'm not a pessimist."

"Okay."

"I'm not."

"Going to admit you're hoping I share some of my pancakes with you?"

"It doesn't look like a skimpy order," she said, watching the butter melt into the soft, fluffy pancakes.

"Best I share rather than have you fight me for them."

"Just a bite. That's all I need."

"You won't stop at a bite."

"Two bites. I promise. I'll stop after two bites."

He lifted his knife and fork. "I assume you want butter and syrup."

"Lots, yes."

He laughed. "You don't have to trade me a bite of your omelet."

"I would," she said. "I'm indulging myself with all this food."

He set the triangle of pancakes, butter and syrup on the edge of her plate. "Enjoy yourself."

"You, too. We can sort out our predicament after breakfast."

"This isn't a predicament. It's my idea of a good time. A pretty town, a rambling country inn and an uptight woman who needs to relax. Can't go wrong."

She figured she could easily think of a hundred ways things could go wrong, but she was adjusting to his presence. She'd finish breakfast, walk back to the inn and then decide what to do. Stay there, find another place in Knights Bridge, return to Boston. She had options. She wasn't trapped.

"Any critters at Harry Bennett's place?" Greg asked, seemingly out of the blue.

Charlotte frowned. "Why would you ask that?"

"Just making conversation."

"No. Not that I'm aware of."

He nodded, swirling a forkful of pancakes in syrup. "Red Clover Inn will be different."

Despite coffee, Charlotte felt a wave of fatigue. Still firmly on UK time, she hadn't slept well last night and almost not at all on her flight. She must have arrived in Boston later than Greg had. Lucky for her, she'd been too tired upon landing to fetch Harry's car and make the drive west. She didn't want to imagine if she'd dragged herself into Red Clover Inn and discovered Greg Rawlings then.

Eric and Christopher Sloan entered the

small restaurant, greeting the staff by name. The two brothers, too, must have flown back across the Atlantic yesterday. They sat at a table near Charlotte's booth.

"Welcome to Knights Bridge," Christopher said.

Eric, in his police uniform, thanked the waiter when he set a mug of coffee in front of him. "I see you two have discovered one of our hot spots," he said, grinning at Charlotte and Greg.

Greg excused himself and took his coffee to the table with the two men. Charlotte seized the moment and dug out enough cash to cover her breakfast and a tip and scooted, giving a quick wave as she made her exit.

Out on the street, in the June sunshine, she decided there was every chance in the world that she'd fallen asleep in her booth and had dreamed that episode in the restaurant. She'd get to Red Clover Inn, and there'd be no rental car in the driveway, no Greg Rawlings camped out in one of the rooms and no threadbare towel, still damp from his shower, tossed on the bathroom floor.

But was that what she wanted?

Probably not, since she'd fantasized about something along these lines on her long flight across the Atlantic.

And it didn't matter, anyway, because there was no denying she'd just had breakfast with him. Now that the reality was upon her, did she want to stay, or did she want to turn around and go back to Harry's house? She could amuse herself in Boston for a few days and then head to Washington. It was the smart option, wasn't it?

Not asking Greg Rawlings if he was armed or accusing him of having had too much to drink, not helping him upstairs to his room, not dancing with him at the wedding — those would have been smart options, too.

Charlotte groaned to herself and walked down the street, passing a handful of small, widely spaced homes before arriving at Red Clover Inn. Although it was within walking distance of the village, it felt out of the way, but Knights Bridge itself felt out of the way — part of its attraction. She took in the rambling inn's classic New England lines with its white clapboards, black shutters and front porch, shaded by twin maple trees. She'd been up for hours but the morning dew still glistened on the lush grass. From what she could tell, the property consisted of the inn itself, a detached garage, a shed, stone walks and an adjoining field dotted with — no surprise — clover.

"How can I leave now?" she asked herself aloud.

She dreaded the idea of driving any distance after so much traveling the past few days. Down to England for the wedding, back to Edinburgh, on to Boston and finally on to Knights Bridge. It was a lot, even by her standards.

She went in through the back door. From what little she'd seen so far, the inn was a bit faded and in need of updating but it had loads of character and potential. She continued down a hall to the front entry, where she'd left her suitcase. She'd thought she'd get settled before going to breakfast but the need for coffee even more than her hunger had won out. She remembered plopping her suitcase on the floor and stretching and yawning before heading back outside and over to Smith's. Had Greg heard her yawn?

He was right. He *would* have scared the hell out of her if he'd appeared at the top of the stairs. For sure she'd have thought he was a figment of her imagination.

She grabbed her suitcase and started up the carpeted stairs. It was just nine o'clock in the morning, but it felt later, she knew, because of the time change — it was already two in the afternoon at home in Scotland. She was relieved she didn't get winded or spike a headache climbing the stairs and yet also frustrated that it had even entered her mind. *Just because you've been cautioned against diving doesn't mean anything is wrong with you.* It was an ongoing argument she'd had with herself since her recovery from her April accident.

She set her suitcase on the floor at the top of the stairs. She felt a pang of loneliness and wished Samantha were in town, but she knew not to drag herself into the past or leap into the future. Best, for now, to stay firmly in the present.

The long hall was carpeted with a well-worn runner. She observed doors with traditional gold numbers on them. She checked the one closest to her. It was unlocked. *Good,* she thought. She didn't want to have to go downstairs and rummage around for a key. She peeked inside — small, tidy, a view of the backyard. Not bad but she'd prefer a room with more windows. Since, except for Greg's room, she had her pick, she kept going. She'd investigate the end rooms first.

She came to an open door down the hall. Sunlight streamed through the windows, the curtains billowing in the spring breeze. The bed was unmade, a towel thrown on the back of a chair, a duffel bag open on a luggage stand. It wasn't as if there were a housekeeping staff to clean the room while Greg was at breakfast. He must have made a quick exit when he'd guessed she'd gone to Smith's and decided pancakes and coffee were in order.

Charlotte pictured him in his threadbare towel.

"Gad."

She exhaled, about-faced and hurried back down the hall, as if Greg might return and catch her checking out his room. She stopped at an end room on the opposite side of the building. Its door was unlocked, any key presumably at the reception desk she'd passed downstairs. Not a problem right now. She went in, and she immediately knew she'd found her room. It had simple furnishings and smelled fresh and clean. Anything fussy and musty and she'd have given up and bolted.

She retrieved her bag and set it on a luggage stand. She didn't feel like unpacking just yet. Instead she walked over to the windows, one with a view of the adjoining field, the other overlooking the backyard with its shade trees, shrubs and perennial flower garden.

Charlotte smiled, pulling back a sheer curtain as she watched a robin perch on a birch branch below her. She didn't need to leave in the morning. She'd be fine here for a few days. It had to be impossible not to relax in such surroundings — even with a sexy DS agent down the hall.

Greg was on his third cup of coffee and doing fine now that the caffeine was kicking in. The pancake-and-syrup buzz was taking effect, too. The Sloans were fighting jet lag, as well, but they figured they'd snap back quickly because they'd never really gone fully on UK time. They both had to be back at work today. Christopher in particular looked bleary-eyed, but he didn't complain as he sucked down coffee.

But there was only so much to say about jet lag, and the conversation shifted to Red Clover Inn. "Things okay at the inn?" Eric asked.

Greg nodded. "Yes, thanks. I was sort of expecting Charlotte but she wasn't expecting me. It's okay. We'll work it out."

"We didn't know she was on her way until last night," Christopher said. "Justin texted us from his honeymoon that Charlotte had been in touch with Sam and was en route."

Eric slathered a triangle of toast with homemade strawberry jam. "Sam figured Charlotte would spend the night in Boston or we'd have warned you. When did she get in?"

"Early. Ninety minutes ago. She did spend the night in Boston but she got on the road before dawn."

"I didn't think about the time change," Eric said.

"No problem." Greg meant it. How could Charlotte be a problem? "We'll be fine. It's a big place. I appreciate the chance to kick back here for a bit."

Christopher pushed aside his plate, not a bite of his full breakfast left. "The inn's great, isn't it? Sam's as excited about its possibilities as Justin is."

"I think she has fantasies of becoming an innkeeper," Eric added.

"Probably easier to hunt for pirate treasure," Greg said.

The eldest Sloan nodded. "Yeah, no kidding. It's weird having just Christopher and me in town. The rest of the family's still in England — except for our grandmother. She's your next-door neighbor, Greg. She didn't make it to the wedding."

"She claims she has a bum knee," Christopher said, picking up his coffee mug. "It's not enough to keep her off a plane, but it's her call. She got some of her friends together and we did live video from the wedding. I think we caught some of you and Charlotte dancing."

"Blackmail material," Greg said with a grin.

Eric laughed. "Neither one of you looks like the type that can dance, but you did just fine."

"I don't think I met your grandmother when I was in town last winter." Greg knew how perilous it could be to get into discussions about grandmothers. "She's in good shape except for her knee?"

"She's not climbing trees anymore but she's still sharp as a tack," Christopher said. "She and the previous owners of the inn were friends. I think their deaths and then the fights between their kids got to her, but that's life, right?"

"True enough," Greg said.

"Let us know if Gran bugs you and you need us to intervene," Eric said.

"No worries. An eighty-year-old grandmother isn't a problem."

"Eighty-three," Christopher said. "Ask her. She'll tell you."

Eric nodded. "Gran's a tough old bird. Have to watch her getting into trouble while Pop's out of town. He thinks she's up to something. I promised him we'd look out for her and he and Mom should enjoy their trip."

The two Sloans both obviously had great affection for their grandmother. They paid their tab and left, and Greg returned to his table. The waiter had cleared Charlotte's dishes. Greg eyed his plate. A few more bites of pancakes had soaked in the pure maple syrup, but they were cold now and he was so full he swore he wouldn't eat for another month.

He paid up and went out into the New England morning. A fine New England morning it was, too. He decided to take a walk and get some sunlight in his eyes and burn off his pancakes, and also to let Charlotte have time to settle in. He wouldn't mind being in the inn alone — he could handle the mice and bats without her help — but he had to admit he'd hate to see her leave. He'd really hate to be the one to drive her out.

Probably should tell her that his kids were coming, though.

Greg put that thought aside. All he needed was to trip over a curb or run into a tree because he had his mind on Charlotte Bennett instead of where he was going.

SEVEN

Edinburgh, Scotland

Samantha pushed ahead of Justin when they reached the cobblestone courtyard where Charlotte's apartment was located in a quiet section of New Town with its eighteenth-century-planned streets and large parks. It wasn't far from the Edinburgh Royal Botanic Garden, their actual destination.

"I have a key," Samantha said, trying not to rush.

If Justin considered their detour an intrusion on their honeymoon or the act of a meddlesome cousin on her part, he hadn't said. They had taken their time driving the rest of the way to Scotland, arriving at their hotel late yesterday, in time to check in, wander through Old Town and have a quiet dinner. They'd had a leisurely morning, enjoying each other and their surroundings. They had only one full day in Edinburgh and Justin had let her decide on their itinerary. Samantha doubted he'd had a visit to Charlotte's apartment in mind.

He eased in next to her. "You live in New England, Sam. What good does having a key to your cousin's apartment in Edinburgh do you?"

"You never know."

He smiled. "As good an answer as any."

"I've always had a key. Charlotte gave me one when she moved in. She'd just started at the institute. They contracted her to work with my parents on the sunken U-boat project. I was working with Duncan Mc-Caffrey at the time."

"So it was before he fired you."

She glanced back at her husband, realized how much she loved thinking of him that way. "Right before, yes." And then Duncan, a respected treasure hunter in his early seventies, had died in a tragic accident, before she'd had a chance to prove herself to him. "Not the best period of my life."

"If Duncan hadn't fired you, you'd have continued treasure hunting with him and his crew and ended up marrying some adrenaline-junkie diver."

"Not answering."

But it was true. Because of Duncan and her need to prove she hadn't betrayed him, she'd ended up in Knights Bridge and had

124

met Justin.

"Ah. Here we go." Samantha paused as they came to the right apartment, tucked off the courtyard. It had its own entrance in the narrow gray-stone building. She unlocked the door and pushed it open. "Cousin Charlotte's home, sweet home, as much as any place is or ever has been home for her."

"It's not what I expected," Justin said as they entered the small apartment.

"What were you expecting?"

"I don't know but not pink walls."

"She'd say they're rose-colored."

He glanced at her. "They're pink."

"Maybe the place came that way. I don't remember."

"You'd remember if Charlotte's Scotland apartment had pink walls." Justin surveyed the cheerful, feminine furnishings. "I think your cousin's a secret romantic."

"I never would have put these colors together," Samantha said, noting the cream-colored shelves and coffee table, green sofa, and accents of yellow and other shades of pink, all the colors showing up in the area rugs and window treatments. "But they work, don't you think?"

"Yep. Sure. They work."

"You don't care."

He shrugged. "I expected more blues since she's a marine archaeologist."

"Now that you think about it," Samantha said with a smile.

"I admit I never considered how Charlotte might decorate her apartment."

"I wish you two had had more of a chance to get to know each other, but there'll be time. My family might not all live in the same town, but we see each other regularly. She's really great."

"Like a sister to you," Justin said.

Samantha brightened. "Yes. Just so." She started toward the adjoining kitchen. "Charlotte might have some good ideas for the inn. And — look, bird prints on the wall. I'd never have expected that. Fish, maybe."

"I'm a carpenter. Doesn't mean I want pictures of hammers and screwdrivers on the walls."

"Good to know. If the prints were marine birds, they might not be such a surprise." Samantha paused in the doorway between the living room and kitchen. "I don't feel sneaky coming in here, you know. Charlotte said we could stay at her place while we were in town."

"Decent of her."

"You'd already booked us at the Waldorf. It's the perfect start to our Scottish honeymoon. It's so elegant."

"Historic, too."

"You don't care if it's elegant or historic provided it has a bed."

"As if elegant and historic matter to you, Mrs. Sloan."

"Not on this trip," she said, smiling. "I used to sleep on the sofa when I visited Charlotte. I haven't visited in a while. Too long. Maybe I should have been more attentive to her after she dumped Tommy."

"But you were happy she dumped him," Justin said.

"Yes, but it was a difficult time for her. She was embarrassed because she waited until the absolute last second, but no one cared about that. It wasn't a big wedding and even Tommy's family seemed as relieved as we Bennetts were."

"The two weren't meant to be."

"That's the bottom line. It was something Charlotte had to see for herself. I think Tommy saw it, too, if not when he was waiting for her to walk down the aisle, at least eventually. He told my parents he has no hard feelings. Just one of those things."

"Yeah."

Justin sounded dubious, but Samantha took his hand and gave it a squeeze. "Unlike us. The universe threw us together and after a wild start, here we are on our honeymoon."

"In your cousin's apartment," he said with a wink.

She laughed and cut through Charlotte's tiny, efficient kitchen into the bedroom. It was half the size of the living room, with cream walls and a duvet cover in a mix of cream, dusty purple and rose, the colors coordinating with those in the living room. Samantha hadn't had any idea Charlotte had such color sense. She'd expected utilitarian beige, gray or white.

"Why are we here again?" Justin asked behind her.

"We're trying to find out what's up with her."

"With Charlotte," he said, as if he needed clarification.

"Yes. Something's not right with her."

"If she wanted you to know, don't you think she'd tell you?"

"Sometimes people want you to make an effort and find out what's going on with them. Need you to, anyway."

"You two are close."

"If this was one of your brothers —"

"There wouldn't be pink walls."

Samantha appreciated his humor — needed it, as he'd obviously realized, as she checked her cousin's apartment for signs she was going off the deep end. "I had visions of arriving and discovering she'd moved out weeks ago and someone else was living here."

"She wouldn't have told you?"

"A year ago, I'd have said yes, even after Tommy. Now? I don't know. I asked her to be my maid of honor in April. She said yes right away. No hesitation. But something was off then, too. I was just so busy with the wedding and my work and then the inn that I didn't push her for an explanation."

"Ever think whatever's up with her is none of your business?"

"No."

Justin grinned. "Didn't think so."

"You don't see any sign she has a stalker or someone's blackmailing her — anything like that — do you?"

He shook his head. "No, but Eric's the police officer in the family."

"But he's back in Massachusetts and you two have a similar nature."

"What would that be?"

"Rock-solid, hardheaded, suspicious Sloan."

"Don't forget blue eyes. Eric and I both have blue eyes."

"You are the perfect man for me, Justin

Sloan," Samantha said. "You have been since you think you rescued me from that fire in your abandoned cider mill."

"I did rescue you."

She waved a hand. "A matter of interpretation."

It was a familiar discussion, one they both enjoyed and would likely have for decades. Now his nineteenth-century cider mill was *their* abandoned cider mill. The prospect of transforming it filled Samantha with genuine excitement, something she couldn't have imagined a year ago. But then lightning — literally — had struck, bringing Justin Sloan to her.

What did Charlotte think of Knights Bridge now that she'd arrived?

She'd scowl at Samantha for thinking about her on her honeymoon.

"You can't break into Charlotte's medical records," Justin said.

"I know. A shame." Samantha sighed. "My folks are worried about her, too. My cousin Isaac said Charlotte didn't seem her usual kick-ass self at the wedding."

"She seemed kick-ass to me. She got Greg Rawlings to bed."

Samantha spun around at Justin. *"What?"*

Justin leaned against the door frame. "Not that kind of bed. Into his room. He was dead on his feet. Ian Mabry saw them and told me."

"And I missed it?"

"It was the night before the wedding, Sam."

"Ah. Right. I was pacing, wondering if I would trip walking down the aisle to meet you."

"Did you consider not showing up?"

"No. Not for an instant. As a Bennett event, our wedding was quiet — and it was perfect, everything I'd ever dreamed of. Especially you."

"Is that why you're coming up with black-mailers and stalkers right now? Missing the Bennett drama?"

"Hmm. Gee. Let me think. Blackmailers and stalkers or visiting the Royal Botanic Garden with you and then walking back to our beautiful hotel for drinks and dinner. Which would I prefer? Want to take a guess?"

Justin stood straight and walked over to her, then slipped his arms around her. "Not bored, are you?" he asked softly.

"Not even close. You weren't worried, were you?"

"No." He kissed her on the lips, then the forehead. "I appreciate that you care about your family. It's one of your charms."

"Most of your family is just hours away in England."

"One of the hazards of a destination wedding. Brandon and Maggie will leave us alone. They'll have enough to do keeping their eye on Tyler and Aidan. Good thing they're staying with Heather and Brody. It'll take them to manage the boys, too."

"Your nephews are adorable."

"Adorable and busy. They researched everything they could do in London. My folks have their own itinerary. My dad will keep my mother from calling us, and Adam — he could be staying down the hall from us at the Waldorf and we'd never know it."

"A quiet guy but also a rock-solid, hard-headed Sloan."

"Funny how you fit right in. The Bennetts will leave us alone?"

"They don't even know we're in Scotland."

Justin grinned. "Smart woman."

Samantha laughed. "I know my family."

They returned to the living room. She gave up on finding any obvious clues at Charlotte's apartment but at least she was less concerned that Charlotte was in imminent trouble. They locked up and headed out of the courtyard, resuming their leisurely walk to the botanic garden.

"You're a good cousin, but Charlotte will be fine in Knights Bridge." Justin encircled Samantha's waist with a thick arm. "She's in a good place with good people."

"Yes, she is."

The Royal Botanic Garden Edinburgh was Samantha's favorite place in Edinburgh. Its seventy acres of lush gardens and walks never failed to enthrall and soothe her, but today, visiting with Justin for the first time, on their honeymoon, was extra special. There was so much to see in Edinburgh. The famous castle overlooking the city was a short walk from their hotel. They'd have time to head up there in the morning before they left the city.

"On my very first visit to the gardens, I imagined coming here on my honeymoon, with the man I loved." She smiled at Justin. "And here I am."

"It's a good place to start a honeymoon."

Arm in arm, she and Justin wandered the grounds, ending with the ten magnificent Victorian glasshouses for which the garden was so famous. They traveled through a variety of miniclimates, from tropical to semiarid, with their displays of orchids, palms, water lilies, cacti and countless other plants.

By the time they had settled at their table on the outdoor deck at the contemporary cafeteria and had ordered tea and cake, Samantha was again thinking about her cousin. "I'm obsessing," she admitted. "I know Charlotte will manage if Greg Rawlings is at the inn. I wasn't worried about her dealing with bats. Why worry about him?"

"I won't tell him you compared him to a bat," Justin said, amused. "Why don't you check in with her? Put your mind at ease."

Samantha snatched up her phone. "I will, and then I'll be done," she said even as she typed.

How are you? Do you love KB?

The waiter delivered their pot of tea, enough for two, then brought the cake, a traditional Victoria sponge cake filled with cream and raspberry jam. "We'll have to take the long route back to the hotel after this," she said.

"Or the short route. There are other ways to burn calories."

She laughed. "So there are."

She saw she had a return text from

Charlotte.

Aren't you on your honeymoon?

Justin and I are having tea at RBGE. You?

I love KB. All fine here. Could have warned me about Rawlings.

Samantha grimaced.

He's there, then?

Yes.

Not a setup. I swear. I didn't know at first. I figured he wouldn't show up.

It's okay. He's amusing himself looking for bats and mice.

Can you relax with him there?

It's a big inn.

It wasn't that big, but Samantha didn't argue. Charlotte seemed fine — but she would, wouldn't she? She wouldn't want to upset Samantha on her honeymoon.

You're sure it's okay?

Positive. Enjoy your honeymoon. Hi to Justin.

Samantha looked up at him. "Charlotte says hi."
"Tell her hi back."
She relayed his response.

Justin says hi.

And goodbye? ;-) Enjoy Scotland. TTYL.

And that was that. Charlotte was gone. Samantha returned her phone to her bag and eyed her cake. "Have you ever seen a cake this perfect? It's almost too pretty to eat."

"But you're going to," Justin said, pouring tea.

"Every bite." She noticed he was studying her as he set the teapot back on the table. "Justin? What?"

"Nothing. It's fine."

"No, tell me. Charlotte's okay. She's a grown-up. She can handle Agent Rawlings."

"Wasn't thinking about them. I was thinking about you. All these times in Scotland and you don't have a kilt, do you?"

"I do not have a kilt, no."

"Never wanted one?"

"Never thought about it. I had one as a toddler. I wore little green kneesocks and saddle shoes."

"There are pictures?"

"Oh, yes. I was cute as hell, I want you to know."

"You'd look good in a kilt now. You could skip the kneesocks. I, however, would not look good in a kilt."

"I differ with you on that one." She smiled. "Wholeheartedly."

He dipped his fork into his cake. "No kilt."

Samantha relaxed, breathing in the familiar scents in the cool Scottish air and relishing the breeze. "Charlotte, Greg Rawlings, your family — they'll all manage without us for ten days."

"Starting now?"

She smiled again, relaxing. "Starting now."

She pretended it was the steam from the tea that was reddening her cheeks, since she had no doubt they'd turned red. Everything about this man made her feel warm, loved and wanted. Tommy had never done that for Charlotte. Worse, he'd undermined her faith in love and romance and their possibilities in her life. Maybe this trip to Knights Bridge would help. Samantha looked at Justin next to her, her emotions welling up as she realized what Knights Bridge had done for her.

He took her hand. "It's supposed to rain later."

"Perfect."

His gaze settled on her. "That's what I was thinking."

"We can laze around at the hotel."

His eyes narrowed, a deep, sexy blue in the graying light. "That's *not* what I was thinking."

EIGHT

Knights Bridge, Massachusetts

Charlotte paused at the entrance to the Swift River Country Store on Main Street, around the corner from Smith's and opposite the oval-shaped town common. Greg had decided to join her to buy groceries and a few necessities. They'd walked together from the inn. They hadn't said much. She was preoccupied with Samantha's unexpected texts from Scotland. Charlotte didn't want Samantha worrying about anything on her honeymoon — *especially not about me.*

Did Samantha suspect something?

"Lost in thought?" Greg asked next to her.

She smiled. "Guilty as charged. I'm just tired from my trip. I haven't flown across so many time zones in a while."

He didn't look convinced. No doubt he was trained in reading people and had experience in detecting BS when he heard it. Charlotte was glad she didn't have anything serious to hide.

She decided not to dig herself in any deeper. "It's a pretty place," she said. "I wonder how different it would be if Quabbin Reservoir hadn't been built. I saw some peeks of it this morning. Beautiful. Hard to believe there once were towns where there's now water."

"This store was open before the valley was dammed and flooded in the 1930s," Greg said. "I learned that when I was here this winter. The locals call it Hazelton's, after the original owners."

"The Hazelton family has some twisting link to one of Harry Bennett's college buddies," Charlotte said. "They went to Amherst College together."

"Your cousin Isaac's starting there this fall. Seems like a smart kid."

"He wants his dad to let him use the Mercedes-Benz."

"Fat chance?"

"I suspect so. The Hazelton-Bennett connection ultimately is what brought Samantha to Knights Bridge."

"I thought it was pirate treasure."

"It was. Samantha and I haven't had a chance to get into all the details on her theories about pirate treasure. I think she was destined to be in Knights Bridge the day she and Justin met." Charlotte smiled. "They're in Edinburgh for the first part of their honeymoon."

"Checking up on you?"

"Why would you say that?"

"Because you're a woman with secrets." He opened the door to the country store and motioned for her to go in first. "After you."

"I hope every woman has secrets," she said, slipping past him.

The rustic store with its worn floorboards and old-time feel seemed to carry everything from groceries to hardware supplies and rain gear. A handful of people were at the register and in the aisles. Charlotte wondered if any of them assumed she and Greg were a local couple running errands on a beautiful June morning. She was a marine archaeologist with an Edinburgh-based institute, in denial about her medical clearance to dive. Greg was a Diplomatic Security Service agent taking a break between assignments. There was no way they belonged together. His crack about her secrets didn't help, but she admitted his sexy presence energized her. He kept her on her toes. She'd kick jet lag fast with him around.

"Don't worry about any problems at the inn," he said as they headed toward the produce section. "I'm handy with bats, mice, and the odd leak and creaky board, and I like to stay busy. You can kick back and relax."

"You're the one who passed out in your booth the other night."

"Dozed off."

"Mmm. Just so you know, I prefer a humane approach with stray rodents."

"That's what you say now. Wait until you wake up in the middle of the night with a bat flapping in your room." He grinned. "Don't look so horrified. I'll hold to the humane line even if you start yelling 'Shoot it, shoot it.' "

"I won't be yelling anything. If a bat's in my room, I'll deal with it myself."

"How?"

"I don't know. Throw a blanket over it."

"Then what do you do with the blanket with the bat in it?"

"Toss it out the window. I'll manage. You aren't seriously concerned about bats, are you?"

"I never joke about bats."

Charlotte shuddered. "Ugh. Well, I can't imagine anything in Knights Bridge would give you pause considering your line of work." She stopped in front of an array of fresh greens. "Do you cook?"

"I get by. You?"

"The basics. I'm not a fussy eater."

"We're going to get along great. Knights Bridge doesn't even have a good pizza place in the village, but we've got Smith's for breakfast and lunch. My kids will think they're roughing it. They arrive Wednesday."

Charlotte didn't hide her surprise. "Kids? Wednesday?"

"I should have mentioned it at breakfast but I didn't get to it," Greg added, grabbing two apples from a bin. "They're coming to visit me." He placed the apples in his basket. "They cook."

"I wouldn't have guessed you're old enough to have teenagers."

"All legal and everything, but I did marry young. Divorce was finalized earlier this year. It was a long time coming."

"I'm sorry."

"Don't be. She's happy, kids are happy. All is good."

"Are you happy?"

"Sun's shining and I'm upright, picking out fruits and vegetables with a kick-ass diver."

Charlotte smiled. He did have a way about him. She examined the various greens. They all looked reasonably fresh. She and Greg didn't have a grocery list and hadn't con-

143

ferred on what to buy ahead of time, but she figured they'd manage. With the store so close to the inn, they could be somewhat spontaneous and easily pick up items they'd missed.

"I'll eat anything but kale," he said.

"I like kale."

"Then you probably also like spinach, which I'll eat."

It was true — she did like spinach. The store had local red-leaf lettuce. She decided on that for now and loaded a head into a bag while Greg added bananas to his basket.

"How's the food in Edinburgh?" he asked.

"Great. I don't cook much. I had scones at a tea shop before I left yesterday."

"I had scones yesterday, too. Don't you feel a little as if we were kidnapped by aliens?"

Charlotte laughed. "That's one way of putting it."

They moved through the aisles, adding a few more basic food items and supplies to their baskets. Greg scooped up two individual frozen turkey potpies, locally made. Charlotte loved the idea of baking them on a cool evening. She could almost smell the buttery, flaky crust. She doubted he was as enthralled with her bag of granola and glass jar of yogurt, also locally made.

They set their baskets on the checkout counter. She started to get out her wallet, but he shook his head. "I'll get this one. You can get the next one. I'll pay for anything for my kids. It'll work out. I'm not into spreadsheets."

"Works for me. Thanks."

They each took a grocery bag as they started out of the store. "I won't get in your way at the inn," he said.

"No problem. I won't get in your way, either."

"It's a big place. You won't even know I'm there." He grinned at her, letting the door swing shut behind them. "We already have proof of that."

"Would you have known I was there if our situations had been reversed?"

"Absolutely."

Probably true. Charlotte squinted in the bright morning sun. She couldn't have asked for a more perfect day to start her stay in Knights Bridge.

"You're not going to sneak off in Great-Uncle Harry's Mercedes-Benz?" Greg asked.

She smiled at him. "Let's see how it goes with the mice and bats."

Across the street, nursery-school children gathered in a circle in the shade of a maple

tree on the common. The common was surrounded with classic homes, businesses,
churches, town offices and a public library.
From what Charlotte had gathered from Samantha, Knights Bridge and its residents
defied stereotypes. It might look as if time
had stood still in the little New England
town for the past century, but it hadn't.
Change had occurred even in the relatively
short time Samantha had been here. Who
could have imagined a treasure-hunting
pirate expert marrying a Knights Bridge
Sloan?

Charlotte started down the sidewalk
toward their street. Greg walked easily next
to her. "I think I got the heavier bag," she
said lightly.

"Damn, I hope so. Jet lag's killing me."

"Ha."

"I can suck it up and carry both bags if
you'd like. Ready to topple over?"

"I'm fine, thanks, although the thought of
a hammock in the shade has a certain appeal."

He sighed. "It sure does."

"I wonder if there's a hammock at the inn,
tucked in a shed or a storage room."

"Let's get these groceries put away and
I'll have a look."

When they reached the inn, they went in

through the front door. "After you," Greg said, letting her go ahead of him down the hall to the kitchen.

"Making sure you're there to catch me if I do topple over?"

"It'd serve you right after the hard time you gave me in England."

"I didn't give you a hard time. I helped you up the stairs to bed." She set her bag on the counter by the sink. The kitchen was spotless and in working order, if dated. "We'd both have been in a mess if you'd toppled over. Fatigue has a nasty way of letting itself be known, no matter how hard we try to deny it."

"Best to deal with fatigue before it deals with you."

"Fortunately, I'm only tired because of my trip."

He set his bag next to hers. "Is that right?"

"You don't believe me?"

"No, Charlotte, I don't believe you."

He sounded matter-of-fact more than offended at the prospect she'd skirted the truth with him. Which she had. She hadn't lied, exactly. She'd simply not told him the full details of her diving accident, her work status or her reasons for being in Knights Bridge. She hadn't told her family, either. She'd barely been honest with herself.

As she unloaded her grocery bag, she watched Greg out of the corner of her eye. He got a pottery bowl down from a cabinet and set it in the middle of the round oak table off to one side of the kitchen. Then he grabbed the apples, bananas and grapes he'd purchased and placed them in the bowl.

"There," he said. "I feel downright domestic."

Charlotte watched him return to his bag of groceries. No, she thought, he wasn't offended, annoyed or put off by what he was convinced were her omissions. He was curious, intrigued and determined to get to the truth. She grimaced, digging into her own grocery bag. By not being straight with him, she'd given him a mission.

Well, too bad.

If she hadn't leveled with her colleagues, friends and family, why would she level with a man who was a complete stranger to her? Everything was a jumble in her head. Facts, feelings, options. Just keeping it all inside her continued to make sense, or at least feel like the only approach that she wouldn't regret later.

And Greg Rawlings was a stranger. They might have had a few close encounters at the wedding and now were sharing a country inn and grocery shopping together, but he was still a stranger. It was Monday. She'd met him on *Friday.*

"What's your place like in Edinburgh?" he asked casually as he walked over to the refrigerator with the potpies.

"It's a small one-bedroom on a cobblestone courtyard near the Royal Botanic Garden."

"Sounds cute."

"It has pink walls," she said.

He opened up the freezer compartment and set the pies inside. "Very cute, then."

She smiled. "It's a sophisticated pink."

"Of course."

"What about you?" Charlotte folded her bag from the country store for reuse later. "I assume the State Department provides housing when you're assigned overseas."

Greg took her bag, folded his and tucked them both next to the refrigerator. "My brother has a spare apartment he let me use in New York last winter. It's not cute." He leaned against the sink and folded his arms on his chest. He looked at ease, casual. "You don't strike me as the type who'd go for anything 'cute.' "

"I don't, do I?"

"Am I wrong? I figure if you were the type who went for cute stuff, you wouldn't mind being called Char or Lottie or something."

"I mind being called Char or Lottie because I'm called Charlotte. I like puppies. They're cute. Kittens. Lambs."

"Everyone likes fluffy baby critters. What about cute dresses? Any of those?"

"You didn't think my maid-of-honor dress was cute?"

"No. A cute dress needs hearts, flowers, lace. Things like that."

Charlotte laughed. "By that standard, no, I don't have any cute dresses. I tend to stick to solids and simple lines. I do a lot of mixing and matching. It's easier when you're on the road a lot."

"And you're on the road a lot?"

"I was when I was working on the project with Samantha's parents." Not a subject she wanted to pursue. "Dare I ask if you have any cute outfits?"

"Sure. You can ask. The answer is none I would describe as cute." He stood straight and winked at her. "But I look cute in everything."

"Sorry, DS Agent Rawlings, I doubt you look cute in everything."

"I'm crushed."

"To be honest, I'm not sure you'd be cute in anything."

He grinned. "I'll leave that one alone and

go see if I can find us a hammock."

He'd sauntered out of the kitchen before Charlotte realized he'd taken her comment to mean he'd be cute in nothing.

She groaned. "Let him have his fun," she said under her breath, grabbing an apple to take upstairs.

Might as well finish unpacking. She was staying, at least through today — and she might stick around even after Greg's kids arrived if he did find a hammock they could hang in the shade.

After she settled into her room, placing her clothes in drawers, organizing her toiletries on the pedestal sink, Charlotte made tea and sat on a cushioned wicker chair on the front porch. Maybe she'd find a book later. She'd noticed bookcases throughout the inn. Right now, she could feel jet lag fraying her at the edges.

She didn't know where Greg was. Still looking for a hammock, maybe.

Just as well.

It was difficult enough to think even without him and his testosterone in the immediate vicinity. He could be one of the reasons she felt frayed, not just fatigue from her trip and the time change.

An elderly woman crossed the driveway

and came up the front walk. She had a cane but seemed sure-footed. She wore a blue sweater, loose jeans and sturdy shoes, and Charlotte had no idea who she was. A neighbor? There was something familiar about her, though, as she stopped at the bottom of the porch steps. "I took a shortcut through the hedges," she said, pointing with her cane toward the side yard. "I live next door. Evelyn Sloan. I'm Justin's grandmother. You're Charlotte, aren't you? Samantha's cousin and her maid of honor?"

Charlotte rolled up out of her chair. "I am, yes. It's nice to meet you, Mrs. Sloan."

"Eric, my eldest grandson, told me you were here, but I recognize you from the wedding photos and videos. I couldn't go." She put her cane back on the walk. "Bum knee."

Charlotte scooted down the stairs. "I'm sorry to hear about your knee."

"It comes and goes. I didn't want to risk a long flight. And call me Evelyn." She squinted past Charlotte up toward the front door. "Where's that FBI agent who's staying here?"

"If you mean Greg Rawlings, he's here somewhere."

"That's his car in the driveway? The little one. I know that big Mercedes-Benz belongs to your family. Samantha came out here in it. Her uncle dropped her off. She thought she could sneak in and out of town with no one the wiser, but it didn't work out that way."

"Lucky for her," Charlotte said.

"True. Eric told me the FBI agent's name but it didn't stick."

"Greg's actually an agent with the State Department's Diplomatic Security Service."

"Same difference," Evelyn said, matter-of-fact. "He was in town this past winter. He's friends with my granddaughter's husband, Brody Hancock."

"I met Brody and Heather at the wedding. For that matter, I met Greg there, too."

"Did Agent Rawlings want the place to himself? He hasn't tried to run you off, has he?"

Charlotte shook her head. "So far, so good. We did a bit of shopping already at the country store."

"If Hazelton's doesn't have it, you don't need it. You don't look as if you'd let him run you off unless you had a good mind to leave." Evelyn leaned on her cane. "I'm not supposed to use it this way. I've had this thing for years. I had lessons in how to use it. It'll be back into the closet with it once my knee settles down. Eric doesn't think a bum knee was good enough reason for me to miss the wedding, but it's not his knee. I plan to visit Heather and Brody in London this fall."

"I understand your son and his wife and a number of your grandchildren are there now."

"My great-grandsons have been texting me pictures of the sights. Aidan sent me one of Westminster Abbey a little while ago. Tyler sent me one of a window box because he knows I like flowers. They're having a ball." Evelyn narrowed her gaze on Charlotte. "You look a bit ragged — excuse me for saying so."

"It's a ways from Edinburgh to Knights Bridge."

"Edinburgh?"

"I live there. I went down to England and back for the wedding."

"Not the best planning, was it? You should have flown from England instead of going all the way back up to Scotland."

Charlotte smiled. The Sloans were a no-nonsense lot. "You have a point, but coming to Knights Bridge was a last-minute decision. I didn't have firm plans when I left for the wedding."

"Don't you work?"

"I was able to take time off." Charlotte

left it there. "Would you like to sit down? I just made tea —"

"No, thank you." Evelyn stared at the porch steps, as if lost in thought. "I don't think any of us would have put Justin and Samantha together, but I believe they will stand the test of time, just as my husband, Ralph, and I did."

"Were people uncertain about you and your husband?"

"Quite uncertain."

"But you weren't," Charlotte said.

Evelyn snorted. "Oh, no. I was filled with uncertainties. Sometimes I think walking down that aisle was the bravest thing I've ever done."

"I can understand that."

"Once Ralph placed that wedding ring on my finger, all my doubts and worries and second-guessing about what my life would be like vanished."

Charlotte knew that wouldn't have happened with her and Tommy. If he'd placed the wedding ring on her finger, none of her doubts about him would have vanished.

Because they weren't doubts.

She'd *known* what he and their life together would have been like. By the morning of their wedding, she'd had no good choices, but the least awful choice was to do what she did and bail on him.

"I'm glad you had a good marriage," she said.

"We were married at my family's home in Amherst," Evelyn said. "It's not far from here. My parents were shopkeepers. They thought I'd go to Smith College and marry an Amherst College boy. I thought I'd move to New York and have adventures. I have no regrets. I've had a good life here in Knights Bridge."

"Are you sure you won't come up and sit a minute?"

"I'm sure. I just . . ." She paused, clearing her throat. "Samantha said you're trust-worthy."

"I like to think I am." Charlotte sat on the top porch step. A breeze stirred in the shade trees on the lawn, creating shifting shadows on the older woman's lined face. "Is there something I can do for you?"

"My life . . ." She took in a breath, standing straighter. "I ran a nursery school here in town for many years. I can tell when a four-year-old is telling a tall tale, and I know it's unfair and unrealistic to trust little ones with secrets. I know my son and my daughter-in-law and my grandchildren. I love them all. They're reliable, straight-forward, the sort you'd want to have at your side when there's trouble. But they wouldn't understand."

"Wouldn't understand what, Mrs. Sloan — Evelyn?"

She raised her pale blue eyes. "I need you to find something for me."

"If I can, of course I will. What are you looking for?"

"A time capsule," she said firmly.

Charlotte tried to hide her surprise. She'd expected something along the lines of a long-lost vase loaned to the inn or a glove dropped on a walk over the winter. But a *time capsule*? "Do you mean an actual time capsule?" she asked. "One of those things you put together as a kid or a newlywed to open in fifty years?"

"Yes, but my time capsule hasn't been opened in sixty-five years."

"I see. Is it here at the inn?"

"I'm sure of it. I just don't know where."

"But if you buried it —"

"I didn't say anyone buried it. I certainly didn't. I don't even know if it was buried."

"Oh." Charlotte had no idea what else to say.

Evelyn's cheeks were a warm red now that she was getting into her reason for this visit, obviously not a comfortable subject for her. "It could be hidden in a cupboard, for all I know. If I knew where it was, I wouldn't need you to find it."

"That makes sense."

"Sorry. That was tart. I know it's here somewhere. My friend and I put it together for our eighteenth birthdays. We were born a week apart. Her parents built this place. She inherited it when they died. She and her husband ran it themselves for a few years but then moved to Myrtle Beach and hired an innkeeper. I visited them in Myrtle Beach several times. Pretty place."

"Your friend didn't take the time capsule with her to Myrtle Beach?"

Evelyn gave a firm shake of the head. "I'm sure she didn't. We planned to bury it together at eighteen, but I had something else to do that day. I don't remember what it was. Nothing important. I forgot all about the silly thing until Betsy — my friend — died. Her husband had predeceased her, and their children went to war over this place. Now *my* family owns it."

"And you didn't expect that," Charlotte said.

Evelyn's thin shoulders slumped. "Not in a million years. I assumed the new owners would be from out of town and they'd tear the place down, and there'd be time . . ." She trailed off, shifting her gaze to the shaded yard. "Last I knew, it was in a large cookie tin. Imported Belgian butter cookies, as I recall."

"The time capsule?"

"Mmm." She turned again to Charlotte. "I'm trusting you not to say a word to anyone about this, whether or not you agree to look for it."

"Of course. I won't. I promise."

"Thank you. I thought you might be up to a bit of an adventure. You're a Bennett after all."

Charlotte didn't know how scouring an old inn for a time capsule two teenagers had put together qualified as an adventure, but she was intrigued nonetheless. "We Bennetts do love our adventures," she said.

"I remember reading about Harry Bennett's excursion to the Antarctic. I was married to Ralph by then."

"Does Samantha know about the time capsule?"

"No. Justin would get it out of her if I swore her to secrecy, and I wouldn't do that — come between the two of them. Besides, they're on their honeymoon. They don't need to be thinking about an old woman's nonsense." She tucked her cane up under one arm. Her knee didn't seem to be troubling her at the moment. "There's nothing exciting in the time capsule. I just don't necessarily want my family stumbling on it."

Charlotte got to her feet. "I'd be happy to look for it for you."

"Good. Thank you." Evelyn set her cane back on the walk. "I should go before our federal agent gets the idea we're up to something. I don't need him on my case, and I'm sure you don't, either."

Charlotte resisted a smile. She didn't point out that Greg was already on her case. "If I find the time capsule, how should I let you know?"

"Bring it to my house. And don't open it. Promise me, Charlotte. Promise me you won't open it."

"I promise."

"Thank you," Evelyn said, although she didn't look particularly relieved or satisfied. "Tell Agent Rawlings my knee was acting up and I'll say a proper hello another time."

She started down the walk using her cane but then tucked it back under her arm as she hustled across the side yard and squeezed through the hedges.

Charlotte returned to her chair on the porch. Her tea was cold. She still was frayed and tired, but having a project — a secret mission — gave her a focus. That it was on behalf of Evelyn Sloan, Justin's grandmother and a woman in her eighties, was a bonus. It beat thinking about her own predicament. Diving, her future, her nonexistent love life, Max's house in Washington, a cousin who was like a sister to her settling in a tiny New England town — why not search for a time capsule?

"What was that all about?" Greg asked, coming out the front door. "Evelyn Sloan, I assume. Eric and Christopher mentioned she lives next door. She looked as if she just paid you to hit somebody over the head."

He sat on a wicker settee at the end of the porch by the field. Charlotte didn't want to lie to him, not only because he'd no doubt see through her given his background but because she didn't do well with lies. They drained her. She'd rather be straightforward and deal with the facts and the truth.

"Yes, Evelyn Sloan is our next-door neighbor," Charlotte said. "We had an interesting chat. Did you meet her when you were in town over the winter?"

"I think so. I was only here for a short time. I didn't meet everyone."

"It is a small town, though." She nodded to her teapot, cup and saucer. "I'd offer you some tea but it's gone cold. Did you find a hammock?"

161

"If I tell you, will you tell me what you and Evelyn Sloan are up to?"

She smiled. "The suspicious Diplomatic Security agent at work."

"The guy who has his own grandmother. You don't have any concerns about her?"

"Her knee seemed fine despite the cane. Whatever was bothering her must have cleared up after her family headed to England."

"Convenient," Greg said. "How was her mind?"

"You mean depression, memory issues, that sort of thing?"

"That's a start."

"I didn't notice any issues but we only spoke a short time."

"That's good." Greg paused, studying Charlotte. "All right. Before you tell me whatever you two discussed is none of my business, I'll quit. I gather she swore you to secrecy, anyway."

"Aren't you glad I didn't wither under your scrutiny?"

He grinned. "You really are a riot, Charlotte. I was just making conversation."

"In that case, are you going to tell me about the hammock?"

"I found one." He got to his feet. "You can help me hang it after lunch."

162

Lunch was canned soup and fruit. Greg couldn't have handled anything else, what with his big breakfast and messed-up internal clock, and Charlotte seemed to be on the same wavelength. After they ate and cleaned up the dishes, he led her out to the side yard.

He had discovered a rope hammock in the shed out back and dragged it between two shade trees, where he'd left it in a heap in the grass. The trees had hooks where presumably this very hammock had hung in the not-too-distant past. He'd brushed off dirt, dust, cobwebs and a few dead spiders from the knots and twists, but the hammock was in good shape. Heavier than he'd expected but he'd managed. Now he had Charlotte's help.

Life could be worse.

"Did you ever have a hammock growing up?" he asked her.

"On visits to the family farm in New Hampshire. My cousin runs it. He's the older son of Harry and Max's youngest brother, who stayed home on the farm while they went to college. They never came back, except to visit. It was a hardscrabble farm

163

in those days but it's doing well now." She dragged one end of the hammock toward one of the trees. "All more than you wanted to know. I'm wired and tired. What about you — did you ever have a hammock as a kid?"

"We had a hammock at a lakeside cabin my family rented a week one summer when I was about twelve. I sneaked up on my brother and dumped him out of it. Dumb move. He's older."

"He had his revenge?"

"He pushed me into the lake first chance he got. It was dusk and I was in my pj's. The water was cold. I can still see him on the dock, laughing his ass off."

"Served you right," Charlotte said. "Where was the cabin?"

"Adirondacks."

"Beautiful country. I don't know it well but I went there with friends during college."

"My brother goes hiking up there every fall. I haven't been back in a long time." Greg pulled his end of the hammock toward his tree. He didn't notice any tears or weak spots in the twists of old rope. "I've never been to Scotland. I hear it's beautiful."

"It is. I love it there."

"When do you go back?"

She shrugged, maybe taking a bit too much interest in her hammock hook. "I booked a return flight in ten days," she said without looking at him. "I figure I can eat the fees and change it if need be."

"Are you on vacation?"

She hoisted her end of the hammock up toward the hook. "Seems stable. Feels like the hammock might have shrunk, though, in which case we're out of luck because it'd be hard to move the tree. What did you ask me?"

"Vacation. Are you on vacation?"

"Hanging a hammock is not working, that's for sure."

Greg watched her fool with the hook, then the hammock. She clearly didn't want to give a direct answer to his question. Now, why, he wondered, was that? He got the loop on his side onto the hook. "Do you have a lot of freedom with this maritime archaeology institute you work for?"

"I do, yes. It's great. Right now I'm between projects."

"Could they give you the ax if you don't come up with a new project?"

"You're blunt, aren't you? No, the 'ax' hasn't been mentioned. No reason for that kind of talk. Shall we get this hammock up? I can hear it calling to me to lie in it."

Greg was 90 percent certain she was skirting the truth — or at least not telling him the whole story — but he let it go. "Funny, it's calling to me, too."

"Don't even think about dumping me out of it."

"Could be fun." He noticed her cheeks turned pink. It could have been from exertion, but he didn't think so. "Let's see if we can get this thing up."

Hitching the hammock to the hooks turned out to be easy enough. It hadn't shrunk, and it was in great shape. Greg enjoyed the work. His first day in Knights Bridge, even with Charlotte Bennett turning up in a forty-year-old Mercedes-Benz, was going just fine, the polar opposite of almost every day of the past year, whether he'd been recovering from a gunshot wound or on the job in places far from his family in New York and his kids in Minnesota. Of course, there'd been no hammocks and no pancakes at Smith's. Also no pretty marine archaeologist with secrets.

"I think we've got this just right," she said. "Too tight, we'll fall out of it. Too loose, our butts will hit the ground when we climb in. Sorry. I'm sure you know that."

"I've never hung a hammock," Greg said.

"Sam and I pretended we were pirates

once and hung sheet hammocks, as if we were on a pirate ship."

"Yo-ho-ho and a bottle of rum."

Charlotte laughed. "That's what we sang." She yanked on her end. "Hook's holding."

She was no slouch when it came to physical work. She was strong, fit and sexy, but Greg tried not to think about the sexy part. He was a guest in Knights Bridge and she was related to a woman who'd just married a Sloan. The Sloan boys had pretty much run Brody Hancock out of town on a rail when he'd gotten crossways of them in their late teens. All was forgiven now, years later, seeing how he'd just married their only sister. Greg didn't need to stir the calm Hancock-Sloan waters by misbehaving.

Besides, he was in Knights Bridge to relax, and he wouldn't relax if he kept noticing Charlotte's dark eyes and slender curves — or trying *not* to notice, not to think about all the possibilities. He also didn't want to cause friction or complicate her life, or his own life. He doubted she needed a fling with a DS agent on his way to a new job in Washington.

She beat him to the hammock and flopped into it with a satisfied sigh. "It's perfect. Oh, my. It is so perfect."

"No argument from me."

He didn't tell her he wasn't looking at the hammock. He was looking at her. She wriggled out of her shoes and kicked them into the grass. The hammock swung gently in the shade. She shut her eyes and sighed with undeniable satisfaction. "I can sense you watching me, Agent Rawlings," she said, her hands folded on her stomach. "Is a spider about to drop onto me?"

"No spider. Just making sure the hammock held."

"Right. Thanks." She opened one eye. "Don't get any ideas about dumping me out of here."

He smiled. "No, ma'am."

She shut her eyes again. "You can have a turn after me. It's great. Peaceful."

"Enjoy."

Greg left her to her nap or meditation or whatever she planned to do in the hammock. Stare up at the leaves, maybe. Look for a bird's nest in the branches. She was down-to-earth, comfortable around intense guys like him but also intense in her own way. He had no doubt she'd put up a good defense if he tried to upend her in the hammock.

He also recognized the signs that she needed this time in Knights Bridge to relax, unwind and deal with whatever it was she had on her mind that she wasn't sharing — not just with him, either. With anyone. He'd been like that when his marriage had started to fail and even when it was clear there was no saving it. He hadn't talked to anyone. He'd just buried himself in work.

He hadn't talked to anyone when he'd been shot, either. He had a tendency to muscle through things. Talking only made him focus more on what was wrong, or so he kept telling himself. Being close-mouthed was one of Laura's gripes about him. It wasn't just because she'd believed talking would help him. It was a way for her to feel a part of his life, especially when he was away. A way for him to show he cared about her and trusted her. She'd tried to convince him that being open demonstrated he had the strength and integrity to admit vulnerability and he wasn't simply a gritty, tough SOB with no self-awareness. He figured either way he lost.

After being shot, he'd doubled down on his no-sharing ways. He hadn't wanted to talk. He'd wanted to recover and get back on the job. That was where he'd put his energy. He'd joked and teased and told everyone he was fine, and soon it was so.

He had a feeling Charlotte was a little bit like that right now.

On the other hand, she could just be tired from her trip and sorting through options for her next project. Since he *wasn't* on the job, he could read into her behavior and speculate.

He glanced back at her as he started toward the front porch.

No. She was tamping down emotions, frustrations, realities she didn't want to face.

Something, anyway.

He went back inside. He escorted a few spiders out of the entry and then headed to the inn's library in search of a book. He'd have his turn in the hammock soon enough.

NINE

Charlotte dozed off and awoke with a start, forgetting where she was. She almost dumped herself out of the hammock, but the June breeze and the smell of flowers helped reorient her. Heart racing, she planted her feet in the grass and sat up. A few yards away, a robin hopped on the lawn. It paused, stared at her a half beat and then flew off to the hedges between the inn and Evelyn Sloan's yard.

Her reaction hadn't been due only to being disoriented awakening from her nap. She'd been dreaming.

"Having a nightmare is more like it."

She leaned against the hammock, swinging in it sideways, keeping her feet planted in the cool grass. She breathed slowly, deeply. In her nightmare, she'd been fighting for air, caught in debris deep underwater with no good options.

She shook off the images — the awful,

claustrophobic, panicky feelings that had followed her as she'd awakened. It wasn't the first time she'd done so. She had experience with shaking off nightmares.

She put on her shoes and walked to the front porch but didn't go up the steps when she saw Greg sprawling on the wicker settee with a book. "I'm going for a walk," she said. "Hammock's all yours."

"Great. I think this cushion has fleas."

"Seriously?"

He grinned. "No. Just getting into my book."

"What are you reading?"

He flipped the paperback over so that she could see the cover. "*Guns of Navarone* by Alistair MacLean. I saw the movie but have never read the book. World War II thriller."

"I gather you didn't bring it with you to Knights Bridge."

He nodded behind him. "Library."

"I'll check it out," Charlotte said. "Are you bored?"

"Nope. I don't get bored." He sat up, his turquoise eyes connecting with her in such a way she felt a rush of heat. He smiled. "I always find something to do."

"You twitch instead of getting bored. I'll keep that in mind." She motioned to the field next to the inn. "I'm going that way to see where the road leads. Don't tell me if you know."

"A Bennett off exploring. Have fun."

Charlotte left him to his book and whatever was next for him and headed across the lawn. When she reached the street, she turned right, away from the village. Why couldn't she have dreamed about her housemate instead of suffocating on a dive? A sexy alpha, alone and bored. Imagine the dreams she could have had.

Except she believed Greg that he wasn't bored.

He was an alpha in search of things to do.

She laughed to herself, glad to be rid of her claustrophobic nightmare. She walked past the field, cheerful wildflowers dotting the tall grass under the midday sun. A shallow, rocky stream bordered the field, running between it and a grove of young deciduous trees on its opposite bank, then through a culvert under the road. She wondered if it was the same stream Samantha had been following when she'd met Justin last fall. Cider Brook. That was its name. It ran past the old cider mill where she'd taken shelter in an unexpected thunderstorm.

Charlotte remembered the texts they'd

exchanged a few weeks later.

I'm not coming to Edinburgh, Charlotte. I'm staying in Knights Bridge.

Because of your pirate research?

Because of a man I met.

Samantha had taken a break from sorting through her grandfather's Boston house to head to Knights Bridge and test her theories about Captain Benjamin Farraday, an infamous eighteenth-century New England pirate. She and Charlotte had been talking informally about her coming to Edinburgh once she'd finally closed out Harry's affairs. Given her background and expertise, Samantha had a number of options — joining Charlotte on a new underwater research project, teaching, researching — but Edinburgh hadn't happened.

Charlotte passed a small apple orchard and another house before the street curved back into the village, intersecting with Main Street. She continued past the country store to her street. It made for a nice walking loop.

She was almost past Evelyn Sloan's house when her neighbor intercepted her on the sidewalk. "I stopped by the inn a little while ago, but I saw that federal agent in the hammock," Evelyn said in a conspiratorial whisper. "I think he's faking being asleep."

"It's a comfortable hammock. I dozed off in there myself before my walk."

"I suppose." She didn't sound convinced. "My grandson Christopher was just here. He said you're a diver. I hate even having my face in the water. I know you use equipment for deep-sea diving, but that makes me hyperventilate, too."

"Do any of your grandchildren dive?"

"Christopher knows how. I don't ask questions about it. I never was one for the water. Ralph would take the grandkids to the lake. Sometimes I'd sit on a rock and watch, but usually I'd stay home and cook dinner for everyone. Samantha dives, too, doesn't she? She must, given her interest in pirates."

"She's an experienced deep-sea diver, yes."

Evelyn shuddered. "I suppose when she and Justin have kids, they'll have them diving. Scares me to think about, so I won't. What about your FBI agent? Does he dive?"

"I don't think so, but he's not —"

175

"He's not an FBI agent. I know. What-ever."

"We only just met. We're not here to-gether."

"That's what Christopher said." Evelyn pulled off a pair of bright pink garden gloves. "Well, he looks as if he's seen it all and done it all. Jaded. I think he knew I was peeking through the hedges just now. I'd be careful searching for my time capsule with him around."

"I'll be discreet," Charlotte said, keeping her tone neutral.

"Any luck yet?"

Charlotte shook her head. "I haven't had a chance to look. It might take more time since I'm not alone at the inn and you don't want Greg to know."

"I definitely don't want him to know. He's used to keeping state secrets. This is differ-ent. He'll be amused. He'll tell his friend Brody and Brody will tell my granddaugh-ter, Heather, and then I'm sunk. My whole gang will know. It's hard to keep a secret with the Sloans."

"You can trust me."

"I'm sure I can." She tucked her gloves into the front pocket of her baggy sweatshirt. "Thank you for taking this on. I was just in my garden. I've got peas that need picking.

I'll bring some by tomorrow."

"I'd love that, Evelyn. Thank you."

She stretched her lower back. She didn't have her cane but her knee didn't seem to be bothering her. "I'm not senile. There's a time capsule somewhere in that inn. Don't do anything to alert my grandsons, either. I dodged Eric in the village this morning. I can tell he's suspicious." She straightened. "I should get moving. Heather gave me a Fitbit for my birthday." She pointed to her wrist, complete with a turquoise Fitbit. "I need to get in my quota of steps."

Charlotte wished her well and continued on to the inn. The hammock was empty. She found Eric Sloan and Greg seated on the front porch, each with a glass of iced tea. "Hey, Charlotte," Eric said. "How was your walk?"

"Lovely. I just ran into your grandmother. She'd been working in her garden."

"Guess her knee's better. Greg says she slipped through the hedges earlier. I have to remind her cat burglars work at night." He set his tea glass on a side table that needed painting. "I hope she's not bothering you."

"Not at all," Charlotte said. "She plans to bring us peas from her garden tomorrow. I don't want her going to any trouble, especially if her knee acts up again."

"Gran doesn't do much she doesn't want to do these days." Eric's tone was amiable, his affection for his grandmother obvious even if he had his suspicions about her recent behavior. "You watch. She never looks caught or guilty. My grandfather used to say it was why she could handle nursery-school children. You need a poker face dealing with four-year-olds."

Greg grinned. "That's for sure."

Eric got to his feet. "Thanks for the tea. I saw Dylan McCaffrey at the country store and mentioned I was headed this way. He asked the three of us to lunch tomorrow. I can't make it, but you two are welcome to go without me. Samantha used to work for his dad."

"Duncan McCaffrey," Charlotte said. "He fired Samantha. She says it was over a misunderstanding."

"It helped bring her and Justin together." Eric turned to Greg. "Dylan's father was a respected treasure hunter. He died shortly after firing Samantha, and she came here in part to set the record straight. It's all these Knights Bridge connections. Don't try to figure them out. You'll tie yourself in knots."

"Sounds like a plan," Greg said. "Lunch is at Dylan and Olivia's place?"

Eric nodded. "Dylan wasn't sure if you

two would be dead on your feet."

"Not by tomorrow," Charlotte said. "Lunch sounds great. I hope you can make it after all."

"Olivia's expecting. That's why she and Dylan couldn't get to the wedding. She's doing well. It was too much traveling for her." Eric motioned toward the porch steps. "I should get rolling. If Gran . . ." He hesitated. "She's always been independent, but she's in her eighties. If she's starting to slip, we want to know. We all care about her, but sometimes it's easier for outsiders to see that something's not quite right with a loved one. Don't hesitate to tell me, okay?"

"Of course," Charlotte said, trying to sound reassuring. "It's nice that you and your grandmother get along so well."

"Yeah. We tease a lot but we do all right. Happy she's still with us. She keeps telling me I'm dragging my heels about getting married. Technically I'm engaged — my fiancée's a paramedic. She's in Boston for training."

"*Are* you dragging your heels?" Greg asked.

Eric laughed. "I guess it'd help to buy her a ring. See you two later. Call if you need anything."

After Eric left, Greg stretched out his legs

179

and tilted his head back at Charlotte. "Still not going to tell me what Mrs. Sloan put you up to?"

Charlotte sat on the porch rail. "She was off just now to get in enough steps on her Fitbit. And who says she's put me up to anything?"

"I do."

"If I did agree to do anything for her, I can assure you it would be innocuous and dull compared to what you're used to."

"Can you assure Eric that his grandmother isn't losing it?"

"I can say unequivocally that Evelyn Sloan seems very much on her game with me. She saw you in the hammock. She thinks you were faking being asleep."

"Me?"

"Ah. Right. You *were* faking it."

"I knew she was looking for you. Whatever she's got you up to, she's enjoying the drama of sneaking around. Plotting with you must be a welcome diversion to picking peas."

"She seems to like working in her garden." Charlotte slid off the rail. "Has anyone ever told you that you have really piercing eyes?"

"Nope. Not in as many words."

"You must scare the hell out of people with just a look."

He stood up. "Not everyone. I think it'd take more than piercing eyes to scare you."

"Think so, huh?"

He grinned at her. "Oh, yeah." He nodded toward the door. "I'll go in and start dinner. I know it's early, but my stint in the hammock got me in touch with how tired I am. I'm making it an early night."

Charlotte fought back a sudden yawn, smiling at him. "Look what you made me do. I'm beat, too. An early night sounds good."

She helped him make a simple dinner of toasted cheese sandwiches and salad. They ate out on the front porch, although the evening air quickly turned cooler than either had expected.

"It doesn't bother me," she said, "but we can go in if you'd like. I know you don't like the cold."

"I'll grab a blanket if I need one."

"It's not *that* cold."

"To you, maybe. I'm not big on freezing." He sighed, settling into his wicker chair. "But this feels good after the hot desert. Do you like Scotland because it's wet and chilly?"

She smiled, picturing her courtyard in Edinburgh. "I like Scotland because it's Scotland." She paused. She didn't want to get too deep into talking about herself. "When we met the night before Samantha and Justin's wedding, you mentioned you'd been shot. Is that true, or was that something you tell women carrying you up the stairs after you've passed out drunk under the table in an English pub?"

"I wasn't drunk and I wasn't passed out."

"You were asleep," she said, skeptical.

He smiled. "That is correct."

"And getting shot?"

"I didn't make it up."

"It happened on the job, didn't it?"

"Overseas. On the job." His tone turned serious. "My team was doing site work. We ran into an ambush and I took a bullet in my shoulder. That's why I was at my brother's apartment over the winter and why I had time to come here in the ice and snow."

"It was a long recovery, then?"

"Longer than I wanted. Worst part was the cat hair in the apartment. I hate vacuuming."

Charlotte sighed. "I bet that wasn't the worst part."

"What happened to me happened."

He sounded sincere, as if his simple words summed up how he felt about what had to have been a difficult ordeal. Charlotte didn't want to press him to talk about the incident

182

if he didn't want to, or if she wasn't the right person. She just had one more question. "Would you say your experience was life changing?"

He didn't answer at once. His gaze, with those penetrating turquoise-blue eyes, was steady, as if he knew there was a backstory to her question — that it wasn't just about him, as interested as she was in his experience. Finally he nodded. "Laura and I gave up any pretense that we wanted to be together, and I went back into the field and got promoted."

"I'd call that life changing."

"Because of it, I'm here now, at this pretty country inn with you."

"It is a pretty inn, and I'm glad you're okay." But Charlotte found herself yawning again, unable to stop, as if the strain of their conversation — finding out he hadn't been kidding about getting shot, imagining his ordeal — had sucked up any reserves she'd had. She waved a hand. "Sorry. It's not you. I'm still on Scottish time but I'll adjust."

"You need sleep. I'll take care of the dishes."

She didn't argue. "Thank you." She got to her feet, aching, she was so tired. "I'll see you in the morning."

"Oatmeal for breakfast okay with you?

Porridge, I guess you'd call it, living in Scotland. I'll set it up and have it ready to go in case you're up early."

"That sounds wonderful. We have oats?"

"We do. I slipped in a can of steel-cut oats at the country store this morning. I'll follow the recipe on the back. I'd look up a recipe for proper Scottish porridge on the internet, but we're in a digital dead zone here."

"There are a hundred ways to make porridge, most of them good as far as I'm concerned." She started for the door. "Dinner was fun."

"We're doing okay as inn mates."

She laughed. "You have an irreverent sense of humor. Let's see how things look in the morning."

"Sleep well, Charlotte."

"You, too, Agent Rawlings."

"You call me Agent Rawlings when you mention things like sleep." He stretched out his thick legs. "Thought you might like to know that before you crawl under the covers."

Charlotte pretended not to hear him and went inside, taking the front stairs up to her room. As she shut her door behind her, she felt a searing sense of isolation that she hadn't expected and couldn't explain. Jet lag, she supposed. It could be disorienting.

She thought of her friends in Edinburgh and her colleagues at the institute. Were Samantha and Justin still in town, or had they left for another part of Scotland? They hadn't left her a precise itinerary, or probably the rest of their families, either.

"Who could blame them?"

She smiled, feeling better as she pulled the curtains and shades in her room.

A bath, a book and bed — her plan for the rest of the evening. With a good night's sleep, all her carnal thoughts about Greg would be out of her head by their porridge in the morning. Still, if she had to dream tonight, she'd rather it be about him and his piercing, knowing eyes than a repeat of her nightmare in the hammock.

With Charlotte gone up to her room and the dishes done, Greg went back outside and walked out to the street to get a decent cell signal. He texted Brody, but the Knights Bridge native and his fellow DS agent didn't know what was up with his wife's grandmother, either.

Want me to check with Heather and whatever brothers are here? I've lost track.

No. I don't want to alarm anyone.

We're up late talking. I'll be subtle.

Not much about Brody Hancock was subtle but he texted back a few minutes later.

Evelyn's been weird since the family bought the inn. They figure it's nostalgia.

It wasn't nostalgia. It was something tangible. Greg was convinced of that much, despite his lack of evidence. He didn't know why he was curious. Jet lag. Fatigue. Looking for distractions ahead of his kids' arrival and his new job in DC. A lot of possibilities that didn't involve Charlotte Bennett.

He typed a response to Brody.

Thanks. Have a pint for me.

Greg returned to the inn and went upstairs. It was still light out and not just because of June's longer days. He'd hit the sack early with his Alistair MacLean novel.

He saw that Charlotte's door was shut.

Probably locked, too, if from habit rather than distrust of him.

He didn't lock his door. If she got in, he'd manage.

TEN

Edinburgh, Scotland
Samantha had visited the maritime archaeology institute where Charlotte worked once, long before Justin Sloan had launched himself into her life. The institute offices were located in a handsome eighteenth-century stone building on a narrow street in Edinburgh's picturesque Old Town. She and Justin had walked from their hotel to Edinburgh Castle, where they'd wandered around for part of the morning, absorbing its long history and enjoying the breathtaking views from its battlements high above the city. They'd have lunch at whatever place struck their fancy and then head north for the next stop on their honeymoon.

"The institute just happens to be on our route," Samantha said, pausing at the front door.

Justin raised his eyebrows. "That's your story, is it?"

"It's true!" She grinned at him. "Close enough, anyway."

"Would you like to stop in and say hello since we're here?"

"I'd feel better if we did. You'll get a real taste of my pre–Knights Bridge life."

They entered a vestibule with a set of stairs straight ahead and open doors to the left and right. Samantha went right, entering the institute's cluttered reception area. The receptionist, a woman in her fifties who'd worked at the institute since its founding thirty years ago, recognized Samantha right off and greeted her warmly. "We heard about your wedding," she said. "Congratulations."

Samantha introduced Justin. "Edinburgh's our first stop on our honeymoon."

"A brilliant choice, not that I'm biased. Alan's in his office, if you'd like to see him. The door's open. Walk right in."

Alan Bosworth, the institute's assistant director and a marine archaeologist himself, rose as Samantha and Justin entered his office off the reception area. It was just as cluttered, with stacks of files and books, rolled-up charts, a dusty desktop computer, a laptop, cameras and at least two printers, one of which was obviously out of use. More charts and photographs of underwater sites consumed the wall space. A window looked out on a small alley. In his early sixties, lanky and eccentric, Alan explained he'd recently returned to Edinburgh after several weeks on a project in southern England, off the coast of Cornwall.

"I missed Charlotte before she took off on leave," he said.

Samantha frowned. "On leave?"

"Leave, yes." He sat on a swivel chair at a sturdy walnut desk, a relic from early last century, dusty and cluttered. "She told you, didn't she? It's not a secret, at least not that I'm aware of."

"I've been preoccupied with my wedding. We decided to stop in on a whim while we're in town. I didn't ask Charlotte when she was returning to Edinburgh. Do you know?"

"Edinburgh? Probably in a fortnight. To work — harder to say. She took an indefinite leave. Understandable given the circumstances but I'm sure she'll be back. I hope so, anyway. It's great she had your wedding this weekend. Always good to see family after a hellish scare." Bosworth tilted back in his chair. "She *did* tell you about that, didn't she?"

"I don't know about a scare," Samantha said.

He winced. "Blast. Me and my bloody big mouth. Her leave has nothing to do with her work here. It's completely voluntary. I've hardly seen her since her scare and I don't have any details. She doesn't like to talk about it." Bosworth wrinkled up his face. "You don't know about any of this, do you?"

Samantha shook her head. She felt Justin stiffen beside her.

"I'm sorry. I didn't realize Charlotte hadn't told you." Bosworth motioned to an overstuffed love seat. "Would you care to sit down?"

"Thanks, but we won't stay long." Samantha calmed her breathing. "What scare, Dr. Bosworth? Can you tell us what you know?"

"Alan. Please. I don't want to speak out of turn. Charlotte must have her reasons for not saying anything."

"Justin and I decided to have our wedding in England and put it together quickly. Charlotte wouldn't have wanted to trouble me with anything going on in her own life."

"That would be like her." Bosworth seemed to absorb his own surprise that his colleague hadn't shared whatever had happened to her with her family. "She was on holiday in April, escorting tourist divers into historic wrecks in the west of Scotland."

"The Sound of Mull," Samantha said, marginally encouraged that she knew that much. "She mentioned it when I called to tell her about the wedding and ask her to be my maid of honor. We emailed a few times but didn't talk again until later in May."

"As I said, I don't have the details. None of us here does. I just know something went wrong on one of the dives and she had a close call."

Samantha inhaled sharply. "Did she have to come up fast?"

"I don't know. She seems fine. A rapid ascent is dangerous, of course, but she's an experienced diver and they'd have had proper equipment and medical people on hand. I don't want to worry you unnecessarily. You saw her yourself at your wedding. Didn't she seem fine to you?"

"Yes, but there are different levels of decompression illness." Samantha didn't go on. Alan Bosworth probably knew more about DCI than she did. "I suppose it's Charlotte's business. Thanks for your time, Alan."

He nodded. "It's good to see you. Give my best to your parents. We all hope Charlotte enjoys her stay in the States and comes back soon. A diving scare can be difficult, regardless of any injuries sustained. You question yourself. You start to wonder if your luck is running out."

"You sound as if you have some experience," Justin said.

Bosworth nodded thoughtfully. "I had a few close calls in the early days. I was lucky not to incur permanent damage — or die." He caught himself. "I don't mean to imply Charlotte's incident was on that scale. I honestly don't know the details."

Samantha thanked him and they left. As she and Justin returned to the quaint street, she digested what Alan Bosworth had told them. "If Charlotte was cautioned against diving again — told she *can't* dive — it'd be a blow."

"A blow to her career?" Justin asked.

"Certainly to the career she has now."

"Think your parents know what happened?"

"If I didn't, why would they?"

"They worked with her and they didn't get married a few days ago."

Samantha waited until they reached an intersection before she gave up and called her father, but he told her that he and her mother had no idea Charlotte had had a diving scare or was on a leave of absence from the institute.

"Tommy mentioned on Saturday that Charlotte had saved a friend of his this spring," her father said. "An amateur diver. I wasn't paying close attention. You know Tommy. He always has something to say. I was focused on the wedding. It was your day."

"Was Tommy involved in the dive that went bad?"

"I don't know. Do you want me to find out?"

"No. Thanks. I'm sure she's okay."

"She looked fine this weekend. Enjoy your honeymoon, kid. I had a feeling you might end up in Scotland. Say hi to Justin for us."

"I will. If you hear anything —"

"It'll keep ten days."

Samantha disconnected and relayed what her father had told her to Justin. "I wonder if this scare is why Charlotte jumped at the chance to stay at the inn."

"Did it strike you as odd?"

"Not really. Not at the time. She needs to see about Max's house in Washington and she's been curious about Knights Bridge. Obviously she has more time on her hands than I realized." Samantha reined in her frustration — and her worry. "I hope she knows she can talk to me."

"What about your uncle Caleb?"

"I'm sure if he knew anything about a diving scare, he'd have said something, wedding or no wedding. If he didn't speak up, Isaac, Keith, Ann or Eloisa would have. They have a nose for Bennett gossip." Samantha glanced up at the gray sky, then shifted back to Justin. "Charlotte wouldn't want me to worry about her even without a wedding and a honeymoon."

"You two have that in common."

"Yes, I suppose we do. Justin . . . Never mind."

"You're worried you two have drifted apart?"

Samantha nodded but made no comment.

"Charlotte was your maid of honor, Sam."

"That's true."

"Maybe she's embarrassed, or this ex-fiancé, Tommy, got inside her head again. She'll work it out. There are a number of possible reasons why she didn't talk to you that have nothing to do with any cracks in your relationship."

Samantha smiled at him. "I need that Justin Sloan common sense right now. Sometimes I wonder if any of us Bennetts have common sense. I've always believed Max did, but you know my family."

Justin tucked a hand into hers. "The Bennetts don't do boring. Common sense is different. Charlotte's in good hands in Knights Bridge."

"Your little town works magic on people."

"*Our* little town," he amended, pulling her close. "Right now, what do you say we dip into a pub for lunch and then head on to our next hotel?"

Eleven

Knights Bridge, Massachusetts

Greg was sure he'd never be able to describe how different Dylan and Olivia McCaffrey's Farm at Carriage Hill was from the world he knew. The cream-colored 1803 antique house was located a few miles from Knights Bridge village, on a country road that dead-ended at a gate to the Quabbin Reservoir and its protected watershed. There were old stone walls, herb and flower gardens, fields, shade trees, and a sign, hand-painted by Olivia, with the inn's logo of blossoming chives.

He glanced at Charlotte as they approached the blue-painted door to a "newer" addition. She looked out of her element, too. "Nothing like your life in Edinburgh?" he asked her.

"Nothing."

Olivia opened the door and welcomed them. Dark haired and green eyed, she was

197

visibly pregnant. She still had a few months to go before her due date. He'd met her only briefly that winter but knew her story. Charlotte did, too. A Knights Bridge native, Olivia had bought her old house with the idea of hosting showers, weddings, girlfriend weekends and such, not opening it to the public on a day-to-day basis as a traditional inn. The only problem had been the wreck of a house and its eyesore yard up the road. She'd contacted the owner in San Diego, one Dylan McCaffrey, former professional hockey player turned multimillionaire businessman in a high-tech entertainment firm launched by his best friend from kindergarten, Noah Kendrick.

In the course of figuring out how he'd come to own a run-down property in a rural town west of Boston, Dylan had discovered unknown-to-him roots in the form of a grandmother, never-married Grace Webster, now in her nineties, who'd fallen in love with an RAF pilot decades ago. Duncan McCaffrey, Dylan's father, was their son. He'd arrived in Knights Bridge in search of his birth mother and purchased her dilapidated property on Carriage Hill Road, but he'd died before he could explain to his own son about his adoption as an infant and the unusual circumstances of his birth.

Down the road, Olivia had just wanted the mattress springs out of retired teacher Grace Webster's former yard. Now Olivia and Dylan were married, expecting their first child.

Olivia, Charlotte and Greg entered a large, homey kitchen. Dylan came in from a mudroom, where a large dog was lapping up a bowl of water. Worth millions, Dylan was clad in jeans and a polo shirt and was just back, he said, from chasing Buster out of the chives. "Buster and I have a gentleman's agreement that he doesn't dig in the gardens and I don't get between him and Olivia," Dylan said amiably. "Buster came with this place. I had to earn my spot. Glad you two could come. Make yourselves at home."

Greg could tell the McCaffreys weren't quite sure what to make of him and Charlotte. "We're not a couple," he said. He was a straight-talking guy. Might as well get that one out of the way.

"Oh," Olivia said, clearly surprised at his comment. "Of course."

"Greg and I got thrown together at Red Clover Inn by accident," Charlotte added, marginally less blunt than he'd been. "We only met this weekend. We were both at Samantha and Justin's wedding in England."

Her comment verged on overexplaining and drawing attention to what was supposed to be a nonissue, but Dylan seized the moment for the grand tour. Olivia stayed behind in the kitchen. Something to do with essential oils. Greg had noted little bottles lined up on a butcher-block island. He'd *heard* of essential oils. Best he could do.

Dylan started by pointing to the mudroom, where Buster was now flopped on the floor, and explaining that the back door opened to a stone terrace and herb gardens. "We'll have lunch out there. By New England standards, it's warm enough to eat outside."

Charlotte loved the idea. Greg didn't argue. Dylan had spent a lot of time on skating rinks but he'd grown up and lived in Southern California. He and Olivia had a house on Coronado Island. As they started their tour, Greg realized he remembered a lot more about his buddy Brody's hometown than he'd imagined.

Dylan took them through the original 1803 part of the house. The main rooms each had a fireplace on the center chimney but they used only the ones in the dining room and living room. Olivia's cozy office was cluttered with paint chips, swatches, all kinds of paper, markers, scissors. A graphic designer, she now spent her time transforming her destination inn to her taste.

"Olivia and her friend Maggie are also launching a goat's-milk venture. Soaps, bath products, that sort of thing."

Hence, Greg assumed, the essential oils.

"I met Maggie at the wedding," Charlotte said. "She's married to Justin's younger brother Brandon, isn't she? They have two boys, if I'm not mistaken. They're in London with Brandon's sister, Heather, and Greg's friend Brody."

"You got it," Dylan said, grinning at her. "I'm impressed. Last I heard they were visiting the Churchill War Rooms."

"I've been," Greg said. "Hell of a place. It'll make an impression on the boys."

Charlotte angled a look at him, as if she hadn't expected that one.

Greg made no comment. He was interested in seeing how she operated among Samantha's new friends. She showed no sign of jealousy, concern or disinterest, and he got no clues — zip, none — on what she was hiding or what she was up to with Evelyn Sloan. His curiosity was a mystery to him, but coffee, porridge and a stint in the hammock hadn't helped curb it. She'd come downstairs before he had and had done most of the work getting the porridge going, but he'd chopped nuts and dried fruit they'd picked up at the country store. A little honey and cream, and they'd been good to go.

Dylan took them upstairs to a handful of guest rooms, decorated in Olivia's distinctive style, with Carriage Hill goat's-milk products in the bathrooms. Each room had a beautiful view, whether of the woods across the road, the flower gardens in the side yard or the backyard herb gardens with wildflower-dotted fields leading to a hill, green against the blue June sky.

"Carriage Hill?" Greg asked, pointing out a back window.

Dylan nodded. "There's a trail to the summit if you're into hiking. It has great views of the reservoir. My grandmother's hometown is underwater now. She remembers sledding down hills that are now islands."

"Fascinating history," Charlotte said, eyeing the decorated pillows on a queen-size bed. "Olivia has quite an eye. Did she make the pillows herself?"

"Most of them. She used old linens. She collects them."

"How fun."

Greg had a mad urge to text Brody that he was talking about antique linens, but he resisted. If his friend had spent the day touring a World War II museum with his wife's family, Greg supposed Brody had his hands full, too.

Also he was sort of interested in the old house and the McCaffreys' plans and multiple interests and talents.

Plus he didn't want to be a jerk. Now that he was resting up, he didn't look back on some points of his behavior the past few days with great pride — although it'd been fun crawling under Charlotte Bennett's skin.

They went back downstairs to the kitchen. Dylan explained that he and Olivia had finally moved into the house they'd built up the road, on the property once owned by his father's birth mother. Duncan had bought her run-down house a few months after she'd moved into a local assisted-living facility. For decades, no one in the small town had known Grace Webster had borne a child. Philip Rankin, the RAF pilot she'd fallen in love with, had returned to England and planned to come back for her, but he'd died a hero early in World War II. His great-granddaughter, Alexandra, had designed Samantha's wedding gown and was engaged to Ian Mabry, the Brit who hadn't thrown Greg out of his pub.

"Grace was all for us tearing down her

old place and building a new house," Dylan said.

"You added a barn, too, as I recall," Greg said. "But it won't be used for cows and horses. It'll serve as the base for your adventure travel business and entrepreneurial boot camp."

Dylan grinned. "And here everyone thought you were bored when you visited town."

"I *was* bored. That's why I remember there was a barn."

Charlotte gave a slight roll of the eyes. Greg wasn't sure if she appreciated his humor, but Dylan and Olivia both laughed. "It can get hard to keep up with the changes here," Olivia said. "My brother-in-law — my sister's husband — is the architect who designed the house and barn. We love how they came out. Mark saw to it they blend in with the landscape."

"He's designed an addition here." Dylan opened the refrigerator, pulled out a tray of cut vegetables and set it on the butcher-block island. "We're about to start work on it."

"We're adding a suite that a live-in inn-keeper or guests can use," Olivia said. "We decided we might as well keep digging and hammering while we were at it. It'll be good to get everything the way we want it, at least for now."

"You two seem to have a lot of irons in the fire," Charlotte said.

"We love it," Olivia said. "Brandon Sloan will be leading a group on a hike in the White Mountains after he gets back from England, the first of Dylan's adventure travel jaunts. Dylan will stay here. Brandon works for his family's construction business — this will be a side venture for him."

"Adventure travel was one of my father's dreams," Dylan said. "Soup and sandwiches okay for lunch?"

"Perfect," Charlotte said. "Thank you."

She and Greg both offered to help, but Dylan and Olivia had things under control and were comfortable moving about the country kitchen. "Maggie would have whipped up something wonderful and joined us if she were here," Olivia said. "I'm glad she's getting this break in England. She and Brandon love to travel, and their boys have a touch of wanderlust, too. Dylan and I can manage soup and sandwiches."

Greg browsed the small, opaque bottles of essential oils corralled on the kitchen island. "Anything for cantankerousness?" he asked.

Olivia laughed. "We have several oils that are recommended for evening out moods."

He grinned at her. "That's a diplomatic way to put it. I have a cantankerous uncle whose moods could use some evening out."

"What about anxiety?" Charlotte asked, lifting one of the small bottles.

"Ah, that's my specialty," Olivia said. "There are several options. If you want to try any of the oils for yourselves, please feel free to take whatever you'd like."

Charlotte set the bottle back down. "I'm adjusting to the five-hour time difference between here and Scotland. A good night's sleep would probably help as much as anything."

"That's lavender oil you just had in your hand. It's a solid option. It can help with sleep as well as anxiety and cantankerousness. Take a bottle. It's a tester. You can let me know how you like it. You can't go wrong, unless you're allergic or something."

"Go ahead, Charlotte," Greg said. "I'll sprinkle some on my pillow, too. It won't turn me purple, will it?"

"No, it won't," Olivia said with a laugh. "Brody warned us you could be obnoxious, Agent Rawlings."

Greg winked at her. "It's an art form."

"I've no doubt."

Charlotte didn't laugh, just tucked a bottle of the lavender oil into her tote bag. They headed out to the terrace for lunch. The big dog was sprawled in the sun and barely stirred at having strangers show up on his territory.

"Meet Buster," Dylan said.

"He adopted us last spring," Olivia added.

Her husband shook his head. "He adopted Olivia. He learned to put up with me."

Yep, Greg thought. Life on Carriage Hill Road was totally different from what he knew. Charlotte, too, probably. And Dylan, although he seemed to have acclimated.

Over lunch, the conversation naturally shifted to Charlotte's life in Scotland and her work as a marine archaeologist. Never good at small talk, Greg observed her with the McCaffreys. She was interesting and obviously dedicated to her work but she was also, without a doubt, trying to hide how uptight she was. He was convinced now that his initial assessment that she was concealing something was on target. He had a feeling Dylan, who, according to Heather, was skilled at reading people, was also onto Charlotte. But she wasn't Dylan's problem, and he said nothing.

Greg realized she wasn't his problem, either, but why let that stop him? He wouldn't go too far. He was just curious. If she told him to go to hell, he'd let it go. His kids were arriving tomorrow. He'd have other things on his mind besides Charlotte's secrets.

As he watched her smile and thank Dylan and Olivia for lunch, Greg realized it wouldn't be that easy to get her off his mind. He couldn't explain it. He'd be smart to accept that she was a momentary distraction while he recovered from his fatigue, coped with nothing much to do in their little town and got his head into his move to Washington. He didn't need to dive in deep with her. He was starting a new job soon, a promotion that would require his focus, time and energy. This wasn't the best time to indulge in the pretense that an attractive marine archaeologist who lived in Scotland was the woman of his dreams.

What if she *was* the woman of his dreams?

Then I really do need to know what she's hiding, he thought, grinning to himself as he helped clear the table.

Then there was whatever she and Evelyn Sloan were plotting. He hadn't brought up their elderly neighbor over lunch, and no one else had, either. He recognized he had a tendency to leap to the worst-case scenario, at least as a possibility if not an inevitability, and particularly when he wasn't on the job. But what did a worst-case scenario look like with Charlotte and their eighty-three-year-old neighbor? He didn't want to think about it and headed inside with the dishes he'd collected. Buster followed him into the mudroom. Dylan met the big dog in the kitchen doorway and gave him a look. Buster yawned, unimpressed.

Olivia came in from the terrace. "Buster, you need to stay in the mudroom. I can't have you underfoot right now with all these essential oils."

He considered her request, then flopped onto the mudroom floor.

Dylan sighed. "See what I mean? He tolerates me."

They all laughed, and Greg welcomed the spark in Charlotte's dark eyes. She'd clearly enjoyed being here, with Olivia and Dylan, getting to know Samantha's new friends, getting a better feel for her new life. Had she wondered if Justin Sloan was another Tommy Ferguson and her cousin had made a mistake in marrying him — or had she wondered if she'd made a mistake in *not* marrying Tommy? Greg didn't think so given what he'd witnessed between the ex-couple in England, but Charlotte could be second-guessing herself for other reasons.

"I'm going to walk back to the village," she said. "It's such a beautiful day, and walking always helps me adjust to a new place, never mind a new time zone. Greg, would you mind taking my tote bag back to the inn with you?"

"No problem."

She handed him her bag and turned to their hosts. "It's great to meet you finally. Thanks for lunch and the tour. It's truly a spectacular place."

After Charlotte left through the kitchen door, Olivia peered out the front window. "Just jet lag?" she asked, glancing back at Greg.

"So far as I know," he said.

She gave a tight shake of the head but didn't elaborate on her misgivings. "I hope the lavender oil does the trick, but she's welcome to try alternatives."

"Samantha didn't mention any difficulties Charlotte was having?" Greg asked, coming straight to the point.

"Not to us," Dylan said.

Olivia scooped up several of her essential-oil bottles. "We've been so busy with the house, new businesses and a baby on the way, Samantha might have deliberately not said anything. She mentioned she and Charlotte hadn't seen each other in a while. Staying at Red Clover Inn came up at the last minute, didn't it?"

"As far as I know. I'm sure she's fine. I'll keep an eye on her. Thanks for lunch."

"Let us know if there's anything we can do while you're here," Olivia said.

"I've got two teenagers arriving tomorrow. I might need you to hand them a paintbrush."

Dylan laughed. "If they get bored, send them over. There's always plenty to do."

Greg thanked them again for the tour, lunch and their company and headed out. The afternoon had turned warm enough to suit him. He even rolled down the windows in his car — convenient when he passed Charlotte on the quiet road.

"You still have your phone, don't you?" he asked her.

"Yes."

"Good. Give me a call if you get lost or tire out and need me to fetch you."

"I won't need you to fetch me," she said, then gave him a forced smile. "But thanks."

"Anytime."

He continued up the road. He blamed her annoyance with him on her tension and her secrets rather than his lame humor. He wasn't used to dealing with people who didn't give a rat's ass that he was a federal agent. Usually it got between them on some level. Charlotte didn't seem to give a damn one way or the other.

It was refreshing, he thought, turning off Carriage Hill Road toward the village.

When he arrived back at Red Clover Inn, he found a metal colander filled with fresh-picked peas on the front steps, with a note.

Dear Charlotte,
As promised, peas fresh from my garden.

Enjoy,
Evelyn Sloan

Greg put the colander in the sink and headed back outside. How could peas from Evelyn Sloan's garden be part of whatever she and Charlotte were up to?

He gave himself a mental shake.

"Peas," he muttered. "Damn."

Maybe he *was* bored.

His book and the hammock beckoned.

Captain Mallory and his men were on the move in *The Guns of Navarone* and Greg was settled in the hammock, enjoying the quiet, when his phone buzzed with a text. He thought it might be Charlotte asking for him to pick her up, but no such luck. It was Brody Hancock in London.

Vic got in touch. He says bring the kids to the lake for a cookout on Thursday or Friday.

By Vic, Greg knew, Brody meant Victor Scarlatti, the retired US ambassador who had a home in Knights Bridge. Vic was Brody's mentor and friend. He and Greg weren't pals. He sat up in his hammock and typed his response.

No way out?

None.

He couldn't be in Singapore or on the moon this week, could he?

He's home on Echo Lake. Said he'll stop by the inn.

When?

Today. Have fun.

213

Greg didn't throw his phone in the bushes, though he figured it would feel good to do it. He was a disciplined agent. He'd been shot. He could deal with Vic Scarlatti. He'd certainly dealt with worse in his years with DSS.

He decided not to whine to Brody, who would be unsympathetic, anyway. The only choice was to change the subject.

You still overrun with Sloans?

Yeah. Heather doesn't notice.

You're an only child. You notice.

A smiley-face emoticon from Brody ended the exchange.

Ten minutes later, Greg was back into his book, rooting for the good guys, when he heard a car in the driveway. He gritted his teeth but didn't move out of the hammock. "Speak of the devil," he said when Vic Scarlatti's shadow fell over him. "Good afternoon, Ambassador."

"Vic. We've been through this."

"Right. When I pulled you out of the snow

214

a few months ago. I almost forgot."

"You never forget, Agent Rawlings."

Greg grinned. "You got that right." He rolled up into a sitting position, his feet on the ground as he took in the retired ambassador. Vic was wiry, with thick iron-gray hair and dark eyes. He had on frayed but expensive khakis and a similarly expensive sweater with an elbow blown out. "Gardening accident?"

"Chasing Rohan."

"You haven't got him trained yet?"

"He's still a puppy. It takes time."

Rohan was Vic Scarlatti's golden retriever, a rambunctious twelve-week-old puppy when Greg had met him. If not for Rohan's escape into the snow, Brody and Heather might not be married now, enjoying each other's company — as well as her family — in London. But Greg didn't believe that. Rohan or no Rohan, Brody Hancock and Heather Sloan would have found each other.

"Why didn't you tell me you were in town?" Vic asked.

Greg frowned. "Why would I?"

Vic shook his head, sighing. "Don't change, Greg. Don't ever change. The world would stop spinning if you did."

"I have no idea what you're talking about."

"Of course you don't. We're *friends,* Greg.

215

Friends."

"Should I expect a present at Christmas?"

"A card if I know where to send one."

"I'll be sure to give you my new address." Greg rocked gently in the hammock, his feet planted firmly on the ground. Vic would never let him live it down if he accidentally dumped himself out of the hammock. "I hear you're doing cookouts now. You must be settling into the life of the retired diplomat. You're a regular country squire these days."

"I've eased into retirement since I last saw you, that's true."

Vic hadn't transitioned quietly or smoothly from forty years in the Foreign Service to his lake house in small-town New England. Last time Greg had seen the retired ambassador, Vic had been grappling with a dark night of the soul about his past, present and future, chasing a golden-retriever puppy, planning major renovations to his lakeside Knights Bridge home and playing Scrabble on his iPad. He looked more relaxed now, more comfortable in his own skin.

"Writing your memoirs these days?" Greg asked.

"Doesn't every retired ambassador?"

"I wouldn't know. I don't keep track once

you don't need DSS. I'm sure your memoirs will be a page-turner."

"Don't patronize me."

Greg put up a hand. "Never."

"I understand you're here with Samantha Bennett's pretty cousin," Vic said.

"Are the two of us firing up town gossip?"

"Word is she can hold her own with you."

"Sounds about right."

"Good for her. Bring her to the cookout. Thursday. It's supposed to be warm. You can wade in the lake and your Montana kids can go swimming."

"Minnesota. What time?"

"Four works but I'm flexible. Nowhere else I need to be. See you then."

"Thanks, Vic. Rohan will be there?"

"He will, indeed. He loves the water."

"So does Charlotte," Greg said. "She's a deep-sea diver."

"Excellent. See you Thursday. Call me if you need anything before then."

Vic about-faced and marched back to his car, more spring in his step than when Greg had last seen him. That was good news, he decided. Vic could be supercilious without even trying, and he'd made mistakes in his life, but he didn't give up.

Greg tucked back into his hammock, glancing at his watch. How long would it take Charlotte to walk back here? Would she take a detour? Did he care? Maybe he should go look for her, or slip through the hedges and have a private word with Evelyn Sloan.

"Maybe you should just read your book," he said, opening to where he'd left Alistair MacLean's intrepid commandos.

Charlotte had no problem finding her way back to Knights Bridge. She felt great when she arrived at Red Clover Inn. She'd had no issues with the distance, jet lag or her diving accident. She'd simply enjoyed walking along the quiet country roads.

She approached the hammock where Greg was sacked out with his World War II thriller open on his abdomen. "How was your walk?" he asked, eyes still shut.

"Lovely."

"New England is beautiful this time of year. No argument from me on that one." He opened his eyes but didn't stir from the hammock. "We could do worse than this place."

"I imagine you have."

"Yep, but no complaints. Have you done worse?"

"Depends on your idea of worse."

"Crawling around in a sunken submarine

would be worse."

"Not if it's work you love," she said.

He studied her, the hammock holding up well to his weight. "Do you love crawling around in sunken shipwrecks?"

"I do."

"As an archaeologist or for fun?"

"Both." She made a point of glancing at the inn, taking a deep breath, absorbing the fresh air and bucolic surroundings. She shifted her gaze back to Greg. "Being here has fired up my domestic side. I wasn't sure I had one after all these years living in tiny quarters on a research ship or out of a suitcase. I did okay with decorating my apartment in Edinburgh. Now I have this mad urge to gather paint chips and fabric swatches."

"Sounds dangerous."

"This place will make a good bed-and-breakfast or guesthouse. So many possibilities."

"I imagine there are, especially compared to a sunken wreck." He sat up, tilting the hammock back so he could lean against it. He shut his book. "Do you see Samantha as an innkeeper?"

"Now I do. I'm not sure I would have without being here. Not that she'll give up on pirates. I love Scotland but I can see why she fell in love with Knights Bridge. Justin has a lot to do with it, I'm sure."

"You Bennetts don't like to settle in one place. I can tell." Greg patted the hammock next to him. "Have a seat if you'd like."

She felt a rush of heat, ignored it. "I'm still wired from my walk."

"Sure."

His tone was neutral but not neutral. It was the only way Charlotte knew to describe it. "Walking helps me adjust to a new time zone. I'll go to bed at a normal time tonight, or at least get close."

"Great. Sleeping in a hammock helps me adjust." He motioned toward the house. "Evelyn Sloan dropped off peas from her garden. I have a feeling she was looking for you. Whatever she's got you up to, you're not going fast enough for her."

Charlotte settled back on her heels, noting the slight stretch in her calves. It gave her something to do while she considered what to tell Greg about their neighbor. Nothing, she decided. "Did she say I wasn't going fast enough?"

"I didn't actually see her."

"They teach you to read fresh vegetables as a DS agent?"

"You bet." He stood up, the hammock swinging, empty, behind him. "Take a turn if you'd like. You don't need to sleep. You can read or stare up at the leaves."

"I think I'll take a shower and see what else there is to read. I swear there are books in every room. Then I'll help shell the peas."

"They're not the kind you shell. I learned that from my grandmother. See? Life is good."

They went inside through the back door. Charlotte glanced at the colander of snow peas in the kitchen sink and read Evelyn's note — she hadn't given away her mission about the time capsule. Greg gave her a suspicious look but said nothing as he made his way to the inn's library.

Charlotte headed upstairs and used her excuse of searching for a book to check the other guest rooms. *Surely* the time capsule wouldn't be in a guest room, but she wanted to eliminate the easy spots first. She needed to be thorough and methodical, as much to convince Evelyn as to get the job done. Having a federal agent ready to pounce was something of a motivation, but it wasn't as if she were searching for anything illicit.

You don't know that for a fact, she reminded herself. Just because Evelyn was in her eighties and looked and acted like a straightforward, honest woman didn't mean she hadn't stepped out of line a time or two in her life. What if the time capsule contained evidence of a past misstep?

Charlotte helped herself to a copy of *Pride and Prejudice* in room ten, the last one she checked for a time capsule. She'd skipped Greg's room but doubted she'd find anything there, either. Jane Austen would do for today.

"You know, I've never read *Pride and Prejudice*," she said, and returned to the kitchen, where she found Greg sorting through the colander of peas. "I watched the BBC version with Colin Firth."

"Guys in tights your thing?"

"Depends on the guy."

"There's that. Thought you might go for guys in kilts."

"Not a bad thought."

"Wet suits?"

She smiled. "Let's make dinner, shall we?"

They did up a stir-fry with chicken and fresh vegetables — including Evelyn's snow peas — and put it over brown rice. They ate on the front porch, catching the sun as it dipped into the west. It was so quiet it was hard to believe they were less than a mile from the village. Charlotte noticed Greg fight back a yawn. She'd done the same. In Scotland, they'd be having a nightcap, or they'd be dead asleep in bed. *Separate* beds, she amended to herself.

"Do you think Evelyn really grew the peas herself?" Greg asked as he set his plate aside.

Charlotte shrugged. "I've no reason to doubt her."

"She didn't just buy them at the country store and use them as an excuse to come by here, check up on you?" Greg thought a moment. "I guess she could have picked them and brought them as an excuse to check up on you."

"This is driving you crazy, isn't it?"

"I've gone from warp speed to a crawl this past week. Indulge me."

"It's called being on vacation. The peas are evidence of Evelyn Sloan being a good neighbor." As far as Charlotte knew, it was the case — even if Evelyn had been hoping for an update on her time capsule when she'd stopped by. "Are you looking forward to your new job in Washington?"

He shrugged. "All right. We can change the subject. Only so far you can go with mysterious snow peas. I don't give much thought to the future these days. It'll be good to be on the same continent as my kids. Beyond that — we'll see."

"Where exactly is the DSS Command Center?"

"Across the Potomac from DC in Rosslyn."

"That's not far from my grandparents' house. The last tenants moved out in May. It's empty now. Do you have a place to live yet?"

"Working on it. Friends offered to let me sleep on their couch."

He clearly had a live-for-today mentality. Charlotte suspected it had been entrenched even before he'd been ambushed last fall. He lifted his feet onto the coffee table. They'd finished eating, so that wasn't a problem. Just the view she had of his legs, his jeans tight across his muscular thighs.

"Is your grandfather's house like his brother Harry's place in Boston?" Greg asked.

"Nothing like it. Harry's house is an elegant Back Bay brownstone. Max's house is a bungalow. He hung on to his New Hampshire farm-boy frugality."

"Was he frugal or cheap? There's a difference."

"Frugal. I didn't necessarily recognize that as a kid. Harry was an adventurer but he and Max respected each other. I think my father would have liked a bit more adventure and a little less frugality while he was growing up, but as he's gotten older, he's started to see his father's virtues."

"And you?"

She smiled. "Max and my grandmother were the best."

"But you ended up becoming a marine archaeologist and working with Harry's son Malcolm," Greg said.

Charlotte settled back in her chair. She felt the evening breeze, the air cool, scented with a hint of some kind of flower. She looked forward to her lavender oil. She'd need something to help her relax after a full day with Greg Rawlings.

"My becoming a marine archaeologist and diver wasn't a rejection of my grandfather," she said, hoping she didn't sound defensive. "What did your father do?"

"Electrician. I did reject that. Flat out. Told him when I was seven I wasn't going to be an electrician."

"That was okay with him?"

"It was fine. Not that he had a choice. He was a smart guy and did well as an electrician, but it wasn't my thing. He didn't have the opportunity to go to college. I did. My brother and sister did, too. No complaints. What about you? This U-boat project's done. What's next?"

"We'll see."

"Do you get to decide or does this institute

you work for decide?"

"A little of both."

He leaned forward, his turquoise eyes leveled on her. "Vague answers, Ms. Bennett."

"That's because I'm not thinking about work. What time do your kids arrive tomorrow?"

"Changing the subject again. Okay. It's not like I'm interrogating you." He sat back. "They arrive in Boston midday. I'll head out in the morning to pick them up. If three Rawlings are too much for you, we can find someplace else to stay."

Charlotte shook her head. "No. Stay here. I can leave."

"You're fine. I'm not looking to mess up your vacation or whatever you want to call it."

"*Vacation* is close enough."

He eyed her a moment. "Having Andrew and Megan here will keep us out of trouble."

"What kind of trouble?"

He stood and picked up their dinner plates. "All kinds," he said, and headed inside.

The screen door had swung shut before it dawned on Charlotte what he'd meant. She groaned. The man's timing was something. He'd waited until she was feeling relaxed and sisterly before reminding her that she was attracted to him — and he to her, even if it was just because she was female and present.

"Gad."

She launched herself to her feet and followed him back to the kitchen.

He had the faucet on, the sink half-full as he added the dishes to the soapy water. He grinned at her. "Nothing sexier than a guy up to his elbows in dish suds, is there?"

"Possibly not."

He shook water and suds off his hands and grabbed a towel, threadbare but serviceable. Charlotte watched his deliberate movements, noted the muscles in his forearms, his blunt nails, the water spots on his shirtfront. And even as she was wondering what it would be like to kiss him, it was happening. She couldn't have said who'd made the first move. With his mouth on hers, the feel of his arms, warm and strong, around her, it didn't matter who'd started the kiss.

He stood back, added more dishes to the sink and switched off the water. "I'd hate to explain to the Sloans how we flooded the kitchen," he said easily.

"I'm too tired to mop the floor, anyway. Well —" Charlotte waved a hand "— that should settle you down while your kids are here."

"Ya think, huh?"

She smiled. "Good night, Agent Rawlings. I'm going up to read about my men in tights."

"I like those little dresses the women wear."

"They wouldn't work on me."

"Bet they'd work just fine." His eyes were warm when he turned to her. "Good night, Charlotte. Hope the lavender oil works its wonders on you."

She went up to her room with her book. She mixed a few drops of the lavender oil in a glass of water and then dabbed some behind each ear and along her collarbones. She breathed in the soothing scent, but she knew it would take some time before she felt soothed. The kiss had stirred her up, physically, emotionally.

She'd be asleep by now at home in Edinburgh, but would Edinburgh ever be her home again? She had no idea. A week ago, she'd told herself that facing the unknown was exciting and energizing, but now it felt unnerving. She felt sneaky for not having told anyone about the accident and her leave of absence from the institute.

Maybe, though, her unsettled feelings had more to do with the scrutiny of her sexy, suspicious fellow guest at Red Clover Inn.

She pulled the curtains, got into the most prosaic pajamas she'd packed and climbed into bed. It was still fairly early but she read only a page before her drooping eyelids defeated her and the lavender oil worked its magic.

A bat swooped low in front of the porch while Greg sat on a wicker chair and read his book. It was well after dark, but he could make out the bat's silhouette as it disappeared into the night. He swore it joined friends above the adjoining field.

He wouldn't mention bats to Charlotte.

Probably wouldn't faze her, though.

But when a mosquito swooped in, he was done. Damn thing was at least half the size of the bat — only a marginal exaggeration. He didn't need to sit out here in the dark and cool air and fight off mosquitoes.

He headed back inside and upstairs in the quiet, rambling inn. He was on bat and mosquito alert, but he didn't see anything lurking in the long second-floor hall.

He checked his room, just in case.

All was quiet.

Maybe he was just looking for a little drama now that his inn mate had retired for the night. Listening to mice scurrying in the walls wouldn't do the trick but chasing a bat might. Was that why he'd kissed Charlotte? The need for an adrenaline rush?

Greg shook his head. *No.* He was attracted to her, and he had been from the moment he'd laid eyes on her the night before her cousin's English wedding. It didn't mean he should act on his attraction or that it'd go anywhere, but it was undeniable.

He washed up, pulled off his clothes and crawled into bed, feeling his fatigue. It wasn't just physical. It was mental, emotional. A tough, dangerous assignment last fall that had ended with him shot and hospitalized. Then had come the grueling months of recovery with the accompanying second-guessing, boredom and uncertainties. Finally he'd gone back to work, on to another tough, dangerous assignment — by his own choice. Now he was taking a break ahead of a new job, a promotion he hadn't asked for and wasn't sure he should have accepted.

He had a good start on *The Guns of Navarone* with its ass-kicking heroes. He wasn't sure how much reading he'd do with the kids here. He yawned as he tried to concentrate on a new chapter. His eyes wouldn't focus. He gave up and shut the book, but he received a text from Laura as he reached to turn off his bedside light.

You'll go inside the airport to meet the kids?

She was worried. He could feel it as he glanced at her text and responded.

Yes.

You won't be late?

No.

I'll follow them on a flight tracker. I'll know when they land.

Andrew and Megan had flown on their own a number of times, including to visit him, their grandmother, uncles, aunts and cousins during his recovery in New York, but they'd never been to Boston. Laura had never liked them flying on their own. Greg told himself it was to her credit she didn't throw hurdles in the way, but he could read the tea leaves with her. She wanted *him* to throw the hurdles. Tell the kids he'd come to Minnesota to see them and they didn't have to disrupt their lives to visit him.

He wasn't playing that game.

Great. Enjoy the time on your own.

There was no immediate response. Then, after a full minute, she texted back.

Enjoy your visit.

He suspected she'd been tempted to shoot off some aggrieved remark to him, read into his words and otherwise take offense where none had been intended, but they'd moved on from those kinds of barbed comments, at least for the most part. They shared two teenagers they loved deeply, unconditionally. That would always be the case.

Greg shut off his light and settled under the covers.

He didn't hear more scurrying in the walls. No bats or mosquitoes got into his room.

Andrew and Megan would get a kick out of the inn. He smiled, thinking of them. He couldn't wait to see them and spend time with them, but he doubted their presence would stop him from wanting to kiss Charlotte Bennett again. Right now, though, all was quiet at Red Clover Inn.

TWELVE

Greg left for Boston shortly after breakfast. Charlotte heard his car in the driveway. She'd slipped downstairs early and made coffee and grabbed cereal that she'd then eaten up in her room. She didn't want to be alone with him after last night's kiss. Best to wait until he got back with his kids. She wasn't nervous about meeting them but she didn't want to do anything to interfere with their time with their father.

What she needed, she decided, was her own agenda — her own things to do.

With Greg safely on his way, she went back downstairs, grabbed her tote bag and walked into the village. It was another sunny, perfect June morning, but clouds, rain and cooler temperatures were forecast for later on in the week. She resisted pancakes at Smith's and continued into the village, crossing Main Street to the common. She checked out the war memorials and enjoyed a few minutes in the shade before heading across South Main to the town's public library, a sturdy late-nineteenth-century building of stone and brick.

Young children were gathered for story hour in a children's nook. It was led by Kylie Shaw, a.k.a. Morwenna Mills, an animated Knights Bridge children's author and illustrator whose wildly popular series about a family of badgers had been inspired by the Swift River Valley.

Charlotte had learned that from Clare Morgan, the librarian. Clare had introduced herself as Charlotte checked out the main sitting room, where an oil portrait of George Sanderson, the library's nineteenth-century founder and benefactor, hung above the mantel of an ornate fireplace. Charlotte was more interested in the old photos taken before the valley had been flooded to create Quabbin Reservoir.

"I understand you're a diver," Clare said. She was in her midthirties or so, slim and fair. She smiled at Charlotte's expression. "I've learned not to be surprised by what people know around here. It's a small town and news travels fast. Samantha told me about you. I moved to Knights Bridge late last year and we've become friends."

"She mentioned you, too," Charlotte said.

"I'm sorry I couldn't make it to the wedding, but I'm glad she had it in the UK, close to her family. Maggie Sloan has been sending me pictures of their London adventures. We're friends — she lives around the corner from me." Clare pointed vaguely in the direction of South Main Street. "Her sons and my son are about the same age."

And, if Charlotte remembered correctly, Clare was newly married to an ER doctor with Knights Bridge roots. Samantha had filled her in on some of the local gossip during their prewedding dress fitting, a good way to manage any jitters — in Samantha's case, more like prewedding excitement. No doubts for her.

Clare pointed to a series of underwater photographs of the massive reservoir. "Divers explored the bottom of the reservoir about fifteen years ago. They filmed a documentary. The project was led by a University of Massachusetts biology professor with help from the state police underwater recovery team. They documented the remains of the four lost valley towns, Dana, Prescott, Greenwich and Enfield. The valley floor was scraped bare to create a pristine bottom for drinking water, but there are all sorts of rumors about what got left behind."

"The mysteries of the deep," Charlotte

said, studying the photographs. She heard the wistfulness in her voice but didn't know if Clare noticed.

"Mmm," Clare said. "The protected wilderness surrounding the reservoir is filled with old stone walls, cellar holes, roads and lanes — the bits and pieces of the lives of the thousands of people who gave up their homes to provide drinking water for metropolitan Boston."

Charlotte heard whoops from the children at story hour and smiled. "I know more about underwater exploration than I do children's stories, I can tell you that."

"Kylie's badgers are a hit with adults, too, but they have a special appeal for children. She's a newcomer, too. She came to town for an artistic retreat and ended up staying."

"Knights Bridge has a way of keeping people here, doesn't it?"

Clare laughed and agreed. She returned to work, preparing for a book club for seniors, she said. Charlotte wondered if Evelyn Sloan was a member but decided not to ask. She didn't want to prompt any unwanted scrutiny of their relationship. Having Greg on her case was enough but at least he was an outsider. She'd gotten a hint from Samantha's first days in Knights

Bridge of how fast news traveled and how easily rumors got exaggerated in the small town, *especially* among the Sloans.

Charlotte wandered into the stacks. From what she could tell, nothing earth-shattering had happened in Knights Bridge sixty-five years ago when Evelyn and her friend had put together their time capsule. Quabbin had finally filled to capacity with the dammed Swift River and Beaver Brook, the last remnants of the valley towns disappearing forever underwater. Amherst, Evelyn's hometown, wasn't as dramatically affected as Knights Bridge had been by the years-long construction of the reservoir and the relocation of the valley's population. New roads were built, other roads discontinued — Charlotte had noticed a photograph of an old country road that ran right into the reservoir, as if it were still 1925 and nothing had changed.

Although she enjoyed her visit to the library, she felt faintly dissatisfied when she left, as if she'd somehow missed clues to what had Evelyn Sloan so determined to find her time capsule and keep it secret. But it was impatience more than anything that had her out of sorts, and also, she thought as she crossed the town common, the knowledge that she'd have to amp up her search.

"Time to go where the spiders live," she muttered to herself.

When she arrived back at the inn, she had leftover stir-fry for lunch and then tackled the main floor for the time capsule. Best to take advantage of Greg's absence since it would be hard to disguise her activities. How to explain digging through closets, cupboards and drawers? He'd see through any of her answers. Looking for playing cards, jigsaw puzzles, something to write with, curiosity, boredom — they all sounded lame to her. She supposed she could say she was paranoid about mice and spiders, but Greg would recognize any outright lie.

And she didn't want to lie to him or anyone else.

Evelyn Sloan would be in much the same position. Even if she could search for the time capsule herself with her bad knee, how to explain herself without making her family suspicious? Staying at the inn allowed Charlotte to slip in her searches with no one the wiser.

If she didn't get caught, she wouldn't have to fib.

The main floor consisted of the kitchen, pantry, dining room, library, living room, an office and reception area, a powder room, and the suite where Justin and Samantha planned to live during renovations. Most of the rooms appeared to have been cleared out, probably before the place was sold to the Sloans. What if someone had tossed out the time capsule assuming it was junk? Charlotte doubted Evelyn's friend Betsy would have hidden it in a main room.

She didn't relish checking the attic and cellar but they could be her best bets. A controlled descent to a sunken wreck with a professional team above and below water was one thing. Sneaking into an old, unknown attic and cellar was quite another. Who knew what she'd find? Spiders, for certain. With the spotty cell service, she couldn't count on calling for help if she got into trouble.

A problem she could put off for now, considering the amount of time even her quick search of the main floor had taken. She'd tackle the attic and cellar her next opportunity.

She discovered a few faded black-and-white photographs tucked in a sideboard in the dining room, under a wooden tray. She spread them out on the table. One depicted two teenage girls standing on the steps of the inn's front porch. Charlotte was positive the one on the left was Evelyn Sloan. Her hair was dark and wavy, one hand on her hip as she smiled at the camera. She wore a sweater and a skirt that came to her midcalf and was cinched at her waist with a slender belt. The girl posed next to her had longer, lighter hair and was dressed much the same — Betsy, Evelyn's friend whose family owned the inn, no doubt, her coconspirator in the time capsule that was now, decades later, such a source of concern.

The other two photographs of the girls had obviously been taken the same day. There was no notation on the backs. Charlotte wondered who'd taken them, what the occasion had been. Had they been tucked into the sideboard in an offhand manner because they weren't important, or the opposite — deliberately, because they *were* important?

Charlotte returned the photographs to where she'd found them and headed out to the front porch with a glass of ice water. She felt like such a snoop that when Eric Sloan appeared on the driveway, she jumped. She was sure she looked guilty. She tried to cover for herself with a smile as she descended the porch steps and met him on the front walk.

"Sorry if I startled you," he said.

"No problem. I was lost in thought."

He was in jeans and a T-shirt and was carrying a bag of spinach. "From my grandmother. I stopped by to check on her. Her knee must be better if she's picking vegetables."

He sounded dubious about his grandmother's knee issues, but Charlotte wasn't going there. She thanked him for the spinach and set the bag on a step. "Would you like a glass of water or iced tea?"

"No, thanks. I'm not staying. Greg's not here?"

"He's in Boston picking up his kids at the airport. I imagine they'll be back here soon. I'm sure he'll appreciate your grandmother's spinach. We enjoyed the snow peas last night."

"She's always loved to garden. My grandfather could take it or leave it. He was a carpenter. He worked on this place, actually. One of his first jobs. That's how he and Gran met. She was in town visiting the family who owned the inn." Eric's deep blue eyes narrowed. "Gran's not being a pest, is she?"

"Absolutely not," Charlotte said without hesitation. She meant it.

"I think she misses Heather since she moved to London. She's the only granddaughter. Gran always liked Brody when he lived in town." Eric grinned. "That's one of us."

"He and Heather seem happy together."

"They plan to come back here and build out on Echo Lake."

"Nice." Charlotte kept her tone light. "Are you sure you won't stay?"

"No, thanks. Give my best to Greg. If his kids are a handful and you need to escape, we can find you another place to stay."

"I'm sure it'll be fine."

"Call me if my grandmother becomes a problem. We can't help but worry about her."

Charlotte smiled. "She seems on her game to me. Again, thanks for the spinach."

"Sure thing."

After Eric left, Charlotte took the bag of spinach into the kitchen and set it on the counter. She filled the sink with water and tossed in the spinach, although it looked relatively clean and picked over. Still, it was something to do now that she was restless, on edge. She considered Eric's visit. What if there was no time capsule? What if his grandmother had made it up or she and her friend had dealt with it forty or fifty or even sixty years ago and she didn't remember? What if she was muddled due to the onset of dementia or something of that nature?

Charlotte shook off the thought. She stuck to what she'd told Eric. Evelyn Sloan was sharp, alert and knew exactly what she was doing — and she had her reasons for wanting to find her time capsule before anyone else did, especially a member of her family.

It was after eight when Greg arrived back at Red Clover Inn with his two teenagers. Their resemblance to their father took Charlotte by surprise, but she didn't know why it should have. She'd known he was a dad. Although visibly tired from their trip, the pair were also wired, excited about spending time with their father in a small New England town.

Andrew hoisted his duffel bag over one shoulder. He was strongly built like his father, with tawny hair and blue eyes. "This place would be great at Halloween. Seriously. You probably wouldn't need fake bats and spiderwebs, right, Dad? You'd have the real thing."

"Tough to get a bat to fly around on cue," Greg said.

"Too bad Brody's not here," Megan said. Her thick curls shared Greg's dark auburn color. "I want to meet Heather."

Her brother snorted. "Jealous because Heather got Brody and you didn't?"

"*No.* Jerk."

Andrew laughed and cuffed her on the shoulder. "Kidding."

Greg made a face as if he didn't get this exchange, which, of course, he did. Charlotte smiled but kept quiet. At thirteen, she'd have had a crush on Brody Hancock, too. Look at her last night, kissing Greg in the kitchen.

"What rooms do we get?" Megan asked. "Can I pick my own?"

"Sure," Greg said. "Any but the ones Charlotte and I have."

"It's really nice to meet you, Charlotte," Andrew said. "Dad already explained that you and he . . ." The boy reddened. "You know."

"They asked if we were together," Greg said, clearly amused. "I answered that at this point, no, we are not."

"It's cool you're a diver," Andrew added.

"Thanks." Charlotte kept her tone carefully neutral. "I enjoy diving."

"I love the ocean," Megan said. "I know I'm from the Midwest and I don't get to the ocean very often, but I still love it. We're only a couple of hours from the ocean here. Are you going to do any diving while you're here?"

"No plans to," Charlotte said, aware of

Greg's eyes on her.

He made no comment and shifted to Andrew and Megan. "I waited until we got here to lay the bad news on you. This place doesn't have Wi-Fi, cable or even a working television. Cell coverage is spotty."

Both teens moaned.

"You'll survive," Greg said. "There are decks of cards in the rooms and board games in the library for rainy days and quiet nights. Playing solitaire always helps me unwind."

"I don't know how to play solitaire," Megan said.

"There's an instruction book in the bookcase at the end of the first-floor hall," Charlotte said. "I found it while looking for a book to read."

"That's another option," Greg said. "Books."

"What kind of books?" his daughter asked.

He shrugged. "All kinds, most of them published before you were born. Before I was born, even."

Andrew grimaced. "I feel like I'm in a time-travel movie."

"The Knights Bridge effect," Greg said. "I'm reading a thriller set during World War II. You'd like it. Charlotte here found a book by Jane Austen. Men in tights, Megan.

Can't go wrong. Go on. Get yourselves settled. We're invited to a cookout on a lake tomorrow at the home of a retired ambassador."

That perked them up. They'd brought swimsuits. Greg shuddered. "Figures."

The kids laughed, running up the stairs. Within seconds, Charlotte heard doors creak open and thud shut as they inspected all the possible rooms. "I'm in room eight," Megan yelled cheerfully down the stairs. "It's adorable."

"I'm in the one that looks like it could be at Hogwarts," Andrew called, less enthusiastic than his sister.

Greg listened to them run around upstairs. "I'll give them a few minutes and then go and check on them," he said.

"When was the last time you saw them?" Charlotte asked.

"March. They've both grown, Andrew especially. They're good kids."

"I've no doubt."

"How was your day? Get into any trouble with our neighbor?"

"I haven't seen her. Quiet day."

"Mmm," he said, then headed upstairs.

Charlotte went into the library, possibly her favorite room at the inn. She'd done a quick search of the shelves for Evelyn's time capsule but hadn't paid much attention to the book titles. She noticed classics — *War and Peace, Moby Dick, The House of Seven Gables, The Great Gatsby* — as well as a dozen mysteries by Agatha Christie, more Alistair MacLean thrillers, a shelf of romance novels, books on New England history and how-to books on everything from card games to cross-country skiing. Charlotte figured she could spend the entire summer here and never run out of things to read.

She moved to shelves stacked with board games.

"It was Charlotte in the library with the candlestick."

She spun around as Greg came into the room. "What?"

"Clue." He walked over to her. "It's a board game. My grandmother loves it. Ever play?"

"Not in a long time."

"Who'd you play it with?"

"My grandfather. My grandmother wasn't into board games. I'd spend a week with them every summer at the family farm in New Hampshire. I think part of Max wished he'd stayed on the farm, but Harry hated it there."

"Only grandchild?"

Charlotte nodded, sitting on a frayed love seat. Greg stayed on his feet, the evening shadows bringing out the angles in his face. He didn't look as tired as he had when she'd first met him, but she thought he'd still appreciate a good night's sleep. Maybe being with his kids reminded him of the life he no longer had with his family.

He sat across from her on an overstuffed chair. "Tommy a fan of board games?"

"What? Where did that come from?"

"A few hours on the road. I get twitchy. You didn't abandon him at the altar because he didn't play Clue or have a family farm, did you?"

She stared at him. She had no idea if he was serious and genuinely interested or just making awkward conversation while he waited for his kids to get settled. Or jerking her chain for some reason she couldn't fathom.

"Sorry," he said. "None of my business."

"You're used to everything being your business, aren't you?"

"On the job. Not in my personal life. Doesn't mean I'm not curious — or that you can't tell me to go to hell."

"Okay," she said, tucking her feet under her on the couch. "Here goes. I decided against marrying Tommy at the eleventh hour because the morning of our wedding I discovered he was a philanderer and marriage wasn't going to reform him, at least not marriage to me. I doubt he'd even mind my telling you. He's rather proud of it."

"Seriously, you discovered this tidbit the morning of your wedding?"

"Yes. I did. The woman he slept with — an amateur diver — showed me pictures from two nights before. She had no good options and neither did I."

Greg made a face. "Ouch. She a friend?"

"No. Not before, not then, not now. She had nothing to do with the wedding. Just with Tommy."

"American?"

Charlotte nodded. "Portland, Oregon. It was cold hard facts — not cold feet — that prompted me to 'abandon' Tommy at the altar."

"He says women flock to him and he can't help himself?"

"Exactly. Maybe they do, and maybe he can't, but that's not what I want in a relationship. *Philandering* is such an old-fashioned word, isn't it? Maybe it's being here that has me using it. Reading Jane Austen."

"It fits the situation," Greg said.

"Being engaged didn't change Tommy.

He'd have had more one-night stands after we were married. Maybe another woman will take that risk one day or simply not care, or maybe he'll find his soul mate and not be tempted to stray again. I don't know and I don't care. I figured out what I was in for late but not too late."

"Good for you. I didn't step out on Laura, if that's on your mind."

"It's none of my business," she said quickly.

"Doesn't mean it's not on your mind." His tone was matter-of-fact, casual, but his eyes were warm as he settled his gaze on her. "Sorry if I spoiled your evening bringing this up, or if I overstepped sticking my nose into your past."

"But I answered willingly. I didn't tell you to go to hell."

"So you did. I figure it's as good a time as any to get the facts out on the table, since we're here together and thinking about kissing each other and such." He smiled knowingly. "Am I right?"

She sat up straight, dropping her feet to the floor, pushing back her hair with her hands — anything to give herself something to do besides melt. She pointed to the shelf of board games. "Clue's tough to play with just two people. Maybe we can get a game going one night while your kids are here."

"Sure thing," Greg said, a touch of amusement in his voice. "It'll help with their screen withdrawal."

"There's a Monopoly game, too. Samantha and I played with Max and Harry once when we were teenagers. Max won. Harry burned out early. Samantha and I hung in until the bitter end."

"Max didn't have mercy on you?"

She grinned. "None."

"Good. Then you'll be up for a game with the Rawlings clan."

Andrew and Megan were done for the night. They wanted to stay up in their rooms and would be down in the morning. They both said they liked the inn — it was an adventure — and Greg decided not to mention bats and mice.

When he returned to the library, Charlotte had disappeared. He'd thought he'd heard her on the stairs when he was saying good-night to Megan but had talked himself into thinking it was Andrew. She could still be on Scotland time but he wondered if she was upset about something. He felt bad for bringing up the jackass ex-fiancé.

"Not that bad," he muttered, heading out to the front porch.

He'd wanted to know if Charlotte was over the guy — if there was baggage she was still carrying about their relationship and that was what he'd been sensing was up with her. In which case he'd back off and give her more space. He'd needed space after his split with Laura, both before and after the actual divorce. It had been a tumultuous time in his life. Any attempt at a serious relationship would have been doomed from the start.

He could see that Charlotte, although not necessarily fully trusting herself when it came to men, wasn't carrying a torch for the philandering SOB she'd left at the altar.

She was over Tommy Ferguson.

For reasons Greg wasn't about to examine after a long day driving to and from Boston, still tired, jet-lagged, with his kids here, he was having a difficult time not thinking about her. In fact, he *liked* thinking about her. He liked trying to figure her out.

He walked down the porch steps out into the yard. A few stars were overhead. With little ambient light given the reservoir and the small towns that encircled it, the night sky was spectacular out here. He noticed Megan's window was dark. He couldn't see Andrew's since it was around back but expected it was dark, too. They'd both been tired and they didn't have the distraction of social media, texting friends, playing games on their phones. Greg had debated confiscating their phones altogether to help them relax and focus on other things, but he hadn't had to make the decision. Knights Bridge had made it for him, at least in their corner of the small town.

He appreciated having his kids under the same roof with him but hated that it was unusual rather than normal. Why couldn't he have a normal life? Ambassador Scarlatti liked to tell him that he wasn't wired for normal. Vic wasn't, either.

Greg wanted Andrew and Megan to have a good time together while they were here, together.

He would focus on that, he decided, heading back inside the inn when the mosquitoes found him.

THIRTEEN

Killiecrankie Pass, Scotland

Samantha looked down at the rocky river quietly coursing through the base of a wooded gorge known as the Pass of Killiecrankie. Justin stood close to her on the dirt trail. They'd stopped at the visitor center and absorbed the information about the pass's history and environment. It was almost noon, sunny and relatively warm for a Scottish late-spring morning. They'd awakened early at their guesthouse in the village of Pitlochry north of Edinburgh and had decided to take advantage of the clear skies and Perthshire Highlands scenery with a hike.

That didn't mean Knights Bridge was far from their minds.

"The Garry River is different from Cider Brook, where we met," Samantha said.

"That was a day to remember." Justin put an arm around her, drawing her close. "But

255

so is this."

She thought she could feel the cold of the river rising up to her, but it could just be the woods and being still after the first leg of their hike. The guesthouse had packed them a lunch, which Justin carried in a day pack. She'd offered to carry it but he'd teased her about keeping her energy for other "activities." They'd hike back up to the visitor center to eat before their trek back to the village.

"You got a text message before we left this morning. Do you want to talk about it?" Samantha asked.

"It was nothing."

"Justin."

He stared down at the river, the steep hillsides covered in oaks and evergreens. Large boulders and rock outcroppings dotted the riverbank and the river itself. A historic Jacobite battle had taken place here in 1689, but it was peaceful now, a popular spot with hikers and tourists.

Finally Justin sighed. "Eric texted me about Gran. Did she say anything to you when we bought Red Clover Inn? Did she express any reservations?"

"Nothing that would prompt a text. She said she'd been friends with the previous owners. Not the quarreling offspring but the couple who died and left the inn to them."

"And her knee? Anything about her knee?"

"Just that it was acting up. She backed out of coming to the wedding but she assured me she was fine — she'd never really expected to go. Do you think she feels left out?"

Justin shook his head. "Not Gran. She's not the type. I don't think her knee kept her from coming to the wedding, or her health in general."

"Maybe she was nervous about being too far from home."

"Maybe, but she says she's planning a trip this fall to see Heather in London. I don't see her going alone, but I'm not interfering as long as she's of sound mind. She's with us all the time. I can see her not wanting to travel with us and having us worry about her and telling her what to do."

"Now, why would she would think you all would do such a thing?" Samantha asked with a smile.

Justin grinned. "As if she's ever paid attention. She could have decided she didn't want to risk jet lag making it harder for her to tell us to go to hell."

"What's on Eric's mind?"

"He says Gran is acting weird. Sneaky,

which isn't like her. He's concerned enough to check in with me but not enough to confront her and risk upsetting her over nothing. He apologized for disturbing our honeymoon. He thinks whatever Gran is up to has something to do with the inn. That's why he got in touch."

"*Do* you know anything?" Samantha asked.

"No," Justin said, shaking his head. "My grandfather and Gran met at the inn. He was on a carpentry job. Gran's family knew the Parkers, the family who owned the inn. She and Betsy Parker were the same age. Betsy married a businessman from Amherst and inherited the inn from her folks when they died. She and her husband ran it for a while but eventually hired an innkeeper and moved to Myrtle Beach. Betsy and Gran stayed friends until Betsy's death."

"Were your grandparents a good match?"

"Yeah, they were. My grandfather died five years ago. He was sick for a while. Heart failure. It was a tough time. We were there for him and Gran as best we could be, but . . ."

He didn't finish and Samantha took his hand. "It was their journey to take as a couple."

"They had a good run together. That's

what they said in those last months." Justin paused, clearing his throat. "It helped but it didn't make it easy."

"She must miss him," Samantha said. "Heather and Brody had a small wedding, with little fanfare. Ours was the first big Sloan family wedding. It's possible Evelyn was worried she'd be reminded of her own wedding and she didn't want to risk getting upset and spoiling things for your family."

"Maybe, but I don't think so. Well, Eric's on the case. He's the eldest grandchild. He and Gran have a special relationship. They're blunt with each other and he sees right through her. She knows she can't manipulate him but that doesn't mean she will tell him what's going on."

"If Eric senses something's up, something's up. Do you want me to get in touch with Charlotte?"

"I want us to have a good lunch and leave Gran to Eric and Christopher."

They walked up to the rustic visitor center and set out their lunch at a picnic table. Last night they'd lingered over a three-course dinner and then a smoky Scotch by the fire, the flames just enough to take the damp chill out of the air. Now it was warm enough that they didn't need jackets or sweaters. Their long-sleeve shirts would do.

They would stay another night at their guesthouse and then continue to their next stop, heading north and west toward the Isle of Skye, one of Samantha's favorite stops in Scotland. But she loved this part of Perthshire with its woodlands and hills broken up by quaint villages, isolated lochs and twisting rivers.

Lunch consisted of ham sandwiches on thick brown bread, apples, buttery short-bread made at the guesthouse and a small insulated container of coffee. Justin unwrapped his sandwich. A hungry man, Samantha thought, although she was probably almost as hungry. "Do you think Charlotte is disappointed you're staying in Knights Bridge?" he asked, lifting half his sandwich.

"She's been nothing but supportive, but we had been talking about doing a maritime project together."

"I can see marine archaeology and pirates going hand in hand."

"They do. We're learning so much about seventeenth- and eighteenth-century ship life as well as the lives of individual pirates through sunken ships that have been discovered. It's not all about gold, you know." She took a bite of her sandwich, enjoying their surroundings. Justin hadn't been easy to talk to in the early days of their relationship.

Sexy, intriguing, a man she'd wanted to know better, but not Mr. Conversation. But all that had changed as they'd come to love and trust each other. "If Charlotte's on indefinite leave from the institute, she might be relieved we aren't planning on working together."

"She wants you to be happy," Justin said.

"And I am happy. I have my pirate research. I don't miss the complexities that historic sunken wrecks involve — all the technical, logistical and legal ins and outs."

"You don't feel you've taken on too many Sloan projects?"

"Definitely not."

Justin set part of his sandwich on the wrapper. "You know they're your projects, too, don't you? Shared. Equal." He smiled. "Don't worry, though. I'm not getting involved with settling the rest of Harry's affairs. You're on your own there."

"Lucky me," Samantha said with a laugh. "Harry was a larger-than-life adventurer in so many ways, but he was also just a guy — a man in love with his wife, doing his best by his sons. Family was important to him. I think Charlotte and I both have been afraid we wouldn't measure up to Harry's example of risk taking and adventure, but he never cared."

"What about his brother Max?"

"They were closer than I realized. They had real respect for each other. I was worried that digging through my grandfather's London apartment and Boston house would turn up things I didn't want to know. The opposite's been true."

"Do you wish Charlotte would move to New England? Could she get a job there?"

"On the East Coast would be great, but we'll see each other and be close wherever she is. I assume she'll return to Edinburgh."

"I could go back there anytime," Justin said, tackling more of his lunch. "You Bennetts don't think twice about getting on an airplane. I can see you have the passport applications ready for our kids before they're even born."

"I love that idea. I can see them here in Scotland with us, but I can also see them in Knights Bridge." She smiled, picturing their little town. "We can take them to story hour at the library, out to the old cider mill — whether or not we get it up and running again."

"It's a great spot. So is this. We need to beat Heather in the baby department. She'll never let me hear the end of it if she has the first kid."

"You're not serious?"

He laughed. "No, I'm not serious. When it's right for us is when it's right."

Samantha let his comment and the possibilities of their life together settle in, such talk, thoughts and imaginings a part of their honeymoon — as well as being in the moment, here, with her husband at a picnic table in the Scottish Highlands. A year ago, could she have pictured this scene? *Not a chance.*

Finally she held up her plump apple. "I have a huge decision. Do I save my apple or do I save my shortbread for the hike back to town?"

"This is the perfect honeymoon if that's your biggest decision of the day."

They decided to split one apple and one shortbread now and save one each for the hike back. They poured coffee and sat next to each other with their backs against the table as they shared the last of their lunch, looking out at the woodland pass where, hundreds of years ago, a bloody battle had raged. Samantha watched a red squirrel scamper up an oak tree.

"I feel guilty not telling Charlotte that we know she's taken a leave of absence. My father or Caleb could tell her if they get in touch with her. I don't want her to think I've been spying on her."

"You have been spying on her," Justin said, getting to his feet.

Samantha grabbed the day pack. "You're no help!"

He grinned. "Relax, okay? Charlotte won't be mad you didn't tell her. She'll think you're on your honeymoon and have other things on your mind. Text or call her if it will make you feel better."

"If anyone can take care of herself, it's Charlotte."

"From what I've seen of her, I've no doubts."

They gathered up their lunch wrappers and remains and tucked them into the pack, in a separate pocket from the apple and shortbread they'd saved. "Max was independent, too," Samantha said. "He didn't have Harry's zest for adventure but he . . . I don't know. I can't explain it."

"He was a Bennett." Justin held out a hand. "I can carry the pack again."

"You're sure?"

"Positive." He took the pack and slung it over his shoulder. "You're preoccupied. I don't want you tripping and losing our last apple and shortbread down the gorge."

"Horrors," she said, laughing. She helped him adjust the pack, feeling the firm muscles of his shoulders. "You've got your grandmother. I've got Charlotte. We're not supposed to have anyone but each other on our minds."

He scooped both her hands into his and pulled her to him. "You're the most important person in the world to me, but I'm glad we have other people in our lives."

"What would we do without family?"

"For ten days?" Justin kissed her lightly. "I think we can manage."

Samantha smiled. "We can, indeed."

FOURTEEN

Knights Bridge, Massachusetts

"This place doesn't look like it burned," Andrew said, hopping up onto a small boulder above Cider Brook, below the small cider mill where Samantha Bennett and Justin Sloan had met last fall.

"The owner's a carpenter and volunteer firefighter," Greg said. "He took care of it."

"He's the guy who got married in England last weekend?"

"That's right."

Greg stood on the bank of the brook above the small pond and stone dam that had been constructed to provide waterpower for the cider mill, built in the mid-nineteenth century. Cider hadn't been made there in decades. Back then, the area, now wooded, had been farmland. Old stone walls that once marked off fields now crisscrossed the mixed hardwood forest. Samantha had ventured out here in search of pirate's treasure and personal redemption when she'd ducked into the mill in the middle of a thunderstorm. It caught fire in a lightning strike. Justin had rescued her, a fact she disputed.

What a pair, the two of them, Greg thought.

The locals had still been talking about Samantha and Justin's fiery — literally — meeting in the old, long-unused mill when Greg had wandered into town briefly over the winter. He didn't think meeting the love of your life in the middle of a fire was that romantic, but as far as he'd been able to tell, he was a minority in that view.

He glanced back at Charlotte as she locked the mill's solid wood door. Samantha had told her where to find the key to the padlock. They'd all had a look inside, but there wasn't much to see, just a wood floor, open beams and a few antique cider barrels. Instead of driving out here with her inn mates, Charlotte had ridden a bicycle she'd found in a shed at the inn. She'd said she'd needed exercise and fresh air. Possibly the truth, Greg thought. It was a beautiful morning. She'd left ahead of them and had managed to beat them here.

"What do the Sloans plan to do with the mill?" Megan asked, stepping onto the stone dam, only a few inches above the water in the millpond.

Greg shrugged. "I don't know. What would you do with it?"

"Turn it back into a working cider mill," Andrew said. "Think they could use hydropower again? There must have been a waterwheel. I wonder what happened to it."

He seemed genuinely interested. Both he and Megan had been up by seven due to their early night. They'd jumped at the chance to have breakfast at Smith's. Charlotte, up at five, had already had breakfast — more porridge, Greg had noticed — and hadn't joined them.

"Are there apple orchards around here?" Megan asked. "They could use local apples."

"They could make hard cider, too," her brother added.

"Cider and hard cider were staple drinks in New England in the nineteenth century," Charlotte said, then smiled. "My grandfather grew up in New Hampshire."

"Charlotte has New England roots," Greg said, addressing Megan and Andrew.

"Strong and deep." She peered into the clear, coppery water in the millpond. "Looks as if the water's only a few feet deep. The brook's probably knee-deep at most. We could jump from rock to rock to get to the other side."

"It's pretty here," Megan said. "It's so peaceful."

"Until the mosquitoes find us," Andrew said. He grinned at Greg. "Good risk assessment, right, Dad?"

"You bet," Greg said.

Charlotte stepped back from the edge of the millpond. "My cousin Samantha came out here last fall in search of evidence a notorious pirate had been this way. Captain Benjamin Farraday. Legend and fact both suggest Farraday could have headed from Boston into interior New England in the early eighteenth century."

"With pirate treasure?" Megan asked, venturing farther out onto the dam.

"That's one of the theories," Charlotte said. "Samantha knows more about pirates than I do. She appreciates the popular myths about pirates but she's a serious scholar. *Treasure hunter* is such a loaded term."

Andrew toed a small stone loose from the mud by the brook. "Do you think there's buried pirate treasure here, Dad?"

Greg watched his daughter on the dam. "That'd be something, wouldn't it?" He kept his tone light despite Megan's precarious balancing act on the old stone dam. "But any treasure would belong to Samantha and Justin Sloan since it's their property. Megan . . ." He took a breath. "Careful, okay?"

She grinned at him. "Sure, Dad."

Andrew tossed his stone into the millpond. Megan held her arms out at her sides, balancing herself as she came within a few inches of where the water flowed over the dam. Greg was about to remind her wet rocks could be slippery, but she stopped short of the water and looked back at him. "Now I have to turn around."

"If you slip, fall into the pond, not the brook," Greg said. "Fewer rocks."

"I'll do that, Dad," she said with a sputter of laughter. She spun around and leaped back onto dry ground. "Easy."

"Good job." Greg turned to Charlotte, who'd squatted down and was dipping her hand into the cold brook water. "Your cousin was out here by herself hunting pirates in a thunderstorm. That's how you Bennetts do things?"

Charlotte shook off her hand and rose. "We're not reckless."

"But you're daredevils, starting with your grandfathers."

"With Samantha's grandfather. Harry was

the daredevil. My grandfather wasn't. Max helped organize Harry's adventures and kept him afloat financially."

"And you're following in Harry's footsteps?"

Charlotte nodded at Megan, who'd jumped onto a partially immersed rock in the middle of the brook. "Your daughter's quite the daredevil herself."

"Megan," Greg said. "Get out of the brook."

"I'm fine." She righted herself as the rock teetered. "It'll be okay if I fall in. The water's no colder than it is in Minnesota."

Greg sighed and turned to Charlotte. "Does she not listen because I'm not there all the time or does she not listen because she's thirteen?"

"Could be a bit of both, or could be because she knows she's fine."

"If she falls in, you can pluck her out. I don't like cold water."

But Megan didn't fall into the cold, rushing brook. Andrew made his way down the bank, searching for frogs. Greg found a flat boulder above the brook and had a seat. Megan jumped into the muck on the opposite bank, her right foot sinking up to her ankle in the mud. She laughed and yelled, kicking muck off her shoe. Then she pulled off both shoes, held one in each hand and stood in the brook, the water flowing fast over the tops of her feet.

She shuddered. "It *is* cold. You'd hate it, Dad. What about you, Charlotte? Do you want to take off your shoes and walk in the brook with me?"

Charlotte laughed, shaking her head. "Thanks, but I'll keep my feet dry for my bike ride back to town."

Megan shifted her attention to Andrew, but he was more interested in his frog hunting. He was almost out of sight among ferns, skunk cabbage and small trees. His sister jumped onto a dry rock in the middle of the brook. Her toes were bright red from the freezing water, but Greg knew she'd never complain, since it'd been her idea to get wet. He observed Charlotte, noticing something different about her as she watched his daughter. It was as if she'd gone inside herself. She was somewhere else, lost in a place that wasn't here, now, at an old cider mill in rural New England.

Megan hopped onto their side of the brook and gave an exaggerated shiver. "I feel the cold more now that my feet aren't in the water than when they were." She sat next to Greg on his boulder and shook out her socks. "I wish I'd brought a towel."

Charlotte pointed up the bank to the dirt driveway. "I'll start back on my bike. Have fun, guys."

It was clearly a strain for her to be cheerful. Thinking about the philandering ex-fiancé? Greg didn't think so. She hadn't struck him as having any regrets about moving on from Tommy Ferguson. Something else had her in its clutches. He knew the signs from tough personal experience. He watched her put on her helmet and push off on her bicycle.

Andrew worked his way through ferns back to the cider mill. Megan put on her socks and shoes. "We won't run out of things to do here in three days, will we, Dad?" she asked.

Greg smiled. "Not a chance."

The ride back to Red Clover Inn was pleasant and didn't take long, and it helped Charlotte get her bearings. She returned the bike to the shed and decided to take the opportunity to check it for the missing time capsule. If not for her promise to keep the search to herself, she'd have enlisted the help of Greg's kids. She'd enjoyed being out at the cider mill with them. Their presence, alas, hadn't stopped her from being hyperaware of their father and his muscular body, his deep turquoise eyes — his knowing looks. He'd guessed something was off with her. She was grateful he hadn't pushed her for an explanation.

Standing by the rock-strewn New England brook, she'd found herself reliving her diving accident. She'd been deep underwater off the coast of Scotland, fighting for her life — for the life of another diver. It had been all she could do not to hyperventilate and pass out in front of Greg and his kids. She'd never expected Cider Brook to trigger such a strong reaction.

Her search of the shed produced nothing but cobwebs, garden tools, a push mower, golf clubs and a few fishing rods. Everything was dusty and not new if not old. A more exhaustive search would take time, but she didn't want to further arouse Greg's suspicions or distract him from his visit with Andrew and Megan should they arrive and catch her digging through the shed.

She locked up, planning to head straight to the shower. When she turned around, Evelyn Sloan was emerging from the hedges. No cane today. "You look chipper," the older woman said. "Adjusting to the time change?"

"I must be. Olivia McCaffrey gave me some lavender oil on Monday. I think it's helping."

"I love lavender. It smells so nice, better than some essential oils I've tried. I've been Olivia and Maggie's guinea pig a few times. They probably have their fingers in too many pies right now, but they'll get it sorted out." Evelyn put a hand on her hip and stretched her lower back. "I just finished working in my garden. I'm most energetic in the morning. Where's Agent Rawlings?"

Charlotte told her.

"He has teenagers? That's a surprise. Well, I hope they enjoy Knights Bridge." She gave a furtive glance behind her before shifting back to Charlotte. "No luck with the time capsule yet, I take it?"

"Not yet. I search when I can. Are you sure you want me to keep this a secret? I can't imagine anyone would open it if you said not to. I could move faster if I didn't have to sneak around."

Evelyn didn't hesitate. "Yes. I'm sure. It has to stay between us."

"All right. No worries. I'll keep my promise."

"Thank you. I checked the internet this morning and the weather in Scotland looks good today. I imagine Samantha and Justin are enjoying their honeymoon. I told them not to send me a postcard. I feel like you're family now, too, since Samantha's your cousin."

"That's sweet."

"I love being called sweet. It doesn't happen every day, I can tell you that."

"Would you like to come inside?" Charlotte asked, motioning toward the back porch.

Evelyn waved a hand. "No, no. I've got my Fitbit steps in for the day. Are you starting to catch on to who is related to whom around here?"

"Getting there."

"Clare Morgan told me she met you at the library yesterday. Kylie Shaw was doing story hour. She's quite a character. She's engaged to a former navy security consultant who's doing some work now for Dylan McCaffrey and Noah Kendrick, his business partner, who's engaged to my grandson Brandon's wife Maggie's older sister, Phoebe." Evelyn smiled. "Did you follow that?"

Charlotte laughed, Evelyn's cheerful, convoluted explanation helping her to let go of the last of her flashback at the brook. "I think so."

Evelyn plucked a dead leaf off an overgrown shrub at the corner of the shed. "Clare replaced Phoebe last fall as library director. Russ Colton — the security consultant marrying Kylie, a.k.a. Morwenna — would get along with your Agent Rawlings, I'm sure, but Russ is in California right now. Los Angeles. He has a brother there."

"Clare, Kylie-slash-Morwenna, Russ, LA. Got it."

"You're confused," Evelyn said with certainty.

Charlotte smiled. "Not hopelessly."

"Clare and her new husband live on South Main in the big Victorian past the library. He didn't grow up in Knights Bridge but he has family here. His grandmother is an old friend. She moved into the local assisted-living facility, but I'd rather — Well, never mind. She loves it there, and that's what counts. Clare was widowed — she has a son by her first marriage."

"She mentioned a son."

Evelyn smiled. "I haven't confused you more, have I?"

"I enjoy learning about Samantha's new friends."

"I hope you'll come back when she and Justin are here. I should get back home. I left a sink full of dishes. Enjoy your cookout with Vic Scarlatti tonight. He has a gorgeous spot on Echo Lake." Evelyn frowned, studying Charlotte. "You are going, aren't you?"

"I didn't . . ." Charlotte caught herself, started again. "I don't know that I'm invited."

"Of course you are. Elly O'Dunn told me. She's Maggie and Phoebe's mother. She has twin daughters, too, Ava and Ruby — they're the youngest. I ran into Elly at the library, too. She works in town. She knows everything that goes on here. Well, not about our time-capsule search. But she told me Vic invited you and Agent Rawlings to a cookout. She may have mentioned his children, now that I think about it." Evelyn paused, as if trying to recollect the details of her conversation with Elly O'Dunn. "Well, it doesn't matter. Elly is Vic's closest neighbor, which isn't saying much out there. You'll see. Give him my best."

Charlotte promised she would — what else could she say? — and Evelyn said goodbye and slipped back through the hedges. Charlotte could hear the rustling of leaves and cracking of small branches. She waited, making sure she didn't hear anything alarming from the other side of the hedges, but all was quiet. She shook off her confusion and went inside and straight up to her room for a shower. She needed hot water and soap after her bike ride and crawl through the shed for the time capsule. She'd eaten a protein bar she had with her on her bike ride. It would do for lunch. The Rawlings clan had packed a picnic lunch for their visit to the cider mill, not that they'd be very hungry after breakfast at Smith's.

When she headed back downstairs, Greg had returned with Andrew and Megan. The teens went upstairs to their rooms while Charlotte made tea in the kitchen. She offered Greg some, but he declined. "Did you find what Evelyn's got you looking for?" he asked casually.

"An artful question," Charlotte said, amused. "I consider my musty copy of *Pride and Prejudice* and a vintage bicycle two good finds. I'll let Samantha know about them after her honeymoon."

Greg leaned against a counter, watching her pour boiling water from a copper kettle into a plain white china teapot. "Evelyn and her friend who owned this place rob a bank back in the day?"

"You're getting ahead of the evidence, Agent Rawlings."

"I can do that. I'm off duty." He turned around to the sink and filled a glass with water. "My mother likes to pretend she's a sweet little old lady. Evelyn doesn't bother pretending. She's tough, smart and devious. I'm telling you. Nothing more dangerous than an old lady on a secret mission. Ask anyone in law enforcement." He drank some of his water and winked at Charlotte. "Kidding."

She set the kettle back on the stove. "The Sloans I've met strike me as straightforward."

"To a fault. My guess is our elderly neighbor isn't used to sneaking around, or to getting someone else to do her bidding. That means whatever she's got you doing must be important, at least to her. She drop off any more vegetables from her garden?"

"How do you know she was here?"

"I don't. I'm guessing because of your manner."

"My manner?" Charlotte held up a hand. "Never mind. Don't tell me. If you go knock on her door, I'm sure Evelyn would give you fresh vegetables."

"I guess we don't need them. We've got Vic's cookout tonight. Did I mention that to you? You're invited."

"So Evelyn told me."

"Small towns," Greg said, as if that explained it. "Where are you off to now?"

She wanted to finish her search for the time capsule and get it out of the way, but it would have to wait with him here, in high-suspicion mode. "The hammock," she said, scooting out the back door before he could comment.

Built in 1912, prior to the breakout of World War I, Vic Scarlatti's house occupied a spectacular spot in the pines and hardwoods on the banks of quiet Echo Lake, a few miles outside Knights Bridge village. "It's breathtaking," Charlotte said as she joined Greg, Andrew and Megan on a stone walk. In the interest of convenience, she'd driven with them out to the lake. The two teens wanted to take a ride in Harry's old Mercedes-Benz, but that would have to wait for another day.

The wiry retired ambassador came down the walk and greeted them. "Perfect weather for a cookout. Glad you could make it. Who do we have here, Agent Rawlings?"

Greg introduced Charlotte first, then Andrew and Megan. Ambassador Scarlatti insisted everyone call him Vic. He led them around to the massive front porch, chatting amiably about his house. "I've owned this place for twenty years but didn't do much to it until I retired. Why renovate when I'm living overseas when I can wait until I'm underfoot? We're still working on the place but you could have stayed in the guest-house." He gestured toward the lake. "It's nice. It's right on the water. Brody stayed there last winter and I stayed there when we had the place ripped apart this spring."

"Thanks," Greg said, "but no way. I don't need a retired ambassador breathing down my neck. No. Way."

Vic snorted. "I'm enjoying life without Diplomatic Security agents breathing down *my* neck."

Despite the teasing, Charlotte could see the two understood and even admired each other.

"Drinks and snacks are set up on the porch," Vic added. "Kayaks and equipment are down on the beach, at least what passes for a beach here. It's too early in the season for swimming for my tastes, but you're welcome to jump in and splash around to your hearts' content."

"Have you ever gone swimming, Vic?" Greg asked.

"I have. I swam all the time as a boy." He stopped as they came to a path, covered in pine needles. "It's not my thing. I don't have enough meat on my bones for swimming in a New England lake, but here I am with a house on a New England lake. I kayak, though."

Greg gave him a skeptical look. "Really?"

Vic didn't skip a beat. "Sure. Absolutely. I

was out for a paddle just last week. I want to take Rohan, but I have a fear of him leaping into the water and turning over my kayak. I'm fairly certain I'd die of hypothermia before I drowned, but the thought of some poor Knights Bridge sod pulling my purple, lifeless body out of the lake . . ."

"Stop, Vic. Damn. The drama." Greg turned to Charlotte and his kids. "Rohan is Vic's golden retriever."

"He's still a puppy," Vic said. "He's incorrigible. He's in the house at the moment."

"I love puppies," Megan said, clearly torn between the dog and the lake.

"You shouldn't kayak alone," Greg said, addressing Vic. "And no, Rohan doesn't count as a companion."

"Yes, yes. I learned crisis prevention and situational awareness from you DS agents."

Andrew and Megan were both biting back laughter at the exchange. Greg sighed. "A little taste of my life, guys. Luckily, Ambassador Scarlatti is more trouble retired than he was on the job."

"Your father is showing off by being patronizing," Vic said.

"Where did you serve as an ambassador?" Andrew asked.

"Paris is the only place I remember now that I'm retired. Everywhere else has faded.

Terribly snobby of me, I suppose, but it's the truth."

"It's not the truth," Greg said.

Vic kept his attention on Andrew and Megan. "Now that I don't have to count on your father to keep me alive, I can ignore him. I developed a fondness for macarons in Paris. What's not to like? Don't try to find one in this town. Stick to apple pie and brownies and such. Now. Enough amusement. Off you go. Enjoy the lake. I'll get dinner on and you can meet Rohan later."

He about-faced and trotted up the stairs to the porch.

"Should I help with dinner?" Charlotte asked Greg.

Greg shook his head. "Trust me, Vic's not doing any cooking himself. Come on. A marine archaeologist must know how to kayak, right? You can show Andrew and Megan. I can paddle a canoe and work a motorboat, but I've never gone kayaking."

"*We* know how to kayak, Dad," Megan said. "It's easy. We can show you."

"Well, I do beg your pardon," he said good-naturedly.

Charlotte followed the Rawlings clan down to the water. It was sparkling under the afternoon sun. Andrew and Megan immediately checked out the three bright-colored kayaks, paddles and life vests lined up on a strip of sandy beach.

Andrew balked at wearing a life vest. "It's quiet water. Nothing will happen."

Greg shook his head. "Wear a vest."

Charlotte hadn't heard such firmness and seriousness from him before. Andrew shrugged and complied without further argument. He and his sister each grabbed one of the two solo kayaks and shoved off into the water.

Greg toed the stern of the two-seater kayak. "Want to introduce me to the joys of kayaking? I'm a quick study."

"Stay centered. Don't lean to one side. Follow what I do with my paddle."

"Sounds kind of sexy."

She sighed. "Greg."

"Made you blush."

"Is this what happens when you're around teenagers?"

"Hop in. I'll push you into the water and then get in."

Within thirty seconds, Charlotte realized he'd been teasing and was, in fact, adept at kayaking. He sat in front. She could have smacked him with her paddle, but the feel of the water under their boat, the late-spring breeze, the gorgeous scenery of woods, water and blue sky — she got caught up in being on the water.

They didn't stay out on the lake for long. Rohan, Vic's adolescent golden retriever, galloped down from the house and barked at the kayakers from the shore. Andrew and Megan got back first, and Rohan leaped into the water to greet them. The kids got the kayaks onto dry land, dropped their paddles and pulled off their vests and played with the puppy, getting him more riled up.

"That dog capsizes us, and I'm blaming Vic," Greg said.

Charlotte laughed. "We'll be fine."

"Easy for you to say. You like cold water."

Clearly not the least bit worried, Greg paddled strongly toward shore. Charlotte found herself relaxing around him and his teenagers as they all returned to the main house.

A cheerful middle-aged woman with un-dyed, gray-streaked red hair had arrived. Vic introduced her as his neighbor, Elly O'Dunn. She'd brought food. "It's stuff out of the freezer, thanks to my caterer daughter, Maggie," she said.

It was clear Elly had an easy relationship with the retired ambassador. She explained she'd had influence on Rohan's training. "Left to Vic," she said, with a smile, "Rohan would be out of control."

Charlotte settled into a comfortable chair on the porch and watched and listened as afternoon turned to evening and the lake glowed orange in the fading sun. Although he'd never married, Vic, she discovered, had a daughter, a respected wine enthusiast who'd recently taken a job at Noah Kendrick's vineyard on California's Central Coast. It was clear Vic wanted her to come back to New England.

Elly explained that her twin daughters were in New York and Hollywood. "I don't think I'll ever see them back here milking goats."

That got Megan's attention. "You have goats?"

"I supply some of the goat's milk for the products Maggie and Olivia are making at the Farm at Carriage Hill," Elly said, obviously proud.

Megan was delighted. "Goats are so cute."

Greg made a face. "Not in my world."

Over dinner, Vic regaled an enthralled Andrew and Megan with raucous tales of the days their father had been assigned to him. "No state secrets have been revealed," Vic added, clearly enjoying himself. "Ah, yes. We did good work and had some good times despite the stresses and strains of our jobs. Damn. I miss those days, but I've come to love the life I have here." He stared out at the lake, shaking his head. "I don't deserve it. That's for sure."

"Damn right," Greg said with a grin.

"I was never cut out for a villa in the South of France or a house in the Hamptons. This place on Echo Lake in little Knights Bridge . . ." Vic raised his wineglass. "To this good life, my friends."

After dinner, Megan sneaked down to the water on her own. Charlotte spotted her and followed her on a path through the pine trees. By the time she reached the water, Megan had walked out up to her knees. "It's freezing," she called happily to Charlotte.

"It's almost dark."

"There's no Loch Ness monster here."

"You can't see obstacles in the water, and we're not familiar —"

"It's a *lake.* It's fine."

Before Charlotte could formulate a response, Megan lost her footing and went under, her arms flailing as she fought for control. Charlotte plunged into the water and grabbed her, yanking her onto her feet. Megan spat out water and gasped, screaming about the cold as Charlotte half carried, half dragged her to shore.

"I stepped off my rock and I couldn't find bottom. I totally panicked. I didn't realize the water was so deep. I'm *freezing.*"

"Are you hurt?" Charlotte asked.

Megan shook her head, shivering, soaked from head to toe. "Don't tell Dad, please."

"Too late. Dad knows," Greg said, emerging from the dark pines. He peered at his daughter. "You okay?"

"Cold and embarrassed."

Her teeth were chattering, her lips purple. "Learn from the experience," Greg said. "You need to take care with unfamiliar water in the dark and you need to have someone with you. The risks aren't worth the benefits. Hypothermia alone can kill you."

"I'm not dead."

He took off his jacket and put it over his daughter's shoulders. "Listen to someone like Charlotte next time. Understood?"

"Understood. I'm sorry."

"I'm glad you're okay." He turned to Charlotte. "What about you? Okay?"

"Fine."

"You look cold and wet to me."

She smiled. "I am cold and wet."

"Let's get you both back to the inn so you can put on dry clothes."

Andrew arrived on the beach as they were starting back to the main house. "Have you ever saved anyone from certain death?" he asked his father.

"It's always best to prevent a life-threatening incident. Come on. It's a beautiful evening but it's getting chilly."

"By your standards," Megan said, grinning now, although still shivering. "I'm only cold because of getting dunked. Thank you for coming after me, Charlotte. Have you ever rescued anyone as a diver?"

"It wasn't the plan but I had to get a trapped diver out of sunken wreckage. It was a close call for both of us."

Megan shuddered. "Scary."

"But you're both okay now?" Andrew asked.

"More or less," Charlotte said, leaving it at that.

"So you're a hero, too," Megan said.

"I did what any other experienced diver would have done. I'm no hero."

Charlotte was keenly aware of Greg's silence as he walked behind her through the pines. When they got back to the house, she helped Elly O'Dunn pack up her car. Vic Scarlatti helped, too. He seemed comfortable in his own skin, but Charlotte gathered that hadn't been the case when Greg had been in Knights Bridge a few months ago. Brody Hancock had grown up on Echo Lake and went way back with Vic. Vic was the reason Brody had ended up in the Diplomatic Security Service.

"Thanks for including me in the cookout," Charlotte told him.

"Anytime. If that Rawlings lot gets too intense for you, you're welcome to the guesthouse yourself. It's comfortable. I used to have an apartment in Manhattan but I've given it up. This place is home."

"Finally," Elly said. "It's about time. You've been coming here for decades."

"You know, Charlotte, around here even if you don't want someone's opinion, you're still likely to get it," Vic said.

"You can say that again," Elly said with a laugh as she climbed into her car.

"Come on," Vic said, slinging an arm over Charlotte's shoulder. "I'll find a couple of old sweatshirts you and Megan can put on for the ride back to town."

FIFTEEN

The evening turned cool and drizzly when they returned to Red Clover Inn and gathered in the library. Greg decided to light a fire. He'd checked with Eric Sloan to make sure the fireplace was safe to use and got the green light. He glanced back at Charlotte as he loaded on the kindling. "You sure you don't want to check the chimney first for stolen loot?"

Andrew and Megan clearly had no idea what Greg meant but Charlotte did. She gave him a cool look as she sank into a chair by the fireplace, leaving the sofa free. "Maybe I already did," she said.

Not a woman easily offended or intimidated, but Greg had already figured that out. He grabbed more kindling out of a copper container in front of the wood box and laid it on the grates in the old fireplace. There was a decent amount of cordwood, whether leftover from the previous owners or brought in by Sloans. It'd get them through the evening, at least.

"It's not that cold, Dad," Andrew said. "It's June. It's practically summer."

"It's cold enough for a fire. Megan's still shivering."

"Am not."

"Fires are romantic," Greg added.

Both kids rolled their eyes. He grinned, glancing at Charlotte. She had her gaze pinned on the fireplace. She and Megan had both changed into dry clothes but Charlotte had put Vic's oversize sweatshirt back on. It was dark green with a moose emblazoned on the front. Greg had no idea why he thought it looked sexy on her.

It was Andrew's suggestion to play Clue. Charlotte joined in, but Greg could tell she only went through the motions. Her mind was elsewhere, and he suspected it was once again somewhere off the coast of Scotland on her dive that had gone bad. He recognized the kind of distracted daze she was in and didn't try to drag her out of it. He wasn't positive what had triggered her inward turn. Being around water, being rested, not having the wedding distraction, Megan's mishap — whatever it was, Charlotte Bennett was caught in the grip of things that troubled her.

Plus she was no damn good at figuring out whodunit in their game.

Greg guessed the identity of the bad guy and the weapon early on, but Megan won when she nailed the room. "It's Professor Plum in the conservatory with the wrench!"

"Rats," Andrew said. "I thought it was the vase."

"There's no vase, Andrew," his sister said.

"Oh. No wonder I lost."

Megan muttered something under her breath. All considered, Greg was pleased by how well she and her brother got along. He appreciated the comfortable banter between them. His kids were doing okay. Their mother deserved the credit for helping them manage their separations due to his work, the ambush that had resulted in his long recovery, their divorce. He'd be closer to their home in Minneapolis with his new job, but he didn't delude himself that the substance of their daily lives would change. Andrew and Megan were getting older and had their own lives. Same for their mother — and for him, he thought, as they put the game away.

"You aren't married, Charlotte?" Megan asked, tucking the weapon cards into their slot.

"Any kids?" Andrew asked.

"No and no."

Megan looked as if she wanted to follow up with more questions. She had match-maker eyes but she didn't pursue the subject. Greg saw no indication Charlotte was worried he might have told his kids about her history as a runaway bride. He was amused by her short, direct answers, but in addition to not being easily offended or intimidated, she didn't embarrass easily, either. She wasn't shy or self-conscious — not by a long shot — but she was private by nature, something he didn't find contradictory.

"When did you start diving?" Megan asked.

"As a kid," Charlotte said. "My parents worked in underwater salvage. So did my father's cousin, Malcolm, Samantha's dad — she's the woman who invited me here and owns this place with her husband. These days I work with a maritime archaeology institute based in Edinburgh."

"That's in Scotland, Megan," Andrew said.

"Jerk." But she grinned, turning back to Charlotte. "We do that to each other sometimes. Treat each other like we're idiots."

"It was possible you didn't know," her brother said, all innocence. "I'm just helping you out."

"That'd be the day." Megan splayed her fingers in front of the fire. "The fire feels good, Dad. I didn't realize how cold I was."

"Hypothermia can do that," Greg said. "I'll put one more log on the fire before we call it a night. Heat this place up good and hot and burn the fight out of you both."

"We're not fighting," Andrew said.

"What do you call it?"

"Being brother and sister." Megan grinned. "That's what Mom says, anyway. You should see us *really* fight."

Greg got a log out of the wood box. "Not while you're here, I hope."

"I don't think we need another log," Megan said. "Really. I'm warm enough."

Andrew raked a hand over his head. "Yeah, Dad. I'm already about to sweat to death."

"I like it warm," Greg said.

His son moaned. "We know."

"Okay, we'll let the fire die down." He set the log back in the wood box. His kids had a point about the heat. Warm was good but he was turning the library into a sweatbox. He glanced at Charlotte, her cheeks pink with the heat in the library. "Should we open a window?" he asked her.

"Can't hurt." She got to her feet, cracked

a window and then sat cross-legged on the floor in front of the fire as she peeled off her sweatshirt to a tank top underneath. "I like watching the flames but it is warm in here."

Greg tore his gaze from her in her tank top. Fortunately, Megan plopped next to Charlotte with more questions. "Is it hard to make a living as a diver?"

"I'm actually a marine archaeologist. That's how I make my living, not specifically by diving. I just wrapped up a project locating and researching sunken World War II German U-boats. It involved a considerable amount of diving."

"What's next now that you're done with that project?" Andrew asked.

"I'm not sure yet." She inhaled, her cheeks going from pink to red, whether from the fire or the questions, Greg didn't know. "The truth is, the diving accident — the rescue I mentioned — might make it too risky for me to dive again. I suffered decompression illness. It occurred on a rapid ascent. It seemed mild, all in all, but it turns out I now could suffer serious complications if I dive again."

"Not like diving into a lake, right?" Megan asked. "Deep-sea dives?"

"That's right. It's the reduction in ambient pressure around the body that causes the problem. Sometimes it's random. Other times there's a triggering event. Diving safeguards have always worked for me. Just not in April."

Greg settled onto the love seat, saying nothing. His daughter frowned at Charlotte. "But you're okay if you don't dive deep?"

"Yes."

"That's good, anyway. You can still be a marine archaeologist if you can't dive, right?"

"To do the kind of projects I have always done, diving is a definite plus and often a necessity. To be a marine archaeologist in some capacity doesn't require diving."

"Are there jobs for you at your institute in Edinburgh if you can't dive?" Andrew asked.

"We'll see. I'm still with the institute." Charlotte smiled. "It'll all work out. I was lucky I didn't suffer a worse case of DCI — decompression illness. I was also lucky I got medical attention early on, since I didn't have severe symptoms that clearly indicated there was a problem."

Megan paled slightly. "Could you have died?"

"No one died," Charlotte said without hesitation. "All's well that ends well."

Greg noticed the vagueness of her response, but Andrew and Megan decided it was too hot in the library and went up to their rooms. "Guess I should let this fire die down before we pass out," he said, shutting the glass doors on the fireplace.

"It feels good after diving into Echo Lake," Charlotte said with an exaggerated shiver. "The water's cold enough as it is but I hit a spring."

"You're used to Scottish waters, though. That must have helped."

She smiled. "No doubt."

He sat next to her on the floor in front of the fire. "Thanks for looking after Megan."

"You're welcome, but she'd have been okay without my help. I just didn't want to take any chances. I didn't know if she'd snagged a tree root or cut herself on a sharp rock."

"Good thinking."

He placed his hands flat on the rug behind him and leaned back, stretching his legs out in front of him. He couldn't remember the last time he'd had a quiet evening in front of a fire. Years, probably. Charlotte looked comfortable, more relaxed after his kids' mini interrogation.

"What's on your mind, Agent Rawlings?" she asked, her eyes on the fire.

"What are your options as a marine archaeologist if you can't dive?"

"There are a number of viable options."

A brush-off answer. He let it go. "Who did you rescue in April? Our pal Tommy?"

"One of his friends. A recreational diver with attitude."

"And Tommy says you were distracted because the guy was a reminder that you'd jilted him. Stirred up all the old history between you two."

"Is that a question or a statement?"

"A guess. I met him, remember?"

She uncrossed her legs and stretched them out in front of the fire, close to his legs but not touching. "The accident happened a year after we ended our engagement. It had nothing to do with our relationship. I wasn't distracted. I helped another diver who was in a dire situation. I came up too fast. It was a close call for both of us, but he's fine and I'm . . ." She paused. "I'm recovered."

"Recovered if you stay on terra firma. You can't dive."

"I didn't say I can't dive. I said there are risks. The alternative to what I did that day was certain death for both of us. I'd say we had a good outcome."

"The guy you saved grateful?"

"Not particularly."

"No surprise," Greg said.

"He blames me for his mistake. Macho guys. Can't ever be their fault."

"I'm macho and it's often my fault."

She laughed. "Thanks for that bit of humor." Her dark eyes connected with his. "Your kids are fun. I enjoyed today."

"Sorry about the tension at the lake. I'm kind of glad Megan took a bit of a risk. She didn't do well when I got shot." He left it at that. "We're checking out the reservoir tomorrow. We'll drive out to Winsor Dam, see what's what. Join us?"

"Can I let you know in the morning?"

"Sure thing. That'll give you overnight to work me out of your system."

"I'm ignoring that comment," she said.

Greg noted she hadn't denied he had a point, but he said nothing further as she said good-night and headed upstairs. He shut the cracked window before the cool evening air could seep into the library and sat back on the floor.

He wasn't sleepy. It would be a good time for a mouse to scurry across the floor. Give him a distraction. A bat swooping into the library would be more work, but he'd handle it. Action beat thinking tonight, he decided. But he lingered by the fire until the flames died to coals. Then he went upstairs and checked on his kids. Both were in bed but awake, reading.

Charlotte's door was shut tight.

He continued down to his room and settled in for the night, alone, with his book.

The next morning, Charlotte woke up at five to fog, drizzle and a silent inn. The dreary weather was forecast to clear by midday, but it didn't bother her. She pulled on jeans, a running top and running shoes and slipped outside without bothering with coffee first. Let the Rawlings family sleep in. She tiptoed off the porch and out to the driveway, then turned right and continued past the field. The cool air invigorated her, chasing away the last of a series of dreams and nightmares. She couldn't remember them all. She didn't want to, either. Lying awake had produced its own problems, chief among them her reaction to Greg. It wouldn't do. She needed to get a grip.

As she reached Main Street and looped back to the inn, she received a text from Samantha's uncle Caleb in London.

All okay in KB?

Charlotte paused in front of the country store and read the message twice, in case

302

she was missing any subtext. She was annoyed with herself for thinking he might be doing anything beyond checking in with her, but that didn't mean he wasn't.

She typed her response.

Just fine. It's pretty.

When do you head back to Edinburgh?

Booked for next week.

What about DC?

Not sure. Soon.

Selling Max's place?

Charlotte noticed Caleb's texts were coming rapidly, as if he'd had his questions stored up and wasn't simply responding to her answers. She continued past the country store, not yet open for the day.

Maybe. How are you?

Sam's new in-laws are visiting. Nice folks.

Enjoy.

Hi to your DS agent. I hear he's there with his kids.

Knights Bridge's news would naturally work its way to the Sloans and through them to Caleb. Charlotte wasn't alarmed, but at the same time, she seldom heard from him. Why now? Because they'd just seen each other at Samantha's wedding? Because she was in the United States — in Knights Bridge? His son Isaac was headed this way soon for college.

Charlotte decided to keep her response simple. Yes. She didn't explain further. Hi to your gang.

You bet. Bye. Hope I didn't wake you.

She slipped her phone into her jacket pocket. An unusual exchange, for sure.

No one was up when she arrived back at the inn. She made coffee and toast and took them out to the front porch. She sat on a wicker chair. Her robin was hopping in the dew-soaked grass. Charlotte picked up her coffee mug. She didn't hear the sound of a single car as she took the first few sips of her coffee and contemplated Caleb's texts.

He knows about my leave of absence.

Had to be, she thought, although her confidence in that assessment grew shakier as she ate her toast. Samantha could have found out in Edinburgh but Caleb, a maritime historian, had his own ties to the marine archaeology community in the UK. Samantha's connections were a bit more dated because of her treasure-hunting work with Duncan McCaffrey and her months going through pack rat Harry's London apartment and Boston house.

Had Samantha's parents, Malcolm and Francesca, found out about the leave of absence? They hadn't seemed to know at the wedding, but Charlotte had avoided any discussion about her work.

"Who talked?" she asked, gazing out at the quiet, green landscape.

Tommy Ferguson knew about the accident but not about the extent of her injuries, and he had no reason to know about or be interested in her leave from the institute.

She sighed. She had a good idea who the source was.

She found a spot with just enough signal to send a text. She typed a message to Alan Bosworth in Edinburgh, debated a moment and then hit Send.

My family knows I'm on leave, not just on vacation.

Thirty seconds later, he blithely admitted her cousin had stopped by the institute with her new husband.

I'm afraid I spoke out of turn. I didn't realize they didn't know.

Of course, Alan didn't know everything about her situation, either. Charlotte reined in any irritation with him. It wouldn't be fair, and it wouldn't do any good now, anyway. He knew about her leave, yes, but not about her caution against diving.

No problem. Edinburgh's a great spot for

newlyweds. What are you working on?

Sunken cities. My favorite.

Charlotte smiled as she wished him well. It was Bosworth's standard answer. He loved sunken cities. She ate her toast and finished her coffee. She couldn't flirt with denial any longer. Last night, talking about the accident, telling the Rawlings family about the risks she faced with her diving career, had been a start.

She thought about Knights Bridge. She felt like both a part of the small town, given Samantha's marriage to a Sloan, and an outsider. She was that way in Edinburgh to a degree, too. Insider, outsider. Underwater, there'd never been any question that she belonged, doing deep-sea dives for her work as a marine archaeologist. Now that was done, at least most likely done.

Who was she kidding? Her doctors had been clear about their assessment. She risked her health and potentially her life if she dived again and had a more serious bout of DCI.

Her mood sinking, she decided not to go to Quabbin. Let Greg have time on his own with his kids.

Their outing would give her a solid window on her own to investigate the cellar and attic for Evelyn's time capsule. Charlotte had no illusions that her elderly neighbor had given up on her quest, and nothing like digging through a rambling old New England inn to improve her own mood.

By midday, the sun had burned through the fog and any hint of rain had ended. Greg walked with Megan and Andrew on the top of Winsor Dam, along a narrow road that had been barred to public vehicles since 9/11. On one side was the pristine reservoir, created when the huge earthen dam had stopped the natural flow of three branches of the Swift River and allowed the north-south valley to flood. Aqueducts carried pure drinking water to metropolitan Boston to the east.

Andrew and Megan climbed onto the stone wall above the steep, grassy slope formed by the dam. Elly O'Dunn had told them that when she was a kid, she and her friends used to roll down the dam in blankets or slide down on cardboard. Madness, as far as Greg was concerned. No wonder it was forbidden now. He'd driven the kids through the visiting area, up past the spillway and out to the lookout tower. They'd read about the small valley towns of Dana, Prescott, Enfield and Greenwich, taken by eminent domain to create the reservoir and all now lost to history.

"What's on your mind, guys?" Greg asked, enjoying the sun. Today would be the warmest day he'd had since arriving in Knights Bridge.

Andrew sat on the low wall and squinted up at his father. "Mom has a boyfriend."

"I know." Greg kept his tone casual. "Good for her. I hope she's happy."

"He works in insurance," Megan said. "He likes baseball and hockey."

"He came to one of my baseball games," Andrew added.

More than Greg had been able to do lately. "One of the games you won?"

"Lost but I got a hit."

Greg nodded. He knew the game Andrew was talking about. He kept track of his kids' activities, and he got back to Minnesota to see them when he could. It wasn't as often as he'd have liked. Video chats helped but there was no substitute for being together in person, the way they were now — the way they could have been if he and Laura had worked out their marriage and she and the kids were coming with him to Washington. But that ship had sailed months ago. If he hadn't been shot — if he'd been sent to a place where his family could have joined him — the outcome of his marriage would be the same.

"His name's Richard," Megan said. "He's really nice. We like him."

"Good. I'm glad."

"Dad . . ." His daughter blinked back tears, her lashes sticking together as she sniffled. "We're still your kids. Forever."

"Yep." He brushed a tear away with his thumb. "No question. Ever."

"You don't regret having kids, do you?" Andrew asked, blunt, awkward. "Marrying Mom in the first place?"

For two cents, Greg would have rolled down the dam and risked a fine, scolding, arrest. What'd they do to dam rollers? He sucked in a breath. "It was easier when you two liked to try to bite each other and didn't ask deep questions. Look, I don't spend a lot of time on regret. It doesn't get me anywhere. I regret not having two pieces of Elly O'Dunn's strawberry roulade last night. I didn't even know what a roulade was. But does regretting my masterful restraint help me get another piece of roulade? It doesn't."

Andrew groaned. "Dad, we're serious."

He sighed. "I know, guys. I don't regret

marrying your mother. I don't regret we had kids. You two are the best thing that's ever happened to me. I know Mom feels the same way."

"What if you have another baby?" Megan blurted.

Greg managed not to choke. "Wait — what? Where's this coming from?"

"If you marry someone like Charlotte . . ." Megan paused, her eyes clearing of tears, their deep turquoise reminding Greg of his grandmother. "She's young enough to have children."

"You married young, Dad," Andrew said. "You have time to start another family."

"Add to the family I have, maybe, but that's theoretical only. I'm not . . ." Greg broke off, reminding himself to breathe. Never mind rolling down Winsor Dam, he swore he'd rather face another ambush than have this conversation. "Why are you asking me about Charlotte?"

"Are you two pretending you're not to-gether for our sake?" Andrew asked.

"Yeah, Dad," Megan said. "You don't have to pretend with us."

Greg was sure he'd started to sweat. Bad enough he kept thinking about Charlotte. Now *his kids* were asking about her.

Be strong, pal.

311

He cleared his throat. "I haven't known Charlotte long. It's a coincidence that we both ended up at Red Clover Inn together."

Andrew stood, looking out at the reservoir, blue under the mostly clear sky. "We're not in second grade anymore, Dad. We see how you and Charlotte look at each other."

Not a kid who minced words. Greg supposed it served him right since he'd never been subtle himself. "Right now I'm focused on our time together. Then I'll focus on finding a place to live in Washington and starting my new job. I'm not thinking about relationships."

"Okay," Andrew said. "If you say so."

"I do say so."

Megan giggled. "Sure, Dad."

They took a scenic route back to Knights Bridge. Construction of the reservoir had changed the natural flow of the roads in the area and its economic development, but as a result, at least arguably, Knights Bridge had retained its rural character and quaintness, its out-of-the-way, time-stopped-here feel. When they arrived at the inn, Harry Bennett's old Mercedes-Benz was in the driveway but there was no sign of Charlotte. The bicycle she'd ridden to the cider mill was in the shed. Had she gone on a walk? If so, Greg noted, she'd left her phone on the kitchen counter.

Andrew and Megan offered to make dinner and set off to the country store together.

Greg went upstairs to fetch his book. As he turned down the hall to his room, he heard footsteps behind a door. Too big to be mice. Then the door opened and Charlotte hopped into the hall. She saw him, gasped and then breathed, smiling. "You startled me. I was in the attic."

Cobwebs stuck to her. "Mission accomplished?" he asked.

"I heard mice," she said.

"We checked the traps this morning and released the captives. I'll set out more tonight."

"Great. More mice to catch." She tugged on the cobweb in her hair. "I'm going to take a shower. How was Quabbin?"

"Beautiful. Interesting."

"Nice," she said, disappearing into her room.

Dinner went well. Charlotte insisted on doing the dishes and shooed Greg and the kids out of the kitchen.

They retreated to the library. It was warm enough to leave the windows open. No fire tonight.

While Andrew and Megan set up another game of Clue, Greg wandered back to the kitchen, where Charlotte was rubbing lotion into her hands, the dishes done.

"Andrew and Megan are enjoying their time with you," she said. "You're their hero."

"I'm not. I'm the father who should have been there for them. You up for Clue?"

"Let me sweep the floor and I'll be in."

"I can help."

"One-person job."

He returned to the library. They waited for her, but she declined to join them for the game. Andrew dealt the Clue cards and Megan fiddled with the weapons while Charlotte said good-night.

"You didn't get bit by a spider up in the attic, did you?" Greg asked her as he glanced at his cards. Well, Colonel Mustard wasn't the culprit. "Spider bites can knock you for a loop."

"I wasn't bitten," she said. "I'll see you all in the morning. Have fun."

Greg sensed her reluctance to leave. "Want to guess the perpetrator, weapon and room?"

"Mr. Green, conservatory, candlestick."

She smiled and retreated. He could hear her footfall on the stairs and turned back to the game. "Think she's right?" he asked the kids.

Not even close, as it turned out. It was

Miss Scarlet in the drawing room with the knife. Andrew won and gloated, but Megan won the next game. They gave up on a third and headed upstairs.

As he glanced at Charlotte's room, Greg noticed a light under the door and wondered if she was up reading Jane Austen or staring out the window, thinking about the few minutes underwater in April that had changed her life.

SIXTEEN

Andrew and Megan cooked breakfast on what was turning out to be another pleasantly warm day in Knights Bridge. Blink, he told his kids, and they'd miss summer there altogether. "Just like Minnesota, Dad," Andrew said, grinning.

"I'll get out there before school starts," Greg said.

"Even with the new job?"

"Yes. Even with the new job." No caveats, he thought. He'd do it. "We'll figure out good dates for you to come to Washington."

The kids decided to eat on the front porch. Charlotte was already out there with her coffee and accepted Megan's invitation to join them. Megan made Greg sit outside while she and Andrew brought out plates, silverware, napkins and the food — scrambled eggs, sausage, toast, yogurt and local strawberries.

"A feast," Charlotte said with a smile.

Over breakfast, Greg threw out some ideas for the day, but Andrew and Megan wanted to stay in town and laze around. It was their last full day in Knights Bridge. "We can take turns riding the bike," Megan said.

"There's a second bike in the shed. I don't know what shape it's in." Charlotte plucked a fresh strawberry from a serving bowl. "I see a lazy day with the Rawlings clan includes physical activity."

Greg made no comment. Andrew and Megan insisted on doing the cleanup themselves, without adult supervision, but they managed to slide their father a knowing look as they gathered up dishes and went back inside. "They can see right through me," he told Charlotte as he grabbed a couple of strawberries.

"I've no doubt, but I think I probably missed something."

He sat back, his chair at an angle from her. "Probably."

He didn't think he'd communicated *that* much of what he was thinking to her, but he noticed spots of color appear in her cheeks. Maybe it was the warm day. She mumbled something about getting more coffee, asked him if he wanted any — he shook his head — and slipped inside, the screen door creaking shut behind her.

No, not the warm day.

Greg ate his strawberries. He was about to head inside when Vic Scarlatti called to invite them swimming. "The water won't be any warmer than it was the other day, but we're hitting eighty degrees today," Vic said. "This is New England. We need to seize the moment. Get here when it suits you. I'm just sitting on the porch playing Scrabble on my iPad."

Greg found Charlotte out back, admiring newly blossoming flowers, and invited her to join them at Echo Lake, but she was reluctant. "I don't want to intrude on your time with your kids. You're starting a high-pressure job. You need a good break, too."

"You just don't want to jump in that cold lake water."

"I'm not intimidated by a cold New England lake."

"Good. Did you bring a swimsuit?"

"Always. You?"

"Never but I have shorts that'll do should I get brave enough to take a dip. Get your suit on and meet us in the driveway at noon if you want to ride with us, or at Vic's if you want to ride your bike."

"Riding with you sounds good. Thanks."

He didn't know what to make of her more subdued, cooperative mood. Thoughts of him in shorts? He grinned, going around front to find the kids. Megan was in the hammock and Andrew was arriving back from his turn on the bike. There had been another bike in the shed but it had a flat tire and rusted brakes.

Echo Lake for a picnic and swimming was met with actual applause by the youngest two members of the Rawlings family.

They kept the picnic simple by stopping at the country store for sandwiches, chips, fruit and drinks.

Vic greeted them in the driveway. No shorts for him — Greg doubted Vic owned a pair. He motioned toward the lake. "I opened up the guesthouse. Figure you might like to have access to it for your swimming and picnic. Typical New England weather. We're lighting fires one day, swimming the next."

"Going to jump in the lake with us, Vic?" Greg asked.

"Not a chance. I have important work to do up at the house."

"Thought you were playing Scrabble."

"An assistant secretary of state is calling me at noon."

Greg supposed it could be true but he wouldn't put a little posturing past Vic.

"Have fun, guys," Vic said as they trooped

down to the lake.

Rohan galloped down to the beach with them. The golden retriever was more eager to get in the water than Greg was. He'd put on the one pair of shorts he'd packed but was in no rush to get wet. They got beach chairs and towels out of the guesthouse and set them up, but Andrew and Megan weren't into sunning themselves. They peeled off their outer layers and charged into the water.

Charlotte had slipped into the bathroom at the guesthouse and emerged in a simple one-piece black suit that managed to take Greg's breath away. He sat on a chair in the sun. Damn, she had long, fit legs. And the curve of her hips and breasts, the taut abdomen.

"If you stare at me in my wet suit, your kids will notice," she said.

"I'm staring at you in your dry suit. Think they've noticed?"

"As you pointed out earlier, they can see right through you. They notice everything."

"Yeah. Easy to think they're just swimming but they're plotting. They go home tomorrow, you know."

Charlotte nodded. "Great idea to have a quiet day. Are you going in the water?"

"Someone's got to set up the picnic."

"Sure, Agent Rawlings."

So much for subdued, he thought as he watched her ease into the water. No squeals and drama from her. She dived into the still lake, her strokes smooth and strong as she disappeared underwater. Greg didn't detect any hesitation or obvious physical limitations from her diving accident, but that didn't mean she wasn't struggling with the aftereffects. He knew from personal experience about hiding the truth. During his recovery, he hadn't wanted to tell the people closest to him about the emotional turmoil and pain he'd been in, not because he was in denial but because he didn't want to make anyone else uncomfortable.

Charlotte came up for air, dived again. After a few minutes, she flipped onto her back and floated in the sparkling water. "Coming in, Greg?" she called to him.

"Sure, why not?"

The air was warmer but the prospect of swimming next to her had a decisive appeal. He stood up from his chair and pulled off his shirt. He didn't think about his scars until his daughter gasped. *"Dad!"*

Andrew stopped still in the water. "Man, Dad, that's a serious scar."

"What? That's where I got shot. Rough day on the job. All patched up now."

He got close enough to the lake's edge for the water to seep over his toes. It was cold but he'd steeled himself. Andrew and Megan cheered him on, and he decided against easing his way into the chilly lake inch by inch. Just go for it. Dive in. Do his kids proud by not being a wimp in front of Charlotte, a professional diver. Didn't matter that she wore wet suits on the job.

He grinned at her. "Never should have let you go in first."

He didn't wait for her response. He dived into the lake. He'd been sitting in the sun and the shock of the cool water on his warm skin had him stifling a yell when he surfaced. Andrew and Megan noticed, of course, and were highly amused.

Charlotte appeared next to him, up to her shoulders in the water. "I'm standing on a nice, flat rock," she said. "No lake-bottom gunk."

"Is *gunk* a professional-diver word?"

"It gets the point across. The water here is beautiful. There aren't any other houses on the lake?"

"Brody grew up over there," Greg said, pointing up the lake, out past Vic's place. "The house was razed after he moved out at eighteen. He and Heather plan to build a house there."

"Lovely."

"Some of the land across the lake is protected."

Her gaze drifted to his scar. "You're healed?"

"A hundred percent."

"That's good," she said softly.

"No scars from your accident?"

"Not visible, no."

She slipped underwater and glided toward shore. In a moment, she raced out of the water, the breeze striking her wet body as she grabbed a towel and pulled it around her. Greg tried to be subtle sneaking a look at her in her wet bathing suit, but she noticed. Probably Andrew and Megan did, too. They were old enough. He watched them laughing, throwing sticks for Rohan, getting the puppy worked up. He liked to see their independence, their self-confidence, their hope in their futures. He liked the young adults they were becoming. He just didn't want them to grow up too fast.

He got out of the water before Andrew and Megan did. He grinned at Charlotte, stretched out on a towel in a sunny spot in the grass. "I could shake off like Rohan."

"That would be something to see." She tossed a towel to him. "Is there anything about you that's subtle?"

"Not much." He caught the towel and dried off, chest first. "You're straightforward yourself, you know."

She nodded out toward Megan and Andrew in the water. "They don't seem to miss their screens as much as they thought they would."

"I wish we could have a longer visit but they have a packed schedule at home," Greg said, watching his kids in the quiet New England lake. "We'll see each other again soon. It'll be easier now that I'll be in Washington."

He went inside to change into dry clothes. When he came out of a downstairs bathroom, Charlotte was coming out of a bedroom, also in dry clothes. "Your lips are blue," he said. "That tells me the water's as cold as I think it is."

"I hit that same spring again as the other day."

"Ah. That must be it. Not just missing your wet suit. Come on. Let's unpack lunch."

They found an old quilt and spread it out in the grass a few yards from the water for their picnic. Vic wandered down from the main house, without his iPad, and happily accepted Charlotte's invitation to join them.

"There's plenty of food," she said.

"I knew you'd bum lunch off us," Greg added.

Vic directed his attention to Charlotte. "You're far too nice to be influenced by him. Ignore him."

Greg grinned, handing Vic a drink. "It's half lemonade, half tea, and reasonably cold. You could use a picnic table out here."

"I'll put it on the never-ending list of things this place needs," Vic said.

He and Greg sat in chairs, but Charlotte stayed on her towel. Andrew and Megan emerged from the water, followed reluctantly by Rohan, who shook off without spraying the food. He settled down next to Vic, a sign, Greg thought, that life wasn't as chaotic on Echo Lake as it had been that winter.

Charlotte passed out sandwiches, and the first lakeside picnic of the season was on.

The kids wandered along the edge of the lake while Greg gathered up the remains of the picnic. Charlotte helped but they both told Vic to relax and enjoy himself — the least they could do since he'd opened up his place to them. Rohan lay sprawled next to Vic in the shade. They looked content, but Greg couldn't help but feel that Vic was isolated and alone out here, the consequences of his life dedicated to his career instead of to his relationships. Projecting, maybe, given the state of his own relationships.

He'd just tied up a trash bag when he received a text from Eric Sloan.

Have you seen my grandmother?

Greg frowned and showed the text to Charlotte, who was wiping off the guesthouse counter. She shook her head. "I haven't seen her. You?"

He shook his head, typing his response.

Not today. What's up?

Can't find her. Car's in her driveway. She didn't show up for her library book club.

Unusual behavior for her?

Yes.

Charlotte set her sponge in the sink and

turned to him. "Tell Eric to look for her at the inn."

Greg did so.

Check the inn. On our way.

"I need to get there," Charlotte said. "I can ask Vic to drive me to town."

"No. We'll go together."

He went outside and whistled for Andrew and Megan. They hadn't seen Evelyn Sloan on their bike rides that morning. "You guys can stay here," Greg said. "I need to go back to the inn with Charlotte."

But once he explained why, they insisted on going, too.

Vic got to his feet, his face lined with concern. "There's no reason for Evelyn to be out here, but I'll check with Elly. She always knows what's going on in town. Evelyn's told her family for years that when the time comes, she's going off into the woods to die like an old dog. I don't know if dogs do that, but it's what she says." He waved a hand. "Nothing you need to repeat to her grandsons. They know."

"Agreed," Greg said. "Thanks, Vic."

When they arrived back at the inn, Eric Sloan met them on the front porch. "I've

327

checked the downstairs rooms. Nothing so far. Christopher's checking Gran's other haunts in the village. He'll text me if he finds her. It's not like Gran to forget or blow off her book club. Wherever she is, she took her cane with her. It's not at the house."

Charlotte inhaled deeply. "She asked me to do a favor and look for something for her that she thinks is at the inn. It's obviously important to her."

"What, she told you not to tell us?"

"That's right. She's very eager to find it."

"And you're not moving fast enough for her," Eric said with a sigh, his worry evident. "She could be anywhere in the inn?"

Charlotte nodded. "Anywhere."

Charlotte wasn't surprised when no one asked her for details on what Evelyn had dispatched her to find. It was clearly time to zero in on finding *her.* Christopher, Evelyn's firefighter grandson, arrived to help. He and Eric conferred briefly but decided they'd clear the inn, her house and both yards before launching a formal search for their grandmother.

A dozen scenarios flashed into Charlotte's mind at once as she headed into the cellar to search. Megan and Andrew decided to join her. It was the last place anyone would expect an elderly woman who loved gardening to wander, but an elderly woman searching for a missing time capsule? Charlotte ignored the tightness in her throat. The cellar, the attic, closets — anywhere in the sprawling inn became possible. But her grandsons and Greg would check every corner of the adjoining properties, regardless of Evelyn's reasoning. They couldn't get tunnel vision. Her whereabouts could have *nothing* to do with the time capsule.

As Charlotte stood on the painted concrete floor by two commercial washers and dryers, Greg came down the steep stairs and joined them in the cellar. "I took a quick look down here while you guys were at the reservoir," she said. "I haven't had a chance to do a thorough search."

"Does Evelyn know where you've searched?" Greg asked.

Charlotte shook her head. "The cellar's big. It's divided into a laundry room, furnace room, storage rooms, closets. There's a bulkhead by the oil tank. When I was down here, it looked as if it hadn't been accessed in decades. It's encased in cobwebs."

"So Evelyn wouldn't have come in that way," Greg said, glancing into the adjoining furnace room. He looked above him, touching a rope clothesline strung loosely between two beams. "Have you called for her?"

"Yeah," Andrew said. "No answer."

"All right. Let's take a look."

Megan started for a door but walked into a cobweb. "Gross," she said.

"Nothing like a face full of cobweb," her father said. "You can wait in the kitchen if you want."

"No. I'm fine. Come on, Andrew. Let's see what's in here." She turned the doorknob and looked back at her brother. "It's unlocked. You first or me first?"

"You first."

"*Me* first," Greg said. He glanced back at Charlotte. "I'll stay with Andrew and Megan."

He wasn't concerned about foul play, she realized. He simply didn't want his kids to walk into an emergency situation. Evelyn Sloan could be injured, ill or worse — *especially* if she'd ended up down here. Greg pushed open the door, and Charlotte saw that it opened into a storage room lined with shelves filled with old coolers, canning jars, lamps, boxes of stray cords and other stuff that amounted to junk.

No Evelyn.

Charlotte edged toward the south side of the cellar that abutted the field. She pulled on a string dangling from a naked lightbulb in a socket above her. It didn't offer much light compared to the fluorescents by the stairs, but at least it was no longer as dark as a dungeon.

The Rawlings clan eased in behind her. "Different from one of your sunken shipwrecks," Greg said. "Or not that different?"

"Different wildlife for sure," she said, realizing he was trying to keep a light tone with his kids there. She smiled at them. "The mysteries of the deep either way." But she stopped, nodding to a shut door in a dark corner. "This door was padlocked when I got the lay of the land down here the other day. It's not now."

Greg stood next to her. "I'm going to take a look, okay?"

"Sure."

"Dad," Andrew whispered, "I hear something."

"Me, too," Megan said, also in a whisper. "It's not mice."

Charlotte heard it, too — a moan, she thought. "Evelyn? It's Charlotte Bennett. Are you in there?"

There was no response.

Greg pushed open the door. "She's here," he said.

Charlotte could see Evelyn crumpled on

the floor just inside the door. She was on her side, lying among old magazines and a cardboard box she'd obviously turned over on herself. Another naked lightbulb gave off dim light. There were more boxes on shelves in what appeared to be a large closet.

"I'll get her grandsons," Andrew said, not waiting for an answer as he withdrew.

Megan squeezed in next to her father. "I have first-aid training."

But he was already checking Evelyn's vitals, speaking softly to her. Charlotte got Megan's help pulling magazines out of the way so that they could open the door wider.

"No, no," Greg said when Evelyn tried to move. "Just be still for now. Let's wait for the pros."

She sank her head onto a *Life* magazine from the 1970s. "Eric and Christopher?"

"On their way."

She shut her eyes. "Damn," she said, sighing.

Her cop and firefighter grandsons arrived. Charlotte, Megan and Greg got out of the way as the two Sloans checked Evelyn to make sure nothing was broken and she wasn't in any other physical distress. She rallied, complaining, arguing, unhurt and obviously grateful, just in need of water.

Megan had run upstairs and returned, out

of breath, with a jug of water. She handed it to Christopher.

Evelyn took a few sips. "I accidentally knocked over a box of magazines while I was looking for a pressure cooker."

"A pressure cooker, Gran?" Eric snorted. "You haven't canned in years."

"I remember Betsy had a pressure cooker. I was inspired. I'm going to have a bumper crop of tomatoes. You boys love my home-made tomato sauce."

Greg glanced at Charlotte, his expression telling her he knew the tale about the pressure cooker was not the truth. Evelyn didn't seem to care it was an blatant fib. Who was going to contradict an eighty-three-year-old woman who'd just been trapped in an old cellar?

Christopher handed the water jug back to Megan. He was a good-looking guy, and she went red. Charlotte wasn't sure Greg noticed. If he did, he gave no sign of it. Christopher shifted back to his grandmother. "You went to a lot of trouble breaking into this place for a pressure cooker," he said.

She sniffed, sitting up straighter. "I did not break in."

"There's a broken padlock," Eric said, pointing to the evidence just inside the door.

"Not my doing."

Eric and Christopher clearly knew better, but they helped her to her feet and got her up to the kitchen. Charlotte followed them and Greg, Andrew and Megan upstairs. She figured Evelyn trusted her with her secret given that she'd lied in front of her.

Evelyn didn't want to sit at the kitchen table and drink more water but her grandsons insisted. "Just for a minute," Christopher said. "Catch your breath. Make sure you're all right."

"I'm *fine.*"

"No bruises?" Eric asked.

"None that I don't deserve. Good thing I'm not afraid of spiders," she said with a shudder. "I could do without small, dark spaces, though. Don't tell Olivia Frost about what happened — Olivia McCaffrey, I mean. She's claustrophobic. She'll hyperventilate."

"We're just glad you're okay, Gran," Christopher said.

"I'm glad your father and the rest of your brothers are in England. I wouldn't get grief from Heather." She made a face. "The whole town will know by nightfall, won't they?"

"Sooner than that," Eric said. "Your book club sounded the alarm about you."

"Oh, no." She moaned. "Those busybodies — I'll never hear the end of it."

Christopher grinned. "Are you kidding? You made their day."

"Think of how much fun they'd have had if I'd needed an ambulance," she muttered.

"You love the attention," Eric said, grinning at her.

"You never were my favorite, you know." But she had his hand clutched in hers as she spoke. "I thought I could slip in and slip out again with no one being the wiser. I remember when Grace Webster took off to her old hideout in Quabbin and got us all in a state looking for her. Now here I am."

"You adventurous old ladies," Christopher said.

Eric kissed her on the cheek. "Leave a note next time."

"I knew someone would find me," she said. "I didn't want to waste energy doing too much yelling and screaming. I usually keep a bottle of water with me. My doctor says you don't always feel thirsty when you're older and to keep track of what I drink."

"Smart," Christopher said.

Eric turned to Charlotte, Greg and the kids. "Thanks for your help."

"Glad it worked out," Greg said.

No one brought up the pressure-cooker

story. Charlotte's gaze connected with Eve-lyn, who sighed heavily and looked up at the three men. "I was searching for a time capsule," she blurted. "Betsy and I put one together for our eighteenth birthdays. We were born within two weeks of each other. I remembered last night that she had a closet in the cellar she always kept locked and thought it might be there." Evelyn paused, glancing around the kitchen. "I left my cane in the cellar . . ."

Andrew and Megan volunteered to look for it and headed downstairs.

Evelyn rubbed a finger on the wood table. "I wasn't looking for a pressure cooker. I'm the one who hacked the padlock. I used a crowbar. You'll find it under the magazines. I remembered how Samantha tackled the padlock when she ducked in the cider mill to get out of that thunderstorm. I figured I could do the same."

Eric grinned at her. "So that's it, Gran. You were waiting for a good-looking guy to come rescue you."

"Agent Rawlings *is* good-looking."

Christopher laughed, shaking his head. "Samantha says she didn't need Justin to rescue her."

"Seems to be a typical Bennett attitude," Greg added.

"Damn, Gran," Eric said. "What's in this time capsule? Anything juicy?"

She took her hand from his and waved it, dismissive. "I don't remember what's in it. I just want to find it before anyone else does. I'm allowed."

"You went to a lot of trouble for something innocent," Eric said. "Sure you didn't put nudie shots of yourself in there? Sparing Pop a stroke?"

Evelyn rolled her eyes. Andrew and Megan returned with her cane. She thanked them and set it firmly on the floor in front of her. "I'm going home. If something really does happen to me, at least I know I won't rot before you come looking for me."

Greg looked at the two brothers. "Did I miss anything or didn't something just really happen to her?"

"Not by Sloan standards," Eric muttered.

But the teasing obviously helped Evelyn return to normal after her mishap in the cellar. She could have easily broken a hip or bashed her head, but Charlotte wasn't fooled, either, as she watched the Sloans head out through the back door. Evelyn Sloan was also using the teasing as a tactic to get everyone off her case.

She wasn't finished with her hunt for her time capsule.

After the Sloans left, Greg turned to Charlotte. "She'll sneak back in here if we don't find that time capsule first."

They fanned out through the inn to search for the time capsule, covering ground that Charlotte hadn't gotten to and rechecking spots where she'd had only a cursory look. Andrew and Megan took the main floors, Greg headed up to the attic and Charlotte went back down to the cellar — with the spiders, she noted. Then again, there were spiders everywhere in the old inn.

After ninety minutes, they had nothing. They gathered in the library for iced tea and the cookies they hadn't eaten on their picnic at Echo Lake.

Andrew sprawled on the floor in front of the unlit fireplace. "What would you do if we find the time capsule?" he asked, wiping a smear of dust off his cheek.

"Give it to Mrs. Sloan," Charlotte said.

Greg sat on the love seat. "She's entitled to a few secrets."

Megan tugged a Monopoly game off a shelf. "Would you tell Chris and Eric you found it?"

"I'd leave that up to their grandmother." Charlotte sank onto a chair upholstered in a soft deep tan fabric, only mildly worn for its obvious age. "I have no idea what's in the time capsule that has her so obsessed. Maybe it's just the idea of it and wanting control."

"Will you open it if you find it?" Megan asked.

"I promised I wouldn't." Charlotte could feel the day's warmth and humidity but someone had opened a window, letting in a light breeze. The inn didn't have central air-conditioning and the window air conditioners and fans she'd spotted in the cellar looked as if they needed cleaning, if they worked at all. But her mind was on Evelyn, and the Rawlings family. This turn in their last day together in Knights Bridge didn't seem to bother them. She smiled, trying to stay focused on the matter at hand. "Doesn't mean I wouldn't be tempted to open it."

Megan set the Monopoly game on the coffee table. "What about you, Dad? Would you open it?"

Greg leaned forward and lifted the lid off the game box and placed it on the floor. "I doubt Mrs. Sloan is hiding state secrets or evidence of a crime, don't you?"

"Yeah," Andrew said. "More likely it's something personal she doesn't want her family to see. I mean, if she and her friend were eighteen when they put the time capsule together — even back then, people could do dumb things at eighteen."

"You can do dumb things at any age," Megan added knowledgeably.

Greg laughed. "That's for sure." He pulled the game board out of the box. "Last time I played Monopoly was with Brody and Heather at Vic's guesthouse. Heather trounced us. She's even more vicious at Risk."

Andrew scooted over to the coffee table. "I want to meet her."

"Me, too," Megan said.

"She says the same about you two," Greg said. "You both did great today with Mrs. Sloan. You focused on the facts and let them drive what you could do, and you listened to Charlotte, Eric, Christopher and me. You didn't get ahead of yourselves or jump to conclusions. You stayed calm and focused."

"Do you think I could be a DS agent?" Andrew asked.

If the question caught Greg by surprise, he showed no indication. Charlotte stayed quiet, watching him unfold the Monopoly board and set out the Community Chest and Chance cards.

"It's not for me to say," he said. "It's for you to decide what you want and commit yourself to it, set goals and work hard toward reaching them. Everything you're doing now will help if you decide you want to go into diplomatic security. Finish high school strong and go to college, participate in extracurricular activities and service, learn about yourself and the world — you'll figure out what makes sense for you. I believe in you. If you work now toward becoming a DS agent, you'll land somewhere worthwhile even if you change your mind."

Megan neatened a stack of pink five-dollar Monopoly bills. "What about me? Girls can become DS agents."

"Of course," Greg said. "Ditto what I just said to your brother."

"Mom would have a fit if we both went into the Foreign Service," Andrew said.

Greg winked at his son. "Maybe I would, too. More so, because I know what you'd be getting into. But I'd support your decision, and so would your mom."

"Well, relax," Megan said. "I'm going to be a botanist. Being here in Knights Bridge convinces me even more. I *love* the gardens at the inn, and Mrs. Sloan said I could come see her garden and pick as many ripe vegetables as I want."

"Lots of time to sort out your lives," her father said, counting out manila-colored hundreds.

Megan shook her head. "Nope. I know."

She stared at the open Monopoly board and the stacks of money, the little houses and hotels, the game pieces. Charlotte recognized the thirteen-year-old's dazed state, the slumped shoulders, the sudden tears in her eyes. The adrenaline dump had run its course, and now she was drained, exhausted. Andrew, two years older, was better at hiding it but she could tell he felt the same.

"Takes a while to play Monopoly," Charlotte said. "I want to take a stint in the hammock before it storms and read my book. Elizabeth and Mr. Darcy are about to meet again."

Greg set his tidied stack of hundreds in the box. "Why don't we wait until after dinner to play Monopoly? We're supposed to get thunderstorms later. Take advantage of the good weather now."

Megan nodded, setting her fives next to the hundreds. "Andrew and I can go pick veggies in Mrs. Sloan's garden. See how she's doing."

"I'm sure she'd appreciate the distraction," Greg said.

Andrew got to his feet, eyeing his father. "We're going home tomorrow. Will you tell us about your new job before we go?"

"Yeah, sure."

"Tonight," Andrew said.

"And not just one-word answers to our questions," Megan added, jutting her chin at her father. "We're not little kids anymore. You can talk to us."

He shrugged. "Fair enough. Then you can tell me about your summer plans. Deal?"

"Deal," his kids said simultaneously.

"Great. Have fun picking vegetables. Just no kale, okay?"

Andrew grinned. "No problem, Dad. I hate kale, too."

As he and Megan left the library, she was lecturing him on kale's healthy attributes and proper ways to cook it and to serve it raw. Greg shuddered. "Kale," he said as if that summed up his opinion.

"I imagine Evelyn has plenty of lettuce, spinach and peas for Megan and Andrew," Charlotte said. "It's nice that Andrew wants to follow in your footsteps."

"Adrenaline from the search. We'll see what happens once he's back in Minnesota."

"Aren't you flattered?"

"I don't want to be flattered. I want him to find what works for him and he's passionate about. I don't want him trying to make up for my absences."

"Is that what you think is going on?"

"I don't know. It's natural for them to be interested in my work." He placed the Monopoly cover back on the box. "Both my kids would make good agents. I didn't sound as if I doubted that, did I?"

"No," Charlotte said. "Not at all."

"It was easier to accept having them follow in my footsteps before I got shot. What if one of your young cousins wanted to be a deep-sea diver?"

"Two do. Two don't want to go near it."

"Let me guess — one of the younger sisters and the second son."

"Eloisa and Keith. Exactly right. Isaac and Ann aren't interested."

"Was it easier to be enthusiastic about Eloisa and Keith diving before your accident?"

Charlotte tucked her feet up under her in her chair. "Who says I was enthusiastic then?" She decided to change the subject. "Did you guys find anything interesting on your search?"

Greg shook his head. "Looks to me as if the family went through the place pretty well before they put it on the market. It was probably more trouble than it was worth to go through the old photographs and magazines. A couple of rooms are missing dressers — I assume they were worth selling. Easier to bundle everything else into the sale price." He stood, peering out the window at the backyard. "I assume Andrew and Megan will get moving if they hear thunder."

"They've got some time before it starts to storm." Suddenly restless, Charlotte launched herself to her feet. "I was going to hit the hammock with my book, but I still have a lot of unfocused energy. Great-Uncle Harry was written up in numerous magazines after he explored the Antarctic a half century ago. I wonder if any of them are in the cellar closet where we found Evelyn. I'd like to take a look."

Greg glanced back at her from the window. "I can go with you and protect you from spiders."

She laughed. "It's not the spiders I'm worried about."

"I'm going to leave it there and not ask."

They went through the kitchen and down the steep stairs to the old cellar, turning on lights as they worked their way back to the closet. "There are hundreds of magazines here," Charlotte said. "There are easier ways to find the spreads on Harry's exploits. I could look online, for one thing."

"That wouldn't be as authentic as digging

in here." Greg flicked old cobwebs off a box. "Easier to get in touch with the passage of time since old Harry's expedition."

Only a few of the boxes were dated, but Charlotte had pried open all of them in her search for Evelyn's time capsule. "I think the date range we're looking for is on this shelf," she said, pointing to a line of a half-dozen boxes.

"*Life* magazine a possibility?" Greg asked, showing her the top row of one box.

"Definitely."

They found boxes of *National Geographic* and *Time* magazines. Greg grabbed them and set them outside the door.

"That should do it," Charlotte said. "It'll be fun to go through them, anyway, regardless of whether we find anything about Harry."

Greg brushed her cheek. "More cobwebs, dust and who knows what." He smiled. "You're something, you know that?"

He leaned in closer, and for a moment she thought he was tackling more dust. Then his eyes held hers, and he whispered her name. She threw her arms around him and smiled. "Here I thought I'd have a quiet few days in the New England countryside."

"I didn't. I knew you were coming."

"Ha."

He threaded his fingers into her hair and drew her closer. "No dust and cobwebs on your lips."

"Yours, either."

Their kiss was lingering, a hint of what could happen between them — a promise, not just a hope. Nothing about being in his arms felt like a mistake, an impulsive act she'd regret later when she came to her senses, returned to her life in Edinburgh, at least what was left of it. Not that thinking straight with his mouth on hers was easy, or even necessary.

He deepened their kiss, ending all her intrusive thoughts.

She heard a door slam shut upstairs — not in anger, she was positive. More like a hurry. Then she heard the rumble of thunder. Andrew and Megan must have come in from Evelyn Sloan's garden.

"A thunderstorm," Charlotte said, standing back from Greg. "Appropriate somehow."

"Yeah." He touched a finger to her lips. "That was okay, wasn't it?"

"More than okay."

"We can bring the magazines upstairs — unless you want to stay down here to do some more digging."

"Nope. I'm good."

They each carried a box upstairs to the kitchen and set them on the floor by the hall to the library. Andrew and Megan were sorting fresh-picked spinach, lettuce and peas they'd heaped on the counter from their haul next door.

"We saw lightning and came in," Andrew said, tossing several spinach leaves into a sink of water. "We made sure Mrs. Sloan got inside before we left."

"She's so sweet," Megan said. "Chris was still there, and he laughed when I said that. But she is sweet, really."

"It was generous of her to let you pick vegetables in her garden," Charlotte said. "I think she's sweet, too, in her own way, but I can understand Chris's point of view. Evelyn strikes me as a solid, interesting woman. He must see that side of her more than the sweet side."

Megan didn't look convinced.

Charlotte took a closer look at the vegetables. No kale. "Is there anything I can do to help?"

Megan shook her head. "Andrew and I will make dinner. A mess of veggies and grilled chicken. Sound good?"

Charlotte smiled. "Sounds great."

"Then shoo," Andrew said, grinning. "Give us room to work."

"No argument from me." Greg peered over his son's shoulder into the sink. "Make sure you two get all the bugs out. A little dirt I can deal with. Something slithering across my plate, no."

His kids threw towels at him. Andrew searched for bugs in the water but couldn't find any. Laughing, Greg grabbed his box of old magazines and headed down the hall. Charlotte followed him to the library with her box. They set them on the floor in front of the fireplace. Thunder rumbled nearby, the late-day light turning gray.

"You can trust me, Charlotte," Greg said softly.

She hadn't expected such a comment. Her breath caught in her throat. "I do. I want to. Yes . . . I trust you, Greg." But her voice was low, barely a whisper, and she didn't know what she'd said aloud, what he'd heard.

"We could do better for a kiss than an old cellar, that's for damn sure. And we will." He opened up his box. "Shall we see what we've got?"

349

SEVENTEEN

Isle of Skye, Scotland

Samantha nursed her smoky Scotch at a boisterous bar where she and Justin had curled up in a booth in a dark, relatively quiet corner. They'd arrived on the picturesque Isle of Skye late yesterday and had spent today checking out the dramatic mountain landscape, one of her favorite spots in Scotland. She'd visited the island with her parents and uncle and his gang, and with Charlotte — and now with Justin, she thought happily. The weather had turned stormy since they'd finished their road trip, but their room was just up the stairs.

Events at home in Knights Bridge had also turned stormy. Samantha had read the texts about Evelyn that Justin received from the two Sloan brothers who were in town this week. "Do you want to call Eric or Christopher?" she asked.

"No. Gran's okay."

It would have been awful if the search for his grandmother had continued into the night, or if it had ended with her hospitalization — or worse. But Samantha didn't need to say that out loud to Justin. He knew. His brothers had interrupted their honeymoon only because they wanted to know if their grandmother had mentioned the time capsule to them or if they'd found it. They weren't concerned about her mental state. They were concerned she'd try again to find it.

"I love the idea of a hidden time capsule, I have to admit," Samantha said.

Justin smiled. "You would."

"Homesick?"

"Not even a little. Gran's good. That's what counts."

Samantha noticed a rugged-looking man in his thirties enter the pub. She recognized him at once and swore under her breath.

Justin frowned at her. "What?"

"I should have picked a place I didn't know. Damn. That's one of Tommy's friends."

"The Tommy at the wedding?"

"Uh-huh. We can sneak upstairs before he sees us."

"Sneaking isn't your style, Sam."

351

She sighed. "No, it isn't."

And the diver — Brian Jones — had already spotted them and wove through the crowd to their table. "Sam Bennett — hey, that is you. Great to see you."

"You, too, Brian. This is my husband, Justin Sloan. Justin, this is Brian Jones, an avid recreational diver."

Justin gave Brian a curt nod. "Good to meet you."

"Likewise," Brian said. "You're married now, Sam?"

"For less than a week," Samantha said. "We're on our honeymoon."

"Oh. Bad timing on my part. Sorry. Have you seen Tommy lately?"

"He stopped by the wedding."

"Seriously? Was Charlotte there?"

Samantha nodded. "She was my maid of honor."

"That took balls on his part. He's in New England now. He's working his way to a new job in Florida. He left . . ." Brian thought a moment. "Must have been Monday."

"What's he doing in New England?" Justin asked casually.

Brian shrugged. "Work. I don't know any details."

Samantha felt the single malt burning

through her. Her stomach ached, but it wasn't the Scotch, she knew. It was Brian, Tommy, her concerns about her cousin. She decided to be frank. "If you're in touch with Tommy, tell him to stay away from Charlotte."

"One thing we all know, Sam, is that Charlotte can take care of herself. I've got no problem with her." His eyes took on a faraway look. "She saved my life."

"That was *you*?"

"Yeah. I was an idiot. Arrogant. I got ahead of myself. I'm not proud. Charlotte nearly died getting my ass out of that wreck. I . . . uh . . . ." He breathed out heavily. "I think about it a lot."

"But you're okay?" Samantha asked him.

"Thanks to Charlotte, yes. Pisses Tommy off that she was the one who saved me. He says there are no hard feelings between them, but I don't know. Well, I have only gratitude toward her. She's something."

Samantha felt mildly guilty for having assumed Brian was there in solidarity with Tommy. His presence appeared to be a simple coincidence.

"Do you know how badly Charlotte was injured in this accident?" Justin asked quietly.

"Not officially. Not the details. I had mild

decompression illness myself. All better now. I haven't seen her since she saved me. She didn't have symptoms at first — must have come as a shock that she was in as rough a shape as she was. I hate to think it was her last deep-sea dive." Brian sniffled, his cheeks bright pink. "Look, you two should be enjoying your evening. I'll leave you to it."

He retreated, not staying for a drink after all. Relieved, Samantha waited until the pub door had shut behind him before she turned to Justin. "Sorry about that. Maybe we should have picked someplace else for our honeymoon."

"Family's with us wherever we go." He moved in closer to her. "I'm enjoying Scotland. And you. No complaints."

She leaned against him, listening to the rain and wind lash the pub windows. She decided to change the subject. Nothing to be gained from discussing Brian Jones, Tommy Ferguson and a diving accident her cousin hadn't wanted to talk about. "What do you think is in your grandmother's time capsule?"

"Something Gran doesn't want us to see."

"Intriguing."

"Her family had more money than my grandfather's family did. I don't think she ever expected to marry a carpenter from Knights Bridge and stay there for the rest of her life."

"Something she and I have in common." Samantha sipped her Scotch, feeling warm next to Justin, and loved, and safe. "I imagine she misses your grandfather."

"He was a great guy."

"Think he'd have liked Scotland?"

"He and Gran visited Scotland when they retired. They loved it. Gramps said he liked the rugged scenery and Gran said she liked the tea and scones."

"Haggis?"

"They both hated it."

Samantha laughed. "Something we all have in common." She felt Justin's arm come around her and settled against him. "I could fall asleep right here."

He kissed the top of her head. "Need me to carry you up to bed?"

"Almost."

But she made it on her own, sinking into the warm double bed with him as the wind and rain continued. "Not much room," she whispered.

"We don't need much room."

EIGHTEEN

Boston, Massachusetts

Thunderstorms rolled through Knights Bridge overnight, lighting up Charlotte's room as if they were determined to warn her she was playing with fire kissing Greg Rawlings and she needed to get her head straightened out. She and Greg had found a *Life* magazine spread on Harry's Antarctic expedition, which had nearly gone down in history as a disaster instead of a triumph. One picture showed him with his two brothers as boys on their hardscrabble New Hampshire farm. Charlotte had stared at the young faces for a long time before heading up to her room.

By morning, the skies had cleared, and Andrew and Megan talked her into driving them and their dad to Boston in Harry Bennett's old Mercedes-Benz. Charlotte noticed Greg said little as they packed up the car and left, but she thought his silence had more to do with Andrew and Megan's imminent departure rather than having her along for the drive to the airport.

Traffic was relatively light into the city. They had time to stop at Harry's bowfront Back Bay house. Charlotte found a parking space on the street instead of slipping in back to the private space off an alley.

"Wow," Megan said, walking up the steps to the gleaming black-painted front door. "I didn't expect a *mansion.*"

Even Andrew, usually more reserved than his sister, was impressed.

Greg gave a low whistle. "I gather Harry bought the Mercedes-Benz new, not used."

Charlotte pushed open the door. "It's in good shape. Harry divided his time between London and Boston and hated to drive."

She stood back while the Rawlings family entered the house. She hadn't been inside it herself in years, but Samantha had told her it hadn't changed. Charlotte gave her guests a tour of the house's four floors. Three years after Harry's death, the classic nineteenth-century Back Bay house felt as if he'd stepped out for an adventure.

As they started back down to the entry, Charlotte broke off and ducked into Harry's office on the second floor. "It's tidier than I remembered," she said, aware Greg had followed her in. "Harry was a notorious pack rat."

"He lived here alone after his wife died?"

"Twenty-five years. Samantha's finished going through his London apartment but she's still sorting through this place. She archives what she wants to save and tags the rest for the dump, sale or donation. Her father and uncle will probably sell the house rather than move in or rent it out."

"It looks as if it needs updating but is otherwise in decent shape."

"Yeah." Charlotte ran her fingertips over a crystal decanter, still containing a few inches of what she guessed was one of Harry's preferred peated single malts. "I used to love visiting when I was a kid. We never stayed long. We'd stop on the way to New Hampshire."

"Quite a family," Greg said. "Is Edinburgh temporary or is it home?"

"I'm on the move so much I sometimes think my suitcase is home. I love Edinburgh and my apartment there, but it's always felt temporary."

"Sounds like a rationalization for some-thing."

"It's not."

"Not saying what you need to say to yourself now that you can't dive and you know your life is changing?"

"I felt that way before the accident." She noticed a framed black-and-white photograph on the wall of Harry and Max, young, vibrant and handsome. "A different time, a different world. Max always said one day Harry would get himself killed on his adventures. He almost did, more than once." Her throat tightened with emotion as she gazed at the long-ago photo. "Ah, Max. The Bennett family's Eeyore. Love you, Gramps. Miss you."

Greg eased in next to her, taking a closer look at the two men in the photo. "Harry and Max must have been quite a pair. They got along?"

"They worked well together. Harry needed Max as someone he could trust unconditionally — someone who would rein him in from time to time, firmly when necessary. Max understood limits. Financial, emotional, mental, spiritual." She smiled, overwhelmed with sudden affection. "And he understood Harry."

"And vice versa? Did Harry understand Max?"

"I think so. I didn't always think so. Max kept Harry alive, solvent and happy, but Harry got Max in the game. He wasn't just on the sidelines. He accepted Harry's risk-taking ways could come to a bad, or at least a premature, end."

"Were they happy when you decided to become a marine archaeologist?"

"I don't know that Harry paid much attention. Max didn't mind marine archaeology. He minded the diving. I can remember his shock. 'A diver, Charlotte? You're going to be a diver? Please tell me I didn't hear that right.' " She laughed at the memory. Just mimicking his voice brought him close to her again. "I told him I was going to be a marine archaeologist who dives. It's not uncommon."

"He eventually accepted your decision?"

"I didn't give him much choice, but yes, he did, just as he grudgingly accepted my dad's decision to get into underwater salvage and exploration."

"Like Harry's son Malcolm, Samantha's father."

"See? You're catching on. My father and Malcolm have always been close." Charlotte felt a sudden wave of awkwardness. "We don't need to waste more time discussing the charms and oddities of my family."

"I'm intrigued by the Bennetts and your place among them," Greg said.

"All families are interesting."

"Yeah. Wait until you meet my uncle

Johnny."

She tilted her head back, studying him. "Do you even have an Uncle Johnny?"

He grinned. "Sure."

"You're not always serious, you know."

"I can be."

The tone of his voice alone sent ripples of awareness through her, but they had to get to the airport. They all piled in the Mercedes-Benz. Charlotte drove, navigating increased traffic and the mad route through the tunnel to Logan. She parked in the central garage and offered to stay in the car while Greg saw his kids off, but Andrew and Megan asked her to join them.

Not wanting to intrude, Charlotte glanced at Greg, but he nodded toward the terminal. "It's okay. Let's go."

Andrew and Megan had no bags to check. They turned on their phones for their boarding passes and chattered with excitement about flying. They couldn't wait to fly to Washington to see their father's new place. "It doesn't have to have three bedrooms," Megan said. "We can sleep on the couch or on the floor. We don't care. We don't need our own rooms."

"You could also put us up in a five-star hotel," Andrew teased.

"Right," Greg said with a strained smile.

"I'll keep you posted."

"It'll all work out," Megan said.

He hugged her. "Yeah, it will. I'm glad we'll be seeing more of each other."

"Us, too, Dad," Andrew said.

Megan hugged her father fiercely, then stood back, sniffling as she smiled through her tears at Charlotte. "Thanks for sharing Red Clover Inn with us. Good luck with your diving."

Andrew nodded. "Yeah. I hope everything works out for you."

Charlotte thanked them and assured them she had loads of options. It was true, even if it didn't feel that way.

Andrew started to shake his father's hand, but they hugged, too. Charlotte hung back while the three walked to the security line. She realized she was old enough to have a teenager herself. In her early twenties, she'd been caught up with her studies and with diving and salvage projects with her father and Malcolm and Francesca. She'd assumed she and Tommy would eventually have children. It had been a vague hope, a dream, maybe, nothing concrete. Tommy wasn't a planner by nature and she'd been focused on their wedding, assuming everything would fall into place after that.

She gave herself a mental shake. Why was

she thinking about Tommy Ferguson?

Once his kids were through the TSA checkpoint, Greg rejoined her. "We're on our own again."

He was subdued as they returned to the parking garage. Charlotte paused as they came to the Mercedes-Benz. "You can drive if you'd like," she said.

"Sure thing."

She tossed him the keys. "It's one awesome car to drive, I have to say."

He slid behind the wheel, and she settled into the front seat, belting herself in, happy to have him drive through the tunnel and west to Knights Bridge. "Thanks for being a good sport and driving us out here and showing us Harry's house," Greg said, starting the car. "He was quite the character. Andrew and Megan had a good time."

"They're great kids."

"You don't live in fear of teenagers." He glanced at her, his turquoise eyes impossible to read. "You don't live in fear of anything, do you?"

"I might not show my fears and I try not to let them dictate what I do, but that doesn't mean I don't have them." She left it at that. "Does it scare you having Andrew and Megan fly on their own, given your work, what you know?"

"They have to live their lives."

"You don't let your work make you paranoid."

He grinned. "I didn't say that."

"Sometimes bad things happen," Charlotte said. "We all know it's true, but we don't like to think the really bad things are going to happen to us. Maybe we can't think that way. We'd never get out of bed if we thought that way."

"You had a tough accident." Greg slowed as they approached the tunnel entrance. "You were deep underwater, in a shipwreck, with a panicked amateur diver. That had to be unnerving."

"I got through it."

He glanced at her. "You don't need to minimize what happened. If you get medical clearance, would you want to dive again?"

"Yes. You've been shot. That had to have an effect on you."

"Not just the injury itself but how it happened." He started through the tunnel. "That was one rough day. I don't pretend it wasn't."

"I'm glad you survived," Charlotte said quietly.

"Yeah, me, too." But his attempt at a light tone didn't take. "It took some time to pick up the pieces of my life and figure out what was next. I could have left the job. I could have tried once more with Laura. Turned out I wasn't done with the job but Laura and I were done. Getting shot didn't finish us off. We were done before then."

"Did things become clear for you right away or over time?"

"Took a while."

"Was it easy?"

"No. Damn. I had to sit in cat hair in my brother's apartment while I figured out my life."

"Now you've been promoted and you're moving to Washington."

"It could have been worse, I guess."

She laughed. "You make light as a coping mechanism, don't you?"

"The promotion's good. If I'd been kicked to the curb, I'd really be making light." Once out of the tunnel, he glanced over at her. "Straight back to the inn?"

Charlotte nodded, leaning back in her seat. "Our books and hammock await."

When they arrived at Red Clover Inn, Charlotte was stunned to discover Tommy Ferguson sitting in a wicker chair on the front porch. She tried to hide her shock as he rose as she approached the steps and absorbed the reality of seeing him in Knights Bridge — in New England.

Before she could say anything, Greg touched her elbow. "I'll go inside," he said quietly, passing her on the steps. He gave Tommy a curt nod and went in through the front door.

Charlotte continued up the stairs to the porch.

"You're looking good, Charlotte," Tommy said, still on his feet. "A few days in this little town are having a positive effect."

"It's a lot of fun."

"Helps to have a good-looking Diplomatic Security Service agent as a roommate."

She ignored his comment. "What are you doing here?"

"I stopped to see you. I got into Boston last night. I'm on my way to Connecticut to meet up with some divers there to talk about having them join me in Florida. Did a slight detour through Knights Bridge. It's not too far out of the way." He flicked a bit of plant debris off the porch rail. "I wanted to tell you at Sam's wedding, but I didn't. I'm getting married in September. It's one reason I took this job in Florida."

Married. Charlotte took a moment to absorb the news. "Congratulations, Tommy. I'm happy for you."

"She's a freelance magazine writer. You don't know her. We met while I was on a dive in Florida in February. She was on vacation. She's not into diving. It's good to have separate interests." He cleared his throat, a rare hint of awkwardness in his expression. "You and I would never have worked forever. You saw that before I did. This works. I guess I wanted to tell you myself, before you heard it."

"My best to you both, Tommy."

"Right. Maybe one day you'll find happiness, Charlotte. I should get rolling. See you around."

"Yeah, sure, Tommy."

She watched him head down the steps and out to the street, where he'd parked his rental car. She'd noticed it when she and Greg had arrived back from Boston, but she hadn't considered it might be Tommy, popping in on his way to Connecticut to tell her he was getting married.

She went inside, noticing her legs were wobbly. It wasn't Tommy, his marriage. It was his need to tell her — the satisfaction he got from rubbing her nose in his happiness.

Damn but she was well rid of him.

Greg was reading his book in the front room. "It's too late for the hammock. Too many mosquitoes, and it'll be dark soon." He nodded toward the front door. "Tommy could have sent you an email about his upcoming nuptials."

"You eavesdropped?"

"More like I overheard. I dropped out of the conversation and fetched my book once he said he was getting married. Tell you what — your fairy godmother was looking out for you the day you jilted that guy." He rolled to his feet. "Come on. I found a bottle of a good-looking Irish whiskey tucked in a cupboard. We can toast bullets dodged in our lives."

NINETEEN

Vic Scarlatti stopped at the inn just as Greg opened the dusty bottle of Irish whiskey he'd found in the dining room sideboard. He had no idea how long the whiskey had been there but it seemed fine to him. He splashed some in the two glasses he'd pulled off another shelf. Charlotte had gone into the kitchen to put together hors d'oeuvres, or something that could pass as hors d'oeuvres.

"Did you knock?" Greg asked Vic, handing him one of the glasses.

"Rang the doorbell."

"It doesn't work."

He shrugged, all innocence. "I know. I thought I heard you holler to come in. Door was open."

No one had hollered, which, of course, Vic knew. Greg grabbed a third glass and splashed whiskey into it. "Welcome."

"I'm on my way to the diner for dinner.

Thought I'd stop in. Good timing since you were pouring whiskey." Vic sniffed the contents of his glass. "It's drinkable?"

"We'll find out. You first."

Vic held up his glass to Greg. "Bottoms up."

Greg waited, watching the retired ambassador take a good swig of the whiskey.

"Whoa." Vic puckered, licked his lips. "That'll grow hair on your chest."

Greg raised his glass. "Cheers."

The whiskey, indeed, was potent, even by Greg's low standards, but also appreciated after seeing his kids off, driving Harry Bennett's Mercedes-Benz with Charlotte next to him and discovering her ex-fiancé on the porch. She'd handled Tommy well and hadn't tried to score points on him. Greg had no doubts she meant it when she said she was past Tommy Ferguson and their wedding-that-wasn't. That didn't mean she was comfortable with thinking about his wedding-yet-to-be.

Vic glanced around the old-fashioned dining room. "I've owned a house in Knights Bridge for twenty years and never realized this place was here."

"Now you're a townie," Greg said.

"I'll never be that, but it's home nonetheless."

Charlotte came in from the kitchen with a small tray of cut-up vegetables, cheese and crackers. She greeted Vic with a big smile that seemed genuine to Greg. "As you can see, we're making ourselves at home here," she said. "In another life, I could be an innkeeper. I can see its attraction for Samantha."

"She'll have fun renovating the place," Vic said. "It's what the Sloans do."

They moved their mini party into the library. Over whiskey and hors d'oeuvres, the discussion turned to the future. Vic, ever the charming, interested diplomat, drew Charlotte out about her plans. "How long have you lived in Edinburgh?" he asked her.

"Three years."

"Beautiful city. I haven't been in far too long. When do you return?"

"I'm booked on a flight next week. You must visit again. Call me when you do."

Vic glanced at Greg, as if to check if he, too, had heard the sudden hollow note in her voice. He had, but he said nothing. Charlotte and Vic talked about the irresistibility of the Royal Botanic Garden, some old castle that loomed over the city and distilleries they'd toured. Scotland had never been on Greg's itinerary but he didn't feel like the odd man out. He enjoyed listening to their conversation, seeing some warmth return to Charlotte's cheeks. She'd made a face on her first try of the Irish whiskey but hadn't choked. She still held the glass in her hand and took the occasional microsip.

"I'm heading to Washington soon to get my grandfather's house ready to put on the market," she said. "I've been renting it out since his death. It's time."

Vic reached for a few veggie sticks. "Fate threw you and Greg together, huh?"

She buried her face in her glass. "Not quite," she said, her voice barely audible.

"Ah. Got it."

Greg made no comment but he had a feeling Vic did get it.

Charlotte set her drink on a side table. "I don't have to be back in Edinburgh on a specific day. I'm not on vacation. Technically I'm on a leave of absence from my job. I have time. You might say I'm figuring out my options for the future. I need to take into account the medical advice on my return to diving."

"Which is?" Vic asked.

"That I shouldn't."

Vic settled back in his chair, throwing one leg over the other, a deliberate move, Greg suspected, to appear casual and interested without ratcheting up Charlotte's evident discomfort. "I see. How's your head?"

"I didn't hit my head."

"I don't mean physical injuries. These major life changes can mess with our heads — how we think about ourselves, our families, our future. We're on this one path with this one destination in mind, and then the universe decides to kick us into a ditch. Or worse."

"That's how Vic viewed retiring to Knights Bridge," Greg said drily.

Vic grunted. "Seems trivial now, doesn't it? It didn't feel that way at the time. I was consumed. Figuratively speaking, I was dangling off a cliff by my fingernails. I felt used up and useless. I finally realized the problem was in here." He tapped his temple with one finger. "In my head. Retiring with no plan is different from getting shot or nearly dying in a diving accident. I do understand that."

"You did almost freeze to death in the snow," Greg said.

"That was my own doing."

"So it was."

Vic sighed, smiling at Charlotte. "These DS agents are merciless."

She laughed, clearly enjoying his company and his frank, self-deprecating humor.

Greg finished his whiskey. He liked Charlotte's laugh. Their kiss and now this talk of the future was launching him out of his complacent focus on the present. Their interlude in Knights Bridge would be coming to an end — sooner rather than later. They'd both be off again, she to Edinburgh once she took care of her business with her grandfather's house, he to his new job at the DSS Command Center. Once he got sucked into his work again, would he even think about these days in Knights Bridge with pretty Charlotte Bennett?

He looked at her dark eyes and had his answer. *Yes. No question.*

Charlotte invited Vic to stay for dinner, but his companion for the evening arrived in the form of Elly O'Dunn. She'd let herself in through the front door. Greg offered her some of the whiskey. "Just a taste," she said. "I mean it. Two sips and I'm good. Three and I'm on the floor. Why don't you two join Vic and me for dinner? Can't beat the turkey club at Smith's."

Greg retrieved a glass from the dining room, poured Elly's "taste" and handed her the glass. "We don't want to intrude."

"Intrude? Intrude on what?" She seemed genuinely mystified, but then her eyes widened. "Oh, good heavens. It's not a *date.*"

Vic made a face. "You could sound less horrified."

She laughed, clearly delighted. "I could, couldn't I?"

"I'm good with leftovers here," Greg said. "But thanks."

Charlotte nodded. "You two enjoy yourselves. I'll be sure to try the turkey club before I leave town."

"I heard about the scare Evelyn Sloan gave everyone yesterday," Elly said. "Have you seen her yet today?"

"We've been in Boston," Charlotte said.

"Eric and Christopher must have her under wraps, but she's an independent woman. One of her friends stopped by the town offices today and said she hasn't given up on that time capsule. Working for the town, I hear things."

"Not just things," Vic said. "Everything."

"Don't I wish. It was awful, the way the adult children fought over this place. I hope there's gold in the time capsule and Evelyn finds it, because it would serve those no-accounts right that they missed it."

"Any idea where it might be?" Charlotte asked.

"Most likely it went into the trash years ago, but this place has more nooks and crannies than any place I've ever known. Good luck. I'd rather try to find Samantha's pirate treasure." Elly finished off her few drops of whiskey and set her glass on the table. She stood straight, frowning. "The son did say something in the midst of all the fighting. He was at the town offices to see about property taxes and mentioned his mother collected old linens. She'd stuffed them into a box, but he and his warring siblings didn't want them. I mentioned Olivia Frost — now Olivia McCaffrey — collected antique linens. She uses them in the guest rooms at Carriage Hill. I never followed up after that. Have you checked all the closets?"

"Yes but not thoroughly," Charlotte said. "I haven't dug through every box."

"Well, I don't know if you could hide a time capsule in a box of linens. I'm sure it'd be a wild-goose chase but thought I'd mention it. If the greedy offspring thought the time capsule held worthless linens, they wouldn't have bothered with it."

Vic was gaping at Elly. Finally he gave himself a mental shake. "No, I'm not dead or dreaming. I'm awake, living in Knights Bridge, talking about old pillowcases." He grinned. "Life doesn't get better. Elly? Shall we leave these two to their whiskey, nibbles and closets?"

She smiled and took his arm. After they left, Greg turned to Charlotte. "Dinner, then closets?"

"We'll run across more spiders in the closets."

"Not in the dinner, at least. I'd rather deal with spiders than mice and bats." He finished the last of his whiskey. "I could deal with a jerk diver, too. Are you upset about Tommy's visit? Did it stir up the past for you?"

"Nothing that dinner, closets and more whiskey won't cure."

Greg ended up going to bed with his book.

It was the decent thing to do, and he was a decent guy.

"Yeah, right."

He finished the last chapter before ten o'clock. Too early to go to sleep, too late to start a new book. He played a game of solitaire on his bed, using a worn deck of cards from a drawer in his nightstand. Something about Vic and Elly's visit, the whiskey or the closet checking — or all three — had gotten to Charlotte and she'd slipped into her room for her bath.

Possibly he was wrong and it hadn't been the visit, the whiskey or the closets. Possibly, he thought, flipping over a seven of clubs that did him no good, it had been him.

Nah. More likely Tommy Ferguson.

Tommy could dive and Charlotte couldn't. Tommy was getting married and she wasn't.

Tommy was a jerk and she wasn't.

The bastard had stopped by because he'd wanted to rub her nose in the perfection of his life without her. To let her know she'd done him a favor by abandoning him on their wedding day.

It'd been payback, pure and simple.

Greg flipped a ten of diamonds. It did him no good, either. He was going to lose this game fast.

Which he did.

He played another one, and he lost it fast, too.

Finally he gathered up the cards and returned them to his nightstand. He crawled under the covers, switched out the lights and listened. No mice scurrying in the walls tonight. Maybe all the activity in the house had prompted them to lie low.

He'd complicated Charlotte's time in Knights Bridge. She had big things to figure out about her life. He didn't — he'd taken the promotion, he'd signed his divorce papers. He'd just needed rest. Maybe he'd been ripe for an attractive, kick-ass woman like Charlotte Bennett.

Not a woman like her. *Her.*

He sighed heavily, but he didn't walk down the hall and knock on her door.

"Being a decent guy."

But he slept in fits and starts, and for the first time since they'd arrived at Red Clover Inn, he was up before Charlotte. He made coffee but waited for her before starting breakfast.

She stumbled into the kitchen, yawning, shirt crooked.

"Rough night?" he asked her from the table. "You look like you just stepped out of the pages of *Princess and the Pea.*"

That got a smile out of her, at least. "On the contrary, I slept well. Too well, maybe. I might have overdone the lavender oil. But yesterday was . . ." she paused ". . . cathartic."

"Cathartic can be good."

"Yes, it can." She yawned again and checked the coffeepot. "Smith's for breakfast?"

"Works for me."

"And then a drive out to Carriage Hill to see if Olivia has the old linens?"

"Scary. I was just thinking the same thing."

They joined Eric and Christopher Sloan

at their table at the small restaurant, but Charlotte didn't mention the linens. The two brothers had obviously had their fill of their grandmother's time capsule. Eric had the day off and planned to work in Evelyn's garden with her to give her some attention and something else to think about. Christopher would stop by later and show her recent pictures of the Sloans in England.

"Can't wait for backup," he said. "Two of us aren't enough to handle Gran."

The Farm at Carriage Hill was bathed in the June sunshine when Greg and Charlotte arrived. They'd taken his rental. He'd done the driving. He'd talked her out of riding her bike.

Olivia greeted them with fresh coffee and open curiosity. It didn't take much explaining before she remembered she indeed had a box of old linens that the eldest sister of the feuding siblings who'd inherited Red Clover Inn had dropped off months ago.

"It was before they put the inn up for sale," Olivia said. "I gather the strife over the inn was difficult for her. She wanted the linens to have a good home, and she'd heard I collected them. I was happy to get them, but I haven't had a chance to go through the box. I was under the impression the family hadn't gone through it, either."

She brought Greg and Charlotte upstairs and opened a hall closet, pointing to an ordinary-looking cardboard box. Greg lifted it off the shelf and carried it into one of the guest rooms. Charlotte grabbed a luggage rack and he set the box on it.

"Dylan's up at the new house," Olivia said. "He'll be sorry he missed this."

Greg grinned at her. "I'll bet."

She laughed, one hand on her swelling stomach. "He knows I can wax rhapsodic over a hand-embroidered Depression-era pillowcase."

"Do you want to do the honors?" Charlotte asked, standing back from the box.

Olivia shook her head. "Please, go ahead."

Charlotte carefully tore open the box. She lifted out a stack of lace-edged white linens, then another of linens with colorful flowers sewn on the ends — appliqué, Greg remembered. At the bottom, buried under the linens, was a metal cookie tin.

"I assumed it contained bits of linen and lace," Olivia said. "I haven't had a chance to open it."

"Evelyn told me she thought the time capsule was in a cookie tin," Charlotte said. "This must be it."

They placed the linens back in their box. "Don't worry about putting the box back in the closet," Olivia said. "Leave it here and I'll go through it. I should have done so ages ago. But then I'd have discovered the time capsule, if that's what this is, without knowing it belongs to Evelyn and she doesn't want the world to see the contents."

"At least not her grandchildren," Charlotte said. "Would you mind if we take it to her?"

Olivia didn't hesitate. "Please do. Trust me, Dylan and I aren't interested in Evelyn Sloan's secrets, assuming this is her time capsule."

Charlotte tucked the tin in one arm. "If it turns out the tin's filled with old buttons and rickrack, we'll bring it back."

"Dylan will be thrilled. He keeps saying I need more old buttons and rickrack."

The two women laughed. Greg followed them downstairs, back to the kitchen.

"I'd offer you more coffee," Olivia said, "but I know you must be in a hurry to see Evelyn. Give her my best, won't you?"

Charlotte promised she would. As Greg went out to the car with her, he texted Eric and gave him the news. He could have sworn he heard the cop Sloan grit his teeth as he typed his response.

I'll call Chris and we'll get Gran to the inn. Get this over with.

True to Eric's word, the three Sloans were at the inn when Greg and Charlotte returned with the cookie tin. They all moved into the dining room. "This is your time capsule, isn't it?" she asked, holding up the tin.

Evelyn nodded, taking a seat at the table. "That's it, yes. It doesn't look as if it's been opened, does it? That's good." She inhaled deeply, exhaled slowly. "Very good."

Charlotte set the tin on the table in front of Evelyn. "Can I get you anything?"

"Water, please," Evelyn said, her voice clear and strong. "I'll wait for you."

The two Sloan grandsons remained on their feet. Charlotte withdrew and returned quickly with a pitcher of water. Greg got a glass out of the china cupboard — no one else was interested in water — and filled it, then set it next to Evelyn.

"Anything else, Gran?" Eric asked, no hint of impatience.

"No, this is perfect, thank you." She took a sip of water as she continued to stare at the tin. "I remember eating the cookies. Well, now I do. I was so impressed because the cookies were imported. I'd brought them to Knights Bridge from home. I never had them after Ralph and I were married. He saw no reason to import cookies when you bake them fresh yourself. He loved to bake."

"Gran," Eric said gently.

She lifted her gaze to him. "I won't get maudlin. Don't worry."

"Good. I was starting to sweat."

She smiled, his teasing clearly returning her to the present and the matter at hand.

"Do you want us to leave the room?" Christopher asked.

"You see, Charlotte? There are sensitive Sloan men. No, Christopher. I don't need you to leave. But thank you for asking."

She opened the tin, a slow process considering it likely hadn't been opened in decades, but she didn't ask for help or even glance up from her task.

Eric leaned against the hall door. "I'm waiting, Gran. I bet Christopher it's a treasure map you're hiding. He bets it's a confession. You and Gramps hit a bank and lost all the loot on a secret trip to Las Vegas."

"Nothing that exciting." She got the lid off the tin and set it on the table. She lifted a yellowed envelope out of the tin. "Matches, please."

Christopher rummaged in the sideboard

and delivered matches and a fireproof candle dish. "You're burning history," he said.

"I believe that's my point."

Eric moved from the doorway. "I always wondered how an Amherst shopkeeper's kid ended up with a Knights Bridge carpenter. Is that in the letter?"

"I didn't know your grandfather when Betsy and I put together the time capsule. I know you're a police officer, Eric, and you can be quite jaded and think everything's your business. However, some things are no one's business."

Her eldest grandson crossed his arms on his chest. "Shouldn't have put it in a time capsule, then."

She picked up the book of matches. "That's precisely why I wanted to find it before anyone else did. I didn't know everything at eighteen. I just thought I did."

"I can check with your old-lady friends and see what they know about what you were like back then," Eric said.

Evelyn sniffed. "Go right ahead. They know nothing about what's in the letter. It's private."

Eric looked as if his head would explode. "If it's private, why did you put it in a time capsule?"

"We were going to open it ourselves in fifty years."

"Now it's been sixty-five years," Eric said.

"I'm aware of that. Things didn't work out as planned."

She placed the letter in the fireproof dish, struck a match on her first try and set the flame to the old paper. Her hand trembled slightly. Christopher stood close. "I don't want you setting the drapes on fire."

"Or myself," she said. "I'm as dried out as a hunk of old wood. I'd go right up in flames."

Christopher shook his head. "Gran, it doesn't work like that."

She ignored him, watching her letter burn. The flames died down, leaving a pile of black ashes and bits of scorched paper. "There. I'm satisfied." She gave the time capsule a dismissive wave. "You're welcome to the rest of the stuff in there."

"Anything good?" Eric asked.

"Postcards of Winsor Dam, a copy of our last senior-year report cards, a menu, money — a penny, dime, quarter and dollar bill — and newspaper clippings. Betsy added some embroidery she'd done. I didn't do needlework. Never have." She sighed, sitting back in her chair. "Imagine yourselves at eighteen."

"I was hell-raising," Eric said. "What about you, Greg? Charlotte?"

"I don't remember being eighteen," Greg said. "Especially when my kids are around."

"I spent eighteen studying," Charlotte said with a half smile.

"I was a proper young woman," Evelyn said.

Eric snorted. "Easy to say now that you've burned the evidence."

"Isn't it, though?"

But she was spent, and her grandsons got her to her feet to take her home. They offered to clean up the ashes, but both Greg and Charlotte said they'd take care of it. They left the tin and its contents. Evelyn might or might not be back for the rest of her time capsule. She'd dealt with the urgent matter of her letter.

Eric paused while his younger brother helped their grandmother into the hall. "Thanks, Charlotte. You respected Gran's wishes. That means a lot to her."

After the Sloans left, Greg collected the ashes. "A few bits didn't burn but not enough to re-create the letter," he said, addressing Charlotte as she watched him. "Too bad. Now I'm curious what she's hiding. Did you read it? You were alone with the time capsule for a couple of minutes at

Carriage Hill."

"I didn't open the time capsule or read the letter," she said.

"But you wish you had."

"I do admit that, yes."

He studied her. "You're a Bennett and I'm told Bennetts can fib with a straight face."

"Who says that?"

"Brody via Heather via Justin, who is, after all, married to a Bennett."

The day turned rainy and windy and felt more like March than June. Their picnic at Echo Lake might have happened last summer instead of a few days ago. Charlotte was happy to let Greg light a fire in the library. It took the chill and dampness out of the air but it wasn't so cold that they needed a roaring fire to heat up the place. She felt the warmth on her face as she curled up in the love seat.

Greg sat next to her, his thighs grazing hers. She was positive it was deliberate. Not that she minded. "Even without a fire it's hard to believe we were swimming the other day," she said. "I know you're not a fan of cold weather."

"Really cold weather. I'd probably do fine in Scotland."

"Winters can be tough in Scotland. It's

not the cold, wet days that get to me as much as it is the dark. But that," she added, "is why we have cozy pubs."

"It's a short hop from Edinburgh to Portugal for a long weekend."

"That's true."

"Still no firm plans for going back?"

"As I mentioned, I have a return flight booked. It leaves from Boston but I have to scoot to Washington to see about Max's house. I thought I'd stop back here on the way. Samantha and Justin will be back from their honeymoon." She brushed a bit of ash from Evelyn's letter off her thigh. She was ridiculously self-conscious with Greg right next to her. "I keep calling it Max's house but that's only because he lived there alone after my grandmother died. It's not as flashy a place as Harry's house in Boston."

"Max wasn't as flashy a guy?"

"He didn't care about the limelight. I'm not saying Harry cared, either, but it didn't bother Max in the least that he didn't get it. It didn't affect their relationship. I think he liked his quiet life."

Greg watched the fire crackle. "Does having Samantha in Knights Bridge affect your decision making about the house and what's next for you?"

"Not really." Charlotte could feel the

warmth from the fire. She liked having Greg sitting close to her, she had to admit. There was more than one way to stay warm. She focused on the matter at hand. "It feels a little strange having Samantha settled. I'm used to her being on the go all the time."

"The Bennetts seem to do well as a family even if you are spread out."

"We do, surprisingly, maybe. We're used to hopping on planes to see each other, moving every few years — sometimes every few months."

"That kind of lifestyle can be tough on relationships."

She looked at him, noticed the fire reflected in those deep turquoise eyes of his. "Unless the two people involved are both on the go, I suppose. Did you like moving to different assignments?"

"Depended on the assignment."

A circumspect answer. "Are you looking forward to being at the DSS Command Center? Will you finish out your career there?"

"It's what's next. It definitely could be my last stop with Diplomatic Security. It's a good one. No complaints."

"You don't like to lock yourself into a plan, do you?"

"I like to keep my options open. What if I

win the lottery?"

"Do you ever buy a ticket?"

"Never." He grinned, stretching an arm on the back of the love seat. "If you don't go back to Edinburgh, what will you do?"

"I hope this trip will help me figure that out. Not being able to dive changes everything."

"I didn't get the impression your institute would dump you because you can't dive. Did I miss something?"

"No. We'd rework my role. I have options. I just never thought . . ."

"You never thought you'd exchange your wet suit for a desk."

"At least not so soon."

"The gratitude and relief at getting out of a tough spot like the one you were in only lasts so long. At some point, you have to wrap your head around the ways it's changed your life. You have to accept that what's next for you isn't going to be what you planned before you got your butt kicked by life."

"Even if it's something better?"

"Well, from my point of view, there are a lot of options that are better than jumping in a cold ocean to explore sunken shipwrecks."

"Says someone who's never explored a

sunken wreck."

"And never plans to," he said lightly. "What's the marine archaeology version of a desk job look like?"

"Managing, planning, teaching, fundraising, writing, researching. Lots of possibilities."

He smiled. "You don't like to lock yourself into a plan, do you?"

"I deserved that," she said with a laugh. "It's cozy in here. I'm actually getting hot."

"What kind of hot?"

She didn't answer. She put her feet up on the coffee table and leaned back against his arm. "You're not coming on to me because I have a house in Washington, are you?"

"I'm not that bright." He lowered his arm so that it encircled her. "I'm coming on to you because you're funny and smart and kick-ass and you don't mind going toe to toe with the occasional shark."

"Sharks don't have toes."

"Tiger?"

"I'm not an expert on tigers, or sharks for that matter."

"Sunken wrecks."

"You're not a sunken wreck."

"You're not, either."

"A couple of hard-driving types." She tried to keep her tone light, but her awareness of him was impairing her ability to speak and think coherently. "Maybe a fire wasn't the best idea."

"We could have wrapped up in a blanket together."

He wasn't having any difficulty with speaking and thinking, obviously. She saw the spark of humor in his eyes. He pulled her toward him. She half turned, half rolled into the wall of muscle that was his chest and shoulders. Heat surged through her that had nothing to do with the fire crackling a few feet away.

His mouth found hers and she sank into him, into their kiss. She wrapped her arms around him, gasped at the feel of his hands on the overheated skin of her lower back. He parted her lips with his tongue, and she thought she would melt into him.

She moaned, tingling, aching. She might have said his name out loud. She didn't know.

The weeks of tension, uncertainty and loss since her accident fell away. He skimmed his hands up her sides under her shirt, and she angled back just enough that he could reach her breasts. She moaned with an abandon she'd learned not to let loose. Uptight . . . yes, she'd been uptight.

Somehow she'd ended up straddling him.

Every inch of him was hard under her. She wanted to explore, touch, taste him, but her body wouldn't cooperate. She was liquid in his arms. He pulled her shirt over her head and cast it aside. Her bra followed. She didn't even know how it came off.

"Charlotte." His voice was husky, thick. His mouth descended to her breasts. He flicked his tongue on her, sending flames of pure sexual desire through her. "I want you. Tell me what you want."

How was she supposed to speak? She pressed herself into him. "I want you inside me."

It was all he needed to hear. He tore at her pants, then his own, tossing them aside. She glanced up and saw that the library door was shut, but she knew she and Greg were alone. She got his shirt off and ran her fingertips along the muscles on his chest, the scars from where he'd been shot. But he eased his fingers between her legs, and she was lost.

Once he was inside her, she didn't want it to end. Nothing about their lovemaking felt impulsive, crazy, stupid. It felt right, inevitable. She gave herself up to his thrusts.

Yes, yes, yes.

She'd never felt so loved and wanted, and when she came, it was explosive. She clutched him, felt his release as they shuddered together.

And it all hit her. A tsunami of emotions bowled her over, and as she felt the tears welling, she grabbed her clothes, pulled them on. "No regrets, no regrets," she said half to herself. "None. It was wonderful. But I . . ." She stood unsteadily. "I have to go."

Greg reached for his jeans and shorts and pulled them on in one smooth motion. He got to his feet. "I'll see to the fire." He touched his knuckles to her cheek. "Good night, Charlotte."

She ran upstairs to her room, bursting into tears once she shut the door behind her.

It was the physical release of their lovemaking, she knew. It had laid bare all her other bottled-up emotions.

"They can all go away," she said aloud, sniffling.

She cried some more and then washed her face. She put on her nightgown, shivering. She'd left her window cracked that morning, never thinking the air would get this raw by nightfall. She snuggled under her covers.

Now *this* was impulsive, she thought with a rueful smile.

It would have been much warmer to have

Greg with her.

But she didn't go back downstairs to get him. She didn't feel anything like the way she'd felt with Tommy. This was different — real and fun, with no competitiveness, nothing to prove.

She had no tears now. She was drained, but in a positive way.

And she was certain now. She was falling in love with Greg Rawlings.

TWENTY

Isle of Skye, Scotland
Samantha woke up early in their small room, complete with slanted ceilings and a view of the stunning scenery. She took a leisurely shower and pulled on clothes — the warmest clothes she'd brought, since she and Justin were disappearing into the hills for two days of hiking. They'd stop overnight at a bed-and-breakfast to which he'd arranged transport of their luggage.

She zipped up her fleece, aware of Justin watching her from the edge of the bed, where he was pulling on his hiking shoes. "Tommy Ferguson is engaged and moving to Florida and had to stop and tell Charlotte? Seriously? What an ass."

"She's okay, Sam."

"Of course she is. She's a Bennett and she figured out Tommy before the rest of us. I do realize we only know about this because Greg Rawlings told Brody, who told

Heather, who told you. I'm getting used to how things work with your family." She grabbed wool socks and sat next to Justin to pull them on. "Then we have your grandmother, who has now found and opened her time capsule after sixty-five years."

"And burned the evidence," Justin said. Samantha smiled. "We're missing all the excitement in Knights Bridge."

"There'll be new excitement when we get home."

"Never a dull moment in a small town. Now. Before we head into the hills . . ."

"What?"

"I happened to see a painting that intrigued me. I think it'd be perfect for the library at the inn."

Justin frowned. "A painting? Where?"

"At an art gallery in the village."

He tied the laces to his hiking shoe. "I didn't notice an art gallery, never mind a painting. What's it like?"

"It's a watercolor of a fish."

"Sam." He looked up at her. "A fish?"

"Mmm. It's hard to explain but it's perfect."

"What kind of fish?"

"An iconic wild Scottish salmon."

Justin didn't look that enthusiastic. "Okay." He tackled his other hiking shoe.

"We come through here after our hike. What if we stop at the gallery then and have a look? If you still like this painting, I'm on board with buying it. I can just see my brothers' faces when I bring home a painting of a fish from Scotland."

"It's a great painting. You'll see."

"In the meantime, we have —" he glanced at his watch "— less than a minute until our digital blackout. No calls, no texts, no email for the rest of our honeymoon. Eric has our itinerary with hotel numbers for any emergencies, and I trust him only to call in an actual emergency."

"You wouldn't trust your grandmother."

"Not in a million years. Brandon, maybe, but he zeroes in on drama and when last heard from, he was touring the Tower of London with Maggie and the boys. Who knows where they'll end up next. Adam's heading home today. He'd be fine — nothing gets to him — but you never know how jet lag affects people. I'd trust Christopher, too, but he's working long hours. The folks — Pop will make up an emergency to get out of touring another English castle with my mother."

"And Heather is in London. Mmm. Best to leave it to Eric."

"We'll enjoy the beauty of the Scottish

Highlands."

"Then you've noticed?"

"I notice everything when I'm with you, but I especially notice you, Mrs. Sloan."

"I love you, Justin."

TWENTY-ONE

Knights Bridge, Massachusetts
Greg drove out to Echo Lake and found Vic sitting on his porch with Rohan and his iPad. While looking for more whiskey in the cupboards, he'd discovered an old, cracked sepia photograph of Vic's lakeside house. "Thought you might like to take a look," Greg said, handing it to the retired ambassador.

Vic set his iPad aside and sat up straight, studying the photograph. "It must have been taken not long after this place was built. That's almost a hundred years ago. Who's the young couple holding hands on the porch?"

"I thought you might know."

"No idea." Vic turned over the photograph. "No date or inscription. Nothing. Knowing Knights Bridge, the happy couple probably has secrets."

"They do look happy," Greg said.

"Yeah. You can feel the love and romance in the air. Here I am, on my own with Rohan."

Rohan heard his name and perked up at Vic's feet.

"You're not thinking of marrying your dog, are you, Vic?"

"You know, Rawlings, there's a reason you have the reputation you do."

"I hope so. I'd hate to be thought of as a jerk for no good reason."

"Well, you aren't," Vic said. But he laughed, shaking his head. "There are days I miss the job, hanging out with alphas like you, but fewer and fewer." His eyes grew serious as he got to his feet and looked out at the lake. "Adrienne's moving back."

Greg didn't know Adrienne well, just that she was the wine-enthusiast daughter Vic hadn't realized he'd had until she'd looked him up and house-sat for him last winter. "That's great, Vic. I'm happy for you. You weren't hoping to hook the two of us up, were you?"

"That thought gives me heartburn. No." He sighed, staring out at the glistening water. "I don't deserve this second lease on a personal life but I'm getting one, anyway."

"Make the most of it."

"I will. Adrienne will have to look elsewhere for a guy. You're too old for her, anyway."

"Ouch."

Vic grinned. "Payback." Again the seriousness. "Now that I've seen you and Charlotte Bennett together . . ." He left it at that.

Greg walked down a dirt road to Brody's old place on the lake.

Charlotte was already there. She'd left earlier on her bike. "I thought you might follow me out here," she said, angling him a smile. "Good morning."

"Good morning." It was enough for now. They didn't need to talk about last night. He pointed along the lakeshore. "There's some land for sale up past the cove. The dirt road can be extended. Could be a good place to retire when the time comes."

"You and Brody as neighbors?"

"We could go fishing and tell war stories. He and Heather could warn their kids to stay away from me."

"You shouldn't joke about these things, Greg."

"It's a beautiful spot. I'm not sure I'd want to be out here alone. The critters wouldn't get to me. The quiet would, on multiple fronts. I was often alone with my thoughts, with nothing to do, when I was recuperating last winter. It was seldom pretty."

"You're action oriented and not particularly reflective?"

"Yeah. I guess you could say that."

"And you got used to living in the moment and not making a lot of plans. This would be a great place to build a small lake house. Nothing like Vic's."

"Couldn't afford it and I'm not comfortable in big houses. Imagine the vacuuming. Vic has a hell of a wine cellar, though."

"I like him."

"He thinks you're crazy about me."

"Did he say that?"

"No, but I protect diplomats for a living. I can read him."

She laughed. As they left, she glanced back at the lake, shimmering in the late-morning sun. "I can see the appeal of the lake for Brody — and for you, even if you didn't grow up here. It's a place you can put aside a sometimes dangerous, high-pressure career, whether you're between assignments or your career has ended."

"Wouldn't chew our legs off with boredom?"

"There are things to do in Knights Bridge. You'd have friends. Good friends."

"I don't have family here. You do."

"Samantha, you mean — and now Justin."

"He comes with a big family, and if he and Sam have kids . . ."

"Yes. Samantha didn't 'settle' when she decided to stay in Knights Bridge. It wasn't only because of Justin, either. It was because of herself, too."

Charlotte was silent. Greg watched her, and he knew, in his gut, what she was thinking. "You're seeing possibilities for yourself that go beyond 'I need to dive again.' "

"For the first time since the accident," she said softly. "For the first time."

"It's a start."

Greg beat Charlotte back to the inn and therefore to the hammock. Charlotte had ideas about slipping into the hammock with him, but Evelyn Sloan thumped up the front porch steps, using her cane, accompanied by a young woman with a camera dangling from her neck. "This is Amanda," Evelyn said. "She's a reporter for our local newspaper. They got wind of my time capsule and sent her over. I agreed to show her the contents, if that's all right with you."

"Of course," Charlotte said. "Do you want me to call Eric or Christopher?"

"Why? I can handle my own affairs."

Charlotte let it go. "Would you like to chat

405

in the library? I can make coffee."

"No coffee," Evelyn said. "We won't be long."

Amanda, the reporter, couldn't have been more than twenty-five. She looked awkward and tentative, but she followed Evelyn into the inn without comment. Charlotte shut the door behind them.

"The man in the hammock is a federal agent," Evelyn said as they continued down the hall to the library. "Diplomatic Security Service. He protects ambassadors."

"Does he live in town?" Amanda asked.

"Good heavens, no. My granddaughter is married to a federal agent. They're in London."

"I see."

It was clear the reporter didn't "see." Charlotte offered to leave them to their interview in the library, but Evelyn asked her to stay. She plopped onto the love seat, set her cane aside and opened the tin that had become her time capsule. "Sixty-five years is the blink of an eye, you know," she said. "It's something I couldn't imagine at eighteen."

She spread out the contents on the coffee table.

"Now, what about the items you *aren't* letting us see?" the reporter asked.

Flustered, Evelyn looked to Charlotte, but Greg came into the library, shaking his head. "It's a trick question, Evelyn. Don't answer."

"Right," she said. "Our cub reporter here doesn't know anything."

"What could I know?" Amanda asked, a mix of interested and innocent.

Evelyn gave her a steely look. "Nothing."

"There is something, isn't there, Mrs. Sloan? All the contents of the time capsule aren't here. I heard something about this at Smith's when I stopped for lunch. I had a bowl of split-pea-and-ham soup. It was great, but I'd be more in the mood in cold weather. Anyway, I overheard a police officer and another guy. A firefighter, I think. Your grandsons, I believe."

"Eric and Christopher," Evelyn said. "I have four more — three boys and a girl. That's six in all. They're very protective of me."

"So I discovered." Amanda paused. "Your grandsons were talking about your time capsule. I introduced myself and asked them about a rumor I heard at the country store that you burned something that was in the time capsule — something you didn't want anyone to see. They wouldn't confirm or deny the rumor. I appreciate a strong family, Mrs. Sloan. Were they upset you had something to hide?"

"My grandsons? No. They wouldn't care one way or the other. They see everything in their work." Evelyn narrowed her gaze on the young reporter. "That doesn't mean I am saying that I sneaked anything out of the time capsule. I know you're trying to trip me up, just like Agent Rawlings said."

"It is *Agent* Rawlings?" The reporter blushed. "I thought Mrs. Sloan was pulling my leg."

"I'm with the Diplomatic Security Service, ma'am," Greg said politely.

"You're not — Is this part of an investigation?"

"No. I'm not investigating Mrs. Sloan's time capsule."

Amanda looked relieved but also disappointed. She turned to Evelyn. "I'm not trying to trip you up. I'm not that kind of reporter, and this isn't that kind of story. Your time capsule is delightful. It's been wonderful chatting with you. Thank you."

Charlotte walked Amanda out to the front porch. "I would love to know what Mrs. Sloan is hiding, wouldn't you?" the reporter asked, digging out a pack of cigarettes. She stared at the unopened pack a few seconds, then shoved it back in her bag. "I've quit smoking six times this year and it's only June. I left my card on the coffee table. Call me if she decides to come clean about what she slipped out of the time capsule, okay? It would make a great human-interest story."

Charlotte nodded, neutral. "I'll be leaving Knights Bridge soon but I'll be sure Evelyn has your contact information."

"I'm sure it'll go the way of whatever she destroyed. Sixty-five years ago . . ." Amanda smiled. "The imagination does run wild with the possibilities."

She left, and Charlotte went back inside. Greg had opened a window in the library but Evelyn hadn't moved from her position on the love seat. "The paper I burned was a letter I wrote at eighteen to my future self," she blurted.

Charlotte took a breath. "Evelyn . . ."

She held up a hand. "Please. Allow me. Betsy and I asked ourselves where we wanted to be in fifty years. She decided not to write anything down, but I did. I wrote it all down. And I burned it."

Greg leaned against the cold fireplace, not saying a word. Charlotte sat across from the older woman. "Never mind fifty years," she said. "Now it's been sixty-five years."

"Imagine that. We picked fifty because we both thought we'd be alive at sixty-eight.

Not as many people lived into their eighties back then. Those who did seemed ancient. Well —" she smiled faintly "— not for no reason."

Charlotte smiled. "I can see where your grandsons get their sense of humor."

"From their grandfather. I learned to lighten up from him. I wrote about my future — what I thought it would be, wanted it to be, was *desperate* for it to be . . ." She paused, licked her thin, aged lips. "It's not how it turned out."

"That's probably true for most eighty-three-year-olds looking back on themselves at eighteen," Charlotte said.

"Yes, but they don't put it in writing and stuff it into a time capsule for their family to find decades later. Gad. What was I thinking? I remember sitting on the front porch here at the inn scribbling that damn letter to myself. I hated Knights Bridge. The life I wanted — the life I thought I was destined to have — was somewhere else, anywhere else. It would be filled with adventures and riches. Paris, New York, London, San Francisco. And it wasn't."

Charlotte said nothing, aware that Evelyn was lost in thought, her words as much to herself at eighteen.

Evelyn sank against the old cushions on

the love seat, her eyes shining with emotion. "I married a local man and we had a son together. Eventually I opened a nursery school in the village. Then my son married and had six children, and now they're getting married. I expect soon I'll be a great-grandmother. I'm blessed that I'm here, in good health, surrounded by family, even if they can be obstreperous at times. I think deep down when I was writing to my later self, I knew that I was putting it on, writing about someone I never truly wanted to be and a life I never truly wanted to have. I value character, Charlotte. Old-fashioned values of integrity, honesty, hard work, and I see them every day in this little town I disdained."

Charlotte cleared her throat. "I didn't read your letter."

"I know." Evelyn splayed her fingers and looked at the purple veins and brown spots on her weathered hands. "I came here on a lark and couldn't imagine staying. I had nothing but contempt for this town."

"You were only eighteen."

"I knew boys who'd fought in World War II at eighteen." She dropped her hands to her lap and sat up straight. "I was an insufferable snot, is what I was."

Charlotte smiled. "I doubt that."

411

"The life I've had since I wrote that letter to myself all those years ago has been far better than anything I ever imagined. My wild fantasies at eighteen don't compare." She shot Greg a look. "I'm not whistling past the graveyard. Is that even the right saying? You know what I mean. I'm being sincere."

He stood straight. "Did you burn the letter? You didn't exchange it for a parking ticket or something in your purse while no one was looking?"

"I did no such thing. I didn't have my purse."

"Some old Scrabble score card you grabbed in the dining room?"

Evelyn turned to Charlotte. "I can see why he and Brody get along. I burned the letter and I have no regrets for doing so. Not everything is meant for posterity. Ralph was a good husband and a good man. Knights Bridge has been good to me. Life has been good to me." She reached for her cane. "This little town changes people for the better. It isn't always easy, but you have to have faith."

"It changed Samantha," Charlotte said.

"She and Justin were meant for each other." Remaining seated, Evelyn leaned on her cane and studied Charlotte. "You know, seeing you and your federal agent together reminds me of the early sparks between Ralph and me."

Charlotte sputtered into laughter. "You're something else, Mrs. Sloan."

She winked. "I've lived, that's for sure. Justin and Samantha are excited about the inn. Maggie and Olivia have ideas, too."

"That's good, because Sam is terrible with paint and swatches and interior decorating."

"Heather will help with the interior design. Sloan & Sons will do the construction. It will all work out. Innkeepers. Pirate scholar. Carriage Hill can focus on what they do best. Russ Colton will help with security. Adam can redo the stonework."

"You all can make a time capsule as the new owners of this place," Charlotte said.

"I can make suggestions, including about what *not* to do."

"Keep it fun."

"Yes, exactly." Evelyn yawned, obviously worn out. "Walk with me back to the house, won't you? Elly O'Dunn stopped by earlier with some goat's cheese and I made a dip with chives. It's more than I can eat. I'll give you some."

"That sounds wonderful. I'd love to walk with you."

413

TWENTY-TWO

Charlotte made sure Evelyn was settled in her cozy living room with water, cookies and her TV remote. The time capsule and her confession, as she saw it, about her long-missing letter from her eighteen-year-old self had taken an emotional toll. She looked drained but also at peace, with none of the turmoil, impatience and strain that had gripped her since she'd first enlisted Charlotte to find the time capsule.

"Don't worry about me," Evelyn said. "Eric and Christopher will stop by later. I hope I haven't distracted you from your Agent Rawlings."

"He's not why I'm in Knights Bridge."

"But he's not a bad side benefit, is he? You don't have to answer." She shut her eyes. "Thank you, Charlotte."

"Be sure to drink the water, okay?"

"I will. The boys will insist if I don't."

Satisfied Evelyn was okay, Charlotte left

through the front door. It was a warm, pleasant afternoon, but she felt oddly disoriented, as if she'd been plucked from everything she knew in Edinburgh and set down in this small, unfamiliar town. She breathed in the fresh, clean air and cut through the hedges to Red Clover Inn. The Sloans and Bennetts were different in countless ways, but both were solid, tight-knit families. At first, she'd worried Samantha had been too impulsive in marrying Justin and would come to regret staying in Knights Bridge, but no more. Samantha and Justin would return from their honeymoon and pick up where they'd left off with family, friends, work and projects — an inn, an old cider mill, pirates.

And what will I do when I return to Edinburgh?

Charlotte shook off the question and trotted up the steps to the front porch. Greg stood up from a wicker chair, his phone in his hand. "I had to walk up the street to get a decent signal," he said. "I need to be in Washington tomorrow morning for meetings."

She noticed the duffel bag by the door. "You're leaving now?"

"I have a flight out of Boston tonight."

"Everything's okay, I hope."

"Everything's fine. The meetings are unexpected but that's the way it goes sometimes."

"Will you be back here?"

He shook his head. "I dive right into the new job."

Charlotte bit back her surprise, a sudden, crushing sense of disappointment that she couldn't explain. But she wanted to focus on him, since he was the one who had to leave. "I'm sorry you have to cut your break short. At least you got to spend some time with your kids."

He slid his phone into a back pocket. "I need to get rolling. Charlotte . . ." He looked past her, out at the field of wildflowers and tall green grass. Then he shifted to her. "I don't want what we started here to end. I'm not going to Washington and forgetting you."

"Thank you." It seemed like an awkward thing to say, but it was the best she could do. "I know you're going into an intense job."

"You'll be in Washington soon to figure out Max's house. Let me know. Call me."

She nodded. "I will."

He hesitated, chewing on his lower lip. Finally he sighed. "Damn." He raked a hand over the top of his head. "All right. I'll just say it. Listening to Evelyn Sloan talk about her life . . ." He sighed again. "It got me thinking about where I want to be in fifty years, and I want to be with you."

Her throat tightened. "Greg."

He moved closer to her, brushed a lock of her hair off her face. "I'm not great at this stuff, but you're the one, Charlotte. It wasn't love at first sight in England, but I'm pretty sure it was love at second sight when you got me up to bed. Definitely love by the time we danced at your cousin's wedding with you in your maid-of-honor dress, and last night . . ." He smiled. "I'll let last night speak for itself, for now."

"It does, yes, for now." She took his hand, her heart beating rapidly, her throat dry with emotion. "Things have moved fast between us. Maybe it's the Knights Bridge effect."

"Maybe it's us. Where do you want to be in fifty years? I want to be with you, looking out on Echo Lake. Healthy, vibrant, as much in love with you as I am right now." He squeezed her hand, kissed her softly. "It's a great image, Charlotte. Think about it."

And he was gone. Duffel bag in hand, down the steps, out to his rental car and on to Boston and his flight to Washington.

Charlotte went inside and sat in the library. She didn't know what to do with herself. She felt the emptiness of the inn. She shut her eyes, hearing Greg's laughter, seeing his smile, feeling his mouth, his hands, on her.

His emotions had gotten the better of him when he'd realized their time together was coming to an abrupt end. *Lust.* That was it. The unfinished physical business between them.

She opened her eyes and stared at the ceiling. All that stuff about love and Echo Lake fifty years from now was just because he was on a flight tonight instead of having sex with her.

"That's it," she said aloud.

That and the Knights Bridge effect, maybe.

She wandered to Smith's and had the turkey club by herself in a small booth. There were no Sloans at the restaurant tonight. When she walked back to the inn, she noticed Christopher's truck at his grandmother's house. She knew she could have knocked on the door and invited herself in. She could move to Carriage Hill for the night. The McCaffreys would take her in.

She continued on to Red Clover Inn and

418

headed up to her room. She'd take a bath and crawl into bed early with *Pride and Prejudice.* She had only a few chapters left.

As the tub filled with hot water and she peeled off her clothes, her phone vibrated with a text.

Miss me yet?

She smiled, shaking her head.

I will if a bat gets in here.

Damn straight.

Airport?

About to board my flight.

Safe travels. She held her breath, then typed. Miss you.

Knew it.

She laughed, aching for him now. He would get absorbed in his new job. He was that kind of man and it was that kind of work. He'd paid a high cost for his dedication to a job that could be all-consuming.

Knights Bridge could easily become a distant memory.

Charlotte sprinkled the last of the lavender oil into her bathwater. She'd need it if she had any hope of sleeping tonight.

For the first time since she'd arrived in Knights Bridge, Charlotte heard mice scurrying in the walls. She figured it was because the place was so quiet. By morning, she had her plan. She packed, locked up and got back in the old Mercedes-Benz and drove to Boston. She parked the car at Harry's house but stayed only to freshen up while she waited for her Uber car.

By noon, she was on a flight to Washington.

Two hours later, she let herself into her grandfather's bungalow on a quiet, shaded street. Except for Max's grandfather clock, she rented the house unfurnished. The previous tenants had left it in good shape, and she'd had it professionally cleaned and painted for new tenants.

She ran her fingers over freshly painted

wainscoting in the living room. She'd always loved this place. She could see Max sitting by the fireplace, reading a book. A voracious reader, he had been a regular patron at the library. He'd take Charlotte when she'd visited.

Her property manager texted her.

You're here. Great. I have a guy interested in renting the house.

Excellent.

He says you're charging too much. He wants to meet you. Okay with that?

When can he get here?

Between five thirty and six.

Works for me.

Charlotte grabbed a broom and swept the front steps and walk. It was a hot, humid afternoon, but the typical Washington summer weather only reminded her more of Max. In his last years, he'd loved to putter in his garden. After winters in New Hampshire, he said he never complained about the heat. *My heart medicine doesn't hurt, either. I'm cold all the time.*

She sat on the freshly swept steps, sweat trickling down her temples, when Greg came up the front walk. *I'm having a heatstroke. It's like that morning at Smith's except this time I really did conjure him up.*

"I'm for real," he said, amused. "You didn't make me up."

"My prospective tenant?"

He stopped in front of her and squinted at the small house. "This would be a good place for Thanksgiving since it's pretty much like it was when Lincoln was president."

"It wasn't built when Lincoln was president."

"Close enough. Want to show me around?"

"I'm not lowering the rent."

He grinned. "We'll see about that."

She led him inside, through the downstairs with its living room, dining room, sunroom, kitchen, and master bedroom and bathroom. Upstairs were two small bedrooms and a three-quarter bathroom. She debated but decided not to mention that the upstairs would be perfect for Andrew and Megan when they visited.

"It's great," he said when they returned to the kitchen. "I'll take it."

"Where are you staying now?"

"I have a room at a house owned by a friend who just happens to have left town for a few days. Convenient, don't you think?"

"Greg . . ."

He glanced around the kitchen. "No microwave?"

"It broke."

"Easily replaced. I can handle it and you can reimburse me." He smiled, wrapping his arms around her. "I have to be back at work in an hour for another meeting. I'm glad you're here."

"How long did it take you to find out this was my house?"

"Less than four minutes. Don't worry. I'm not going to rent this place if it bothers you to have me here."

"My head's spinning."

He kissed her on the forehead. "Are you hoping that being here in Max's old home will help you figure out what's next for you?"

"Right now I'll settle for thinking straight."

"It could help to talk about your options, how you feel. Not our long suit, I know. Megan and Andrew won't let me off the hook. They're still insisting I talk to them about getting shot. They say they're old enough and I'm not protecting them by not talking."

"Smart kids," Charlotte said.

He nodded. His eyes darkened slightly. "Doesn't mean talking is easy."

"It's not easy to deal with a life-changing incident."

"Yeah. It doesn't matter if it's your fault. The key is that little phrase, *life changing.*"

Charlotte watched as Greg opened cupboards in the kitchen. "Were you at fault when you were shot?" she asked him.

"Felt like it, but no. I'm a guy with a job to do. I'm trained to do it. Safety was and is a priority. Recklessness doesn't work. The fastest way to get people hurt and yourself out of a job is to assume you survive your own stupidity. But that's not what happened when I got shot." He slung an arm around her. "What do you say I come by after my meeting and we have dinner and talk about the next fifty years?" He pulled her close. "Relax. I'm kidding about the fifty years. We can talk about the next five days — the next five hours — the next five minutes.

Whatever you want."

"The next few days is a good start."

"I'm sorry I scared you."

"I'm glad you found me, because I was getting a little unnerved thinking about hunting down a federal agent."

"You'd have come looking for me?"

"Yes." She noticed she hadn't hesitated and smiled, feeling more relaxed. "I need a tenant and you need a house."

He laughed. "You can kick me out if I turn out to be a lousy tenant. We'll talk about that rent price tonight. Where do you plan to stay?"

"Here."

"There's no bed."

"I noticed. I don't mind sleeping on the floor."

Greg winked at her. "The floor works for me, but we can do better."

TWENTY-THREE

Knights Bridge, Massachusetts
Justin and Samantha were the last of the Sloans to return to Knights Bridge from the wedding — except Heather and Brody, of course, who were in London. Samantha had loved every second of her wedding and honeymoon, but she was happy to be back home, sitting out on the front porch of Red Clover Inn on a warm, rainy June day. Charlotte was there overnight, a brief stop on her way back to Edinburgh. She'd insisted on making iced tea and sandwiches and serving lunch in the library. But it was just her and Samantha. Justin had gone next door to see his grandmother.

"Wait until you try the hammock," Charlotte told her cousin. "It's the perfect cure for jet lag."

Samantha curled up on her chair. "I love hammocks. Our two nephews have already been in it. The rain didn't faze them. They must be jet-lagged but you'd never know it."

Charlotte sat across from her. "I swear I can feel the difference here with all you Sloans back in town." Samantha fingered her wedding ring, smiling at the many changes in her life in less than a year. "How was Washington?" she asked.

"I rented Max's house to Greg Rawlings."

"Brody's DS agent friend? The one who stayed here? Charlotte! *That* Greg Rawlings?"

"The same."

"You two . . ."

"He helped me clean up the yard and update a few things. The house needed a new microwave. It's convenient to the DSS Command Center where he works now."

Samantha studied her cousin. She was different. Not as uptight and self-conscious. "You and Greg are . . . what?"

"We'll see."

"I leave the country for a couple of weeks and look what happens."

Charlotte smiled. "I meet a guy who wants to rent Max's house."

"Sure. Right. That's it. You'll go back to Edinburgh and he'll get sucked into his new job?"

"Samantha . . ." Charlotte frowned. "Is

that a painting of a salmon?"

"A wild Atlantic salmon. Gorgeous, isn't it?"

"I love it."

"It doesn't look as good in here as it did on a gray day in Scotland," Samantha said, eyeing the painting on the mantel. She'd placed it there to see if it'd work. And it didn't. She smiled at Charlotte. "It would be perfect for Max's house."

She stood, gazing at the salmon. "Max was an avid fisherman. He didn't take it too seriously. He had a whimsical side when it came to fishing."

"There you go," Samantha said, certain she had the answer. "You have to have the painting. It was Max's hand on my shoulder in Scotland. That's why I bought it."

"Are you sure?"

"Absolutely."

They clinked their iced-tea glasses together in a toast. "To Max and Harry."

Edinburgh, Scotland

Charlotte arrived home on a bright, clear Scottish morning that seemed to draw everyone in Edinburgh outside by mid-morning. She walked to the Royal Botanic Garden and wandered on its meandering paths and through its glasshouses. She had

428

a late lunch at the café, out on the deck. She could have called friends to join her, but she was tired from her trip, prickly, frayed. The familiar surroundings would help her to clear her head and return to UK time.

As her soup and bread arrived, she breathed in the cool air, enjoying the sunshine. For months, she'd been operating on the surface of her life — going through the motions — but being at Red Clover Inn, with Greg, had changed all that. She'd gone deep again with herself, her life. She wasn't just the woman who'd discovered the man she'd been about to marry had betrayed her, and she wasn't just the diver who couldn't dive again.

Had she had a fling with a sexy DS agent and now that was done? It was back to their lives?

She'd promised herself she'd be more careful after Tommy. Falling for Greg didn't feel "careful." It felt impulsive, spontaneous, not well thought out, and perhaps a little crazy and unpredictable.

But *he* didn't feel wrong. That much she knew. Thousands of miles away, he still felt right to her.

After lunch, she walked back to her apartment. She unpacked, checked her fridge, fetched her mail. She settled on her couch, debating the wisdom of a nap. Justin had teased her about her pink walls. She loved them. She loved this place. But while it had been right for her for a long time, was it right for her now?

Her introspective mood lasted through supper alone at a pub and then through the night, back in her own bed. In the morning, she was restless, but it had nothing to do with jet lag or her long flight. It didn't have anything to do with her apartment or her life in Edinburgh. It had to do with *her*.

Rain had moved in overnight. She grabbed her rain jacket and umbrella and went out, grabbing coffee and toast around the corner and eating them as she walked to the institute offices.

She was on a mission.

Alan Bosworth brought her straight into his office. He pulled stacks of folders off a chair and had her sit. He sank onto the creaky chair at his desk. They exchanged small talk about the past few weeks. He'd been busy at the office, couldn't wait to get back in the field. She'd had a good time at her cousin's wedding and got a lot sorted out on her visit home.

"Dare I guess this visit means you've decided what you want to do?"

"Yes." She noted the firmness in her voice. "I want to open an office in Washington. We've been talking about it for years."

Alan looked thoughtful. "Are you giving up on diving?"

She licked her lips. "It's not medically safe for me to dive anymore."

"I wondered. I can understand you'd need time to absorb something like that. I'm sorry."

"So am I, but I did what I had to do that day. I'd do it again."

"You and the diver you rescued both walked away," Alan said. "You're a serious marine archaeologist, Charlotte, and you're a good manager. I can see you opening a new office, but there's work you can do here in Edinburgh, too."

"Thanks. I'm excited about the possibilities in Washington."

"What about shallow-water exploring?"

"That can be something I do on the side if the opportunity arises. It won't be a job."

"You sound as if you've thought this through," Alan said, studying her.

She smiled, relaxing slightly. "I know what I want to do. I haven't thought through all the details."

"Is this mostly a personal or a professional decision?"

"It's a mixture of both. My cousin is staying in New England. Another cousin is starting college there. I wouldn't be surprised if his folks move back to the States."

"There are rumors Malcolm and Francesca Bennett are going back to Florida."

"See? My parents finish up in Australia at the end of the year. Edinburgh . . ." Charlotte glanced around the small office, noting the diving photographs on Alan's wall. "I'd still be with the institute. I'd come back, but my role will have changed. It's already changed — I just needed time to accept it. Everything I've done the past few years since I started here will guide and inform me with what's next."

"All right," Alan said, rising. "We'll talk more. We'd all love to get a Washington office off the ground. Maybe this is its moment. *Your* moment."

"The best is yet ahead and all that?"

"Yes. That's what I believe."

Charlotte smiled, getting to her feet. "It's what I believe, too. Now. I didn't once I got the news about my chances for a worse incident if I dived again."

"You needed to mourn the life you thought you'd have."

They left it at that and he promised to get back to her later in the day with proposed times to meet to discuss a Washington office. He obviously assumed she'd move into her grandfather's house, but, mercifully, they didn't get into details. First things first.

Over the next few weeks, Charlotte huddled with Alan Bosworth and the institute board of directors to work out plans for a Washington office. It would be small to start but with a clear mission and the support of everyone in Edinburgh.

In Washington, Greg got settled into Max's house, paid his rent on time and started his job. She'd never been great talking on the phone, but she loved getting his calls, often, because of the time difference, when she'd settled into bed. But on a raw morning as she had tea and scones at her favorite café near her apartment, her phone vibrated, and she saw his number on the screen.

"Thought I'd catch you early," he said when she picked up. "Don't tell me you're having scones."

"With heaps of clotted cream and raspberry jam."

"Glorified biscuits," he said, as he always did when scones came up.

"Where are you?"

"Work."

At four thirty in the morning? But she thought she'd heard something in his voice. "Work's intense right now?"

"You could say that. But it's good. I get to use my experience to help agents doing the job I once did. And you, Charlotte? How are you?"

"I'm on my way into work. We have an office in mind for me in Washington. I'll even have a part-time assistant."

"You'll need a place to live now that I'm renting your house."

She laughed, but he had to go back to work.

"I'll call you soon," he said. "Don't worry if you don't hear from me."

After she disconnected, she stared at her phone on the table, as if he were still there. Was he going back into the field? On some secret mission he couldn't tell her about? Was she supposed to read between the lines of his early-morning call? On previous calls, they'd talked about everything from their families to work to what color to paint Max's kitchen, since they both agreed it did need painting.

She finished her scones and walked to the institute.

For two days, she heard nothing from Greg

and tried to follow his suggestion and not worry. She wasn't the worrying type, but that didn't mean she wasn't intrigued about what he was up to.

On the third day, she walked back from the institute, feeling a mix of excitement about her work and growing impatient curiosity about what Greg was up to. As she turned into her cobblestone courtyard, there he was, sitting on her stoop.

It was just like their first morning in Knights Bridge. "Did I conjure you up? Are you a figment of my imagination?"

"I'm too jet-lagged to be a figment of anyone's imagination." He leaned back, stretching out his thick legs. He looked tired, although not the bone-deep tired of the night they'd met. He squinted up at her. "This place is cute. A courtyard and everything. Almost broke my ankle on the cobblestones, though."

"You did not."

"Key word is *almost*." He got to his feet. "I've never been to Edinburgh. Thought I'd stop on my way back to Washington. I've been on a work trip that I can't talk about."

"Come on in. I can make you coffee."

"Tea. I'm in Scotland. I can do tea."

"I have shortbread, too," she added with a smile, unlocking her door.

If he had any comments about her rose-colored walls, he kept them to himself. "Nice," he said, scanning her small living room. "Very you."

She filled her kettle in the adjoining kitchen and set it on to boil. "How long can you stay?"

"A few days."

"Then back to Washington?"

He nodded, sitting on the couch. "My schedule won't be as intense as it has been."

"But you like your new job."

"I do."

She went into the living room. "And the house?"

"It's good, too. I have a sexy landlady. I'm dying to sleep with her."

"She happens to be in Edinburgh. Imagine."

Charlotte sat on his lap and draped her arms over his shoulders. The kettle dinged, but the hot water and tea would keep.

"Did you mean what you said at Red Clover Inn?"

"Yes."

"At the time or does it still hold?"

"Still holds. Now. Tomorrow. Decades from now. Everyone warned me to take my time after the upheavals in my life, and I did — by my standards, not theirs."

"You're a deep-end-of-the-pool kind of guy."

"Who's the one who asked a federal agent if he was armed?"

"Ha. Samantha and Justin have invited me to Knights Bridge for Thanksgiving. They said I can bring guests. The more, the merrier. What are your plans? Will you have Thanksgiving with Andrew and Megan?"

"We're doing Christmas."

"Max's house is a wonderful spot for Christmas."

"They'll love it. They want to go back to Knights Bridge, too."

"That can happen. Samantha said we can stay at our inn anytime. That's what it will always be, you know. *Our* inn." Charlotte snuggled against his warm, strong body. "I might have fallen in lust with you in the UK, but I fell in love with you in Knights Bridge."

"Charlotte . . ." He held her tight to him. "I love you, and the answer is yes."

"The answer to what is yes?"

"To your proposal. I'm saying yes to your proposal to marry you."

"I proposed?"

"I read between the lines."

She laughed, rolling on top of him. "Was that your proposal in Knights Bridge? My

437

answer is yes. Yes, I'll marry you, Greg Rawlings."

"It's not just because you want Max's house back now that you're moving to Washington?"

"No. It's because I love you with all my heart."

He wrapped his arms around her and drew her down to him, kissed her softly as he smoothed his hands over her hips. "We'll make the most of my time in Scotland."

Charlotte smiled, a warmth unlike anything she'd felt before enveloping her. This was what true love felt like, she realized. "I've no doubts."

"None?"

"Well. There is the question of kilts. Samantha bought Justin a kilt for Christmas while they were here on their honeymoon."

"Doesn't mean he'll wear it."

"After a few days in Edinburgh, you'll want a kilt."

"We'll see about that. Come on." He eased her from his lap. "We've got time. Let's skip tea and take advantage of the sunshine and go for a walk. You can show me your town."

Charlotte stood, reached for her lightweight jacket. "Samantha also bought a fish painting on their honeymoon that she thought would be right for the inn, but she decided it belongs in Max's house. It really does."

"What's a fish painting?"

"It's a salmon."

Greg frowned. "A painting of a salmon?"

"It's a painting of a live salmon. It's not cooked or filleted or anything."

"Ah." He shrugged on his own jacket. "I'll get used to you and Samantha and your Bennett eccentricities."

He followed her out into the Scottish summer afternoon. They held hands and walked up to the botanic garden. Charlotte pointed out places she knew and relayed the history of the gardens.

"I love being here with you," she said. "I've never loved Edinburgh more than I do right now."

Greg pulled her close as they started down a wide, paved walkway in the picturesque garden. "Edinburgh is great. We can have our wedding here if you want. I promise to stay sober and alert."

"Edinburgh would be a great place for a wedding."

He glanced at her. "I hear a *but.*"

"Imagine a wedding at Red Clover Inn."

He drew her closer and turned her to him. "Mice, bats and a hammock." He lowered his mouth to hers, his kiss a promise of what was to come, for both of them. "We can't go wrong."

AUTHOR'S NOTE

My fictional Knights Bridge is similar to the small town on the edge of the Quabbin Reservoir where I grew up and my mother still lives. Just before I was born, my parents arrived there via the Netherlands and the Florida Panhandle, and I can identify with Charlotte and Greg as to how a place can change people.

I loved creating the scenes in the English Cotswolds and Scotland. It was like being back there! (You can find photos of my visits and a recipe for scones on my website.)

Many thanks to my agent, Jodi Reamer at Writers House, and to my editor, Nicole Brebner, and everyone at MIRA Books for their tireless help and unwavering support during a very busy time in my life. I started writing Charlotte and Greg's story as my husband and I welcomed our third grandchild, Niamh Amalia, who, along with her older brother and sister, is a delight.

As I type this note, I'm deep into ideas for my next Swift River Valley novel. To stay up to date with all my news, please sign up for my e-newsletter on my website — carlaneggers.com — and join me on Facebook and Twitter. I'd love to stay in touch.

Thanks and happy reading,
Carla

ABOUT THE AUTHOR

Carla Neggers is the *New York Times* bestselling author of more than 60 novels, including her popular Sharpe & Donovan and Swift River Valley series. Her books have been translated into 24 languages and sold in over 35 countries. A frequent traveler to Ireland, Carla lives with her family in New England. For more information, visit CarlaNeggers.com